PENGUIN BOOKS

LET IT SNOW

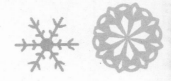

OTHER BOOKS YOU MAY ENJOY

LET IT SNOW

THREE HOLIDAY ROMANCES

JOHN GREEN

MAUREEN JOHNSON

LAUREN MYRACLE

PENGUIN BOOKS

PENGUIN BOOKS

Published by the Penguin Group
Penguin Books Ltd, 80 Strand, London WC2R 0RL, England
Penguin Group (USA) Inc., 375 Hudson Street, New York, New York 10014, USA
Penguin Group (Canada), 90 Eglinton Avenue East, Suite 700, Toronto, Ontario, Canada M4P 2Y3
(a division of Pearson Penguin Canada Inc.)
Penguin Ireland, 25 St Stephen's Green, Dublin 2, Ireland (a division of Penguin Books Ltd)
Penguin Group (Australia), 707 Collins Street, Melbourne, Victoria 3008, Australia
(a division of Pearson Australia Group Pty Ltd)
Penguin Books India Pvt Ltd, 11 Community Centre, Panchsheel Park, New Delhi – 110 017, India
Penguin Group (NZ), 67 Apollo Drive, Rosedale, Auckland 0632, New Zealand
(a division of Pearson New Zealand Ltd)
Penguin Books (South Africa) (Pty) Ltd, Block D, Rosebank Office Park,
181 Jan Smuts Avenue, Parktown North, Gauteng 2193, South Africa

Penguin Books Ltd, Registered Offices: 80 Strand, London WC2R 0RL, England

www.penguin.com

First published in the USA by Speak, an imprint of Penguin Group (USA) Inc., 2008
Published in Great Britain by Penguin Books 2013
This edition published 2014
001

"The Jubilee Express" copyright © Maureen Johnson, 2008
"A Cheertastic Christmas Miracle" copyright © John Green, 2008
"The Patron Saint of Pigs" copyright © Lauren Myracle, 2008

The moral right of the authors has been asserted

Set in Janson MT
Printed in Great Britain by Clays Ltd, St Ives plc

British Library Cataloguing in Publication Data
A CIP catalogue record for this book is available from the British Library

ISBN: 978–0–141–36050–8

www.greenpenguin.co.uk

MIX
Paper from
responsible sources
FSC
www.fsc.org   FSC® C018179

Penguin Books is committed to a sustainable
future for our business, our readers and our planet.
This book is made from Forest Stewardship
Council™ certified paper.

LET IT SNOW

CONTENTS

The Jubilee Express

maureen johnson

For Hamish, who embodied the 'go down the hill really fast, and if something gets in your way, turn' school of teaching me how to deal with a snowy slope. And for all who toil behind the façade of a corporate monolith, for every person who has to say grande latte three thousand times a day, for every soul who's ever had to deal with a broken credit card reader in the holiday rush . . . this one is for you.

Chapter One

*I*t was the night before Christmas.

Well, to be more precise, it was the afternoon before Christmas. But before I take you into the beating heart of the action, let's get one thing out of the way. I know from experience that if it comes up later, it will distract you so much that you won't be able to concentrate on anything else I tell you.

My name is Jubilee Dougal. Take a moment and let it sink in.

See, when you get it up front, it's not that bad. Now imagine I was halfway through some long story (like I'm about to be), and I dropped that one on you. "By the way, my name is Jubilee." You wouldn't know *what* to do next.

I realize Jubilee is a bit of a stripper name. You probably think I have heard the call of the pole. But no. If you saw me, you'd get the idea pretty quickly that I'm not a stripper (I think). I have a little black bob. I wear glasses half the time, and contacts the other half. I'm sixteen, I sing in choir, I attend Mathletes events. I play field hockey, which lacks the undulating, baby-oiled grace that is the stripper's stock-in-trade. (I have no problem with strippers, in case any strippers are reading this. I'm just not one. My major concern, strippage-wise, is the latex. I think latex is probably bad for your skin because it doesn't allow it to breathe.)

My objection is that Jubilee *isn't a name*—it's some kind of a party. No one knows *what* kind. Have you ever heard of someone throwing a jubilee? And if you did, would you go? Because I wouldn't. It sounds like something where you have to rent a large inflatable object, put up bunting, and make a complicated plan for trash disposal.

Come to think of it, it might be interchangeable with hoedown.

My name has a lot to do with this story, and like I said, it was the afternoon before Christmas. I was having one of those days when you feel that life... *likes* you. Finals were over and school was done until New Year's. I was alone in our house, which was feeling very cozy and snug. I was dressed for the night in a new outfit I'd saved for—a black skirt, tights, a sparkly red T-shirt, and my new black boots. I was drinking a little eggnog latte that I'd cooked up for myself. All my presents were wrapped and ready to go. It was all leading up to the big event: at six, I was supposed to go to Noah's house—Noah Price, my boyfriend—for his family's annual Christmas Eve Smorgasbord.

The Price Family Annual Smorgasbord is a big deal in our personal history. It was how we got together in the first place. Before the Smorgasbord, Noah Price was just a star in my sky...constant, familiar, bright, and far above me. I'd known Noah since the fourth grade, but it felt like I knew him in the same way that I know people on television. I knew the name. I watched the show. Sure, Noah was a bit closer than that... but somehow when it's real, when it's your life...that person can feel even farther off and more unobtainable than an actual celebrity. Proximity doesn't breed familiarity.

I had always liked him, but it never really occurred to me to *like* him, like him. I never thought that was a reasonable thing to want. He was a year older than me, a foot taller, broad of shoulder, bright of eye, and floppy of hair. Noah was the whole package—athlete, academic, school-government bigwig—the kind of person you think must only date models or spies or people who have laboratories named after them.

So when Noah invited me to come along to El Smorgasbord on Christmas Eve last year, I more or less ruptured an eye in my excitement and confusion. I couldn't walk straight for three days when I got the invitation. It was so bad that I actually had to *consciously practice walking* in my room before I went to his house. I had no idea if he had asked me because he liked me, or if his mom made him (our parents know each other), or because he lost a bet. All my friends were just as excited, but they seemed to understand it more than I did. They assured me that he had been eyeing me in Mathletes, laughing at my attempts at trigonometry jokes, bringing me up in conversation.

It was all so *crazy*... as weird as finding out that someone had written a book about my life or something.

When I got there, I spent most of the night safely propped up in a corner talking to his sister, who (though I love her) is not exactly deep. There is only so much you can say about your favorite brands of hoodies before you feel the conversational walls closing in. But she can go like a champion. Elise has some Thoughts on the Subject.

I finally took a break just as Noah's mom was setting out another plate and I could make the Oh-excuse-me-but-doesn't-that-look-good excuse. I had no idea what was on it, but it turned out to be pickled fish. I was backing away, but his mom said, "You have to try a piece."

Being a bit of a lemming, I did. But this time, it worked out, because that's when I noticed that Noah was watching me. He said, "I'm so glad you took some." I asked him why, because I really think I suspected it was all a bet. ("Okay, I'll ask her to come, but you guys have to give me twenty bucks if I can make her eat pickled fish.")

And he said, "Because I've been eating it."

I was still standing there with what I assume was a very enchanting expression of total stupidity etched on my face, so he added, "And I couldn't kiss you unless you'd had some, too."

Which is both gross and breathtakingly romantic. He could always have just gone upstairs and brushed his teeth, but he stayed and lurked by the fish for me. We snuck off to the garage, where we made out under the shelf of power tools. That was the start of it all.

So, the particular Christmas Eve I'm about to tell you about wasn't just any Christmas Eve: this was our *one-year anniversary*. It was almost impossible to believe it had been a year. It had all gone by so fast....

See, Noah is always really busy. When he emerged into the world, tiny and wriggling and pink, he probably had to get footprinted and out of the hospital as quickly as possible to get to a meeting. As a senior, a member of the soccer team, and president of the student council, his time had been whittled away to almost nothing. I think in the year that we had been dating we had had about a dozen proper dates with just Noah and me going somewhere by ourselves. About once a month. We'd had plenty of joint appearances. Noah and Jubilee at the student-council bake sale! Noah and Jubilee at the soccer-team raffle table! Noah and Jubilee at the food drive, in the tutoring room, at the homecoming-organizational meeting…

Noah was aware of this. And though tonight was a family event with many people in attendance, he promised me there would be time just for us. He had made sure of it by helping out in advance. If we put in two hours at the party, he promised, we could escape to the back room and exchange our gifts and watch *The Grinch Who Stole Christmas* together. He would drive me home, and we would stop for a while….

And then, of course, my parents got arrested, and all of that went to hell.

Do you know the Flobie Santa Village? The Flobie Santa Village is such a big part of my life that I just assume everyone knows what it is, but I've been told recently that I make way too many assumptions, so I'll explain.

The Flobie Santa Village is a series of collectable ceramic pieces that you can put together to form a town. My parents have been collecting them since the time I was born. I've been staring down those tiny plastic cobblestone streets since I was big enough to stand on my own. We have it all—the candy-cane bridge, Lake Snowbegone, the gumdrop shop, the gingerbread bakery, Sugarplum Alley. It's not small, either. My parents bought a special table to put it up on, and it takes up the center of our living room from Thanksgiving until New Year's. It requires seven power strips to make it all work.

In order to diminish the environmental impact, I got them to turn it off at night, but it was a struggle.

I was named after Flobie Santa Village building #4, Jubilee Hall. Jubilee Hall is the biggest building in the collection. It's the main place that presents are made and wrapped. It has colored lights, a working conveyor belt with gifts stuck to it, and little elves that turn as if they're loading and unloading them. The elves of Jubilee Hall each have a present glued to their hands—so what it really looks like are a bunch of tortured beings doomed to pick up and set down the same gift over and over again until the end of time or until the motor breaks. I remember pointing this out to my mom when I was little; she said I was missing the point. Maybe so. We were clearly coming from different directions on this subject, considering she felt those little buildings were important enough to name her only offspring after.

People who collect the Flobie Village tend to get a little obsessed with it. There are conventions, about a dozen serious Web sites, and four magazines. Some of them try to play it off by saying that Flobie pieces are an investment. And they *are* worth a lot of money, it's true. Especially the numbered ones. You can only buy those pieces at the Flobie showroom on Christmas Eve. We live in Richmond, Virginia, which is only about fifty miles away—so every year on the night of the twenty-third, my parents leave with a car full of blankets, chairs, and provisions and sit in line all night and wait.

Flobie used to make a hundred numbered pieces, but last year they reduced it to ten. This is when things got bad. One hundred pieces wasn't nearly enough, so when the number went down to just one-tenth of that, the claws came out and the fur started to fly. There was a problem last year when people tried to hold places in line—a problem that quickly turned into people smacking each other with rolled-up Flobie catalogs, throwing cookie tins, stomping on each other's lawn chairs, and dumping lukewarm cocoa on each other's Santa Claus–hatted heads. The fight was big enough and ridiculous enough to make the local news. Flobie said that they were "taking measures" to make sure it didn't happen again, but I never believed that. You can't buy that kind of publicity.

But I wasn't thinking about that when my parents drove off to get in line for piece #68, the Elf Hotel. And I still wasn't thinking about it when I was drinking my eggnog latte and whiling away the time until I got to go to Noah's. I did notice that my parents *were* later arriving home than usual. They usually got back from Flobie around lunchtime on Christmas Eve, and here it was, almost four o'clock. I started doing some of the general holiday duties to keep myself busy. I couldn't call Noah...I knew he was busy getting ready for the Smorgasbord. So I added some extra ribbon and holly to his presents. I switched on all the power strips that power the

Flobie Santa Village, setting all the enslaved elves to work. I turned on Christmas carols. I was just stepping outside to turn on the lights on the front of the house when I saw Sam advancing toward our house with his storm-trooper stride.

Sam is our lawyer—and when I say "our lawyer," I mean "our neighbor who happens to be an extremely high-powered lawyer in Washington, D.C." Sam is exactly the person you want to take on a huge corporation or to represent you when you're being sued for a billion dollars. He is not, however, Mr. Cuddles. I was about to invite him in to try one of my delicious eggnog lattes, but he cut me off.

"I have some bad news," he said, ushering me into my own house. "There's been another incident at the Flobie showroom. Inside. Come on."

I thought he was going to say that my parents had been killed. He had that kind of tone. I envisioned huge piles of the Elf Hotel flying off the belt, taking down everyone in sight. I had seen pictures of the Elf Hotel—it had sharp candy-cane spires that could easily impale someone. And if anyone was ever going to be killed by an Elf Hotel, it would be my parents.

"They've been taken into custody," he said. "They're in jail."

"Who's in jail?" I asked, because I'm not super-quick on the uptake, and because it was much easier for me to envision my parents being taken down by a flying Elf Hotel than it was to think of them being taken off in handcuffs.

Sam just looked at me and waited for me to catch up on my own.

"There was another fight when the pieces came out this morning," he explained, after a pause. "An argument about who was holding spots in line. Your parents weren't part of it, but they didn't disperse when the police told them to. They got hauled in with the others. Five people have been booked. It's all over the news."

I felt my legs starting to wobble, so I sat down on the sofa.

"Why didn't they call?" I asked.

"One phone call," he said. "They called me, because they thought I could get them out. Which I can't."

"What do you mean, you *can't*?"

The idea that Sam couldn't bust my parents out of the county clink was ridiculous. It was like hearing a pilot come over the intercom and say, "Hey, everyone. I just remembered I'm no good at landing. So I'm just going to keep flying around until someone has a better idea."

"I did my best," Sam went on, "but the judge isn't budging. He's sick of these Flobie problems, so he's making an example of them all. Your parents instructed me to take you to the train station. I only have one hour, then I have to be back for hot cookies and a sing-along at five. How quickly can you pack?"

This was delivered in the same gravelly tone of voice that

Sam probably used when pounding people on the stand about why they were seen running from the scene covered in blood. He didn't look happy that this task had been foisted on him on Christmas Eve. Still, a little touch of Oprah would have helped.

"Pack? Train station? What?"

"You're going to Florida to stay with your grandparents," he said. "Couldn't get a flight—they're being canceled all over the place because of the storm."

"What storm?"

"Jubilee," Sam said very slowly, having concluded that I was the least-aware person on the planet, "we're about to have the biggest storm in fifty years!"

My brain wasn't working right—none of this was going in.

"I can't go," I said. "I'm supposed to see Noah tonight. And Christmas. What about Christmas?"

Sam shrugged, as if to say that Christmas was beyond his control, and there was nothing the legal system could do about it.

"But...why can't I just stay here? This is crazy!"

"Your parents don't want you alone for two days over the holiday."

"I can go to Noah's! I *have* to go to Noah's!"

"Look," he said, "it's all arranged. We can't reach your parents now. They're being processed. I bought your ticket, and I don't have a lot of time. You're going to have to pack now, Jubilee."

maureen johnson

I turned and looked at the twinkling little cityscape next to me. I could see the shadows of the doomed elves as they worked away in Jubilee Hall, the warm glow of Mrs. Muggin's Cake Shop, the slow but merry process of the Elf Express around the little expanse of track.

The only thing I could think to ask was, "But...what about the village?"

Chapter Two

I'd never actually been on a train before. It was taller than I imagined, with second-"story" windows that I guessed were the sleeping cars. Inside, it was dimly lit, and most of the people stuffed in there looked catatonic. I expected the train to steam and chug and shoot off like a rocket, because I watched a lot of cartoons in my misspent youth and that's how cartoon trains work. This train glided off indifferently, as if it had gotten bored with standing around.

Naturally, I called Noah the moment we set off. This was a slight violation of the I'm-going-to-be-slammed-until-six-so-I'll-just-see-you-at-the-party no-call policy, but never have circumstances been more understandable. When he answered, there was a cheerful clamor in the background. I could hear carols and the clanking of dishes, which was a depressing contrast to the claustrophobic muffle of the train.

"Lee!" he said. "Kind of a bad time. See you in an hour?"

He made a little grunt. It sounded like he was lifting something heavy, probably one of the freakishly large hams his mother always managed to get her hands on for the Smorgasbord. I presume she gets them from some kind of experimental farm where the pigs are treated with lasers and superdrugs until they are thirty feet long.

"Um…that's the thing," I said. "I'm not coming."

"What do you mean, you're not coming? What's wrong?"

I explained the parents-in-jail/me-on-train-in-storm/life-not-really-going-as-planned situation as best I could. I tried to keep it light, like I found it funny, mostly to keep myself from sobbing on a dark train of stupefied strangers.

Another grunt. It sounded like he was shifting something around.

"It'll be fine," he said after a moment. "Sam's taking care of it, right?"

"Well, if you mean not getting them out of jail, then yes. He doesn't even seem worried."

"It's probably just some little county jail," he replied. "It won't be bad. And if Sam's not worried, it'll be okay. I'm sorry this happened, but I'll see you in a day or two."

"Yes, but it's Christmas," I said. My voice got thick, and I choked back a tear. He gave me a moment.

"I know this is hard, Lee," he said after a pause, "but it will be fine. It will. This is just one of those things."

I knew he was trying to calm me down and generally console me, but still. One of those things? This was not *one of those things*. One of those things is your car breaking down or getting stomach flu or your faulty holiday lights sending out a spark and burning down your hedge. I said as much, and he sighed, realizing I was right. Then he grunted again.

"What's the matter?" I asked, through a sniff.

"I'm holding a huge ham," he said. "I'm going to have to go in a minute. Look, we'll do another Christmas when you get back. I promise. We'll find some time. Don't worry. Call me when you get there, okay?"

I promised I would, and he hung up and went off with his ham. I stared at the now-silent phone.

Sometimes, because I dated Noah, I empathized with people who are married to politicians. You can tell they have their own lives, but because they love the person they are with, they end up pulled into the juggernaut—and pretty soon, they're waving and smiling blankly for the camera, with balloons falling on their heads and staff members knocking them out of the way to get to the All-Important Significant Other, who is Perfect.

I know no one is perfect, that behind every façade of perfection is a writhing mess of subterfuge and secret sorrows...but even taking that into account, Noah was pretty much perfect.

maureen johnson

I'd never heard anyone say a bad word about him. His status was as unquestioned as gravity. By making me his girlfriend, he demonstrated his belief in me, and I had picked up on his conviction. I stood straighter. I felt more confident, more consistently positive, more important. He *liked* being seen with me; therefore, I liked being seen with me, if that makes any sense.

So, yes, his overcommittedness was a pain sometimes. But I understood. When you have to take a big ham to your mom, for instance, because sixty people are about to descend on your house for a Smorgasbord. It just has to be done. The rough must be taken with the smooth. I took out my iPod and used the remaining power to flick through some photos of him. Then the power died.

I felt so alone on that train... a weird, unnatural kind of alone that bore into me. It was feeling just beyond fear and somewhere to the left of sadness. Tired, but not the kind of tired that sleep fixes. It was dark and gloomy, and yet, it didn't seem that things would get any better if the lights were turned up. If anything, I would be able to get a much better look at my unpleasant situation.

I thought about calling my grandparents. They already knew I was coming. Sam told me he had called them. They would have been happy to talk to me, but I wasn't feeling up to it. My grandparents are great people, but they are easily rattled. Like, if the grocery store sells out of some frozen pizza or soup they advertise in the circular, and they've gone to the store just for that, they'll stand there debating their next move for a half an hour. If I called them, every aspect of my visit would have to be discussed to the smallest detail. What blanket would I need? Did I still eat crackers? Should Grandpa get more shampoo? It was always sweet, but a little too much for my mind at the moment.

I like to think I am a problem solver. I would distract myself out of this funk. I dug into my bag to see what I had managed to collect as I was rushed out of the house. I discovered that I was woefully unprepared for the trip ahead of me. I had grabbed the bare essentials—some underwear, jeans, two sweaters, a few shirts, my glasses. My iPod was out of power. I had just one book with me. It was *Northanger Abbey*, part of my winter break reading list for English. It was good, but not exactly what you want when you're feeling the creeping hand of doom.

So, for about two hours, I just looked out the window as the sun set, the candy-color pink sky turned to silver, and the first snow began to fall. I knew it was beautiful, but knowing something is beautiful and caring about it are two very different things, and I didn't care. The snow got harder and faster, until it filled the view and there was nothing left but white. It came from all directions at once, even blowing up from underneath. Watching it made me dizzy and a little ill.

People were coming down the aisle with boxes of food—

chips and sodas and prewrapped sandwiches. Clearly, there was a food source somewhere on this train. Sam had shoved fifty bucks in my hand back at the station, all fifty of which would be extracted from my parents once they were breathing free air again. There was nothing else to do, so I got up and made my way down to the snack car, where I was promptly informed that they were out of everything except some floppy microwaved pizza discs, two muffins, a few candy bars, a bag of nuts, and some sad-looking fruit. I wanted to compliment them on being so well prepared for the holiday rush, but the guy working the counter looked really beaten. He didn't need my sarcasm. I bought a pizza disc, two candy bars, the muffins, the nuts, and a hot chocolate. It seemed smart to stock up a bit for the rest of the trip if things were going that fast. I stuffed a five-dollar bill into his cup, and he nodded his thanks.

I took one of the empty seats at the tables braced to the wall. The train was shaking a lot now, even as we slowed. The wind was smacking us from either side. I left the pizza untouched and burned my lips on the chocolate. It was the most action they were going to get, after all.

"Mind if I sit here?" a voice asked.

I looked up to find an exceptionally beautiful guy standing over me. Again, I noticed, and again, I didn't really care. But he did make more of an impact than the snow. His hair was as dark as mine, meaning it was black. It was longer than mine, though. Mine only goes just past my chin. His was pulled back in a ponytail. He looked Native American, with high cheekbones. The thin denim jacket he was wearing wasn't nearly enough protection against the weather. There was something in his eyes, though, that really struck a chord—he looked troubled, like he was having a hard time keeping them open. He had just gotten himself a cup of coffee, which he was clutching kind of intently.

"Sure," I said.

He kept his head down when he sat, but I noticed him glancing at all the food I had in the box. Something told me that he was a lot hungrier than me.

"Have some," I said. "I was just getting stuff before they sold out. I'm not even that hungry. I haven't touched this pizza at all."

There was a moment of resistance, but I pushed it forward.

"I realize it looks like a pizza coaster," I added. "It was all they had. Really. Take it."

He smiled a little. "I'm Jeb," he said.

"I'm Julie," I answered. I wasn't in the mood to go through the "Jubilee? Your name is *Jubilee*? Tell me, what do you use for your routine—baby oil or some kind of nut oil? And does someone wipe down the pole after each use?" conversation. Everything I explained to you in the beginning. Most people call me Julie. Noah called me Lee.

"Where are you headed?" he asked.

I had no cover story for my parents or why I was here. The full truth was a little too much to throw at a stranger.

"Going to see my grandparents," I said. "Kind of last-minute change of plan."

"Where do they live?" he asked, looking at the swirling snow that was beating at the window of the train. It was impossible to tell where the sky ended and the ground began. The snow cloud had crash-landed on top of us.

"Florida," I said.

"Long way. I'm just going to Gracetown, next stop."

I nodded. I'd heard of Gracetown but had no idea where it was. Somewhere on this long, snowy path between me and nowhere. I offered the box of food to him again, but he shook his head.

"That's okay," he said. "But thanks for the pizza. I was kind of starving. We picked a bad day to travel. Guess there's not a lot of choice, though. Sometimes you just have to do stuff you aren't sure about...."

"Who are you going to see?" I asked.

He turned his gaze back down and folded up the plate the pizza disc had come on.

"I'm going to see my girlfriend. Well, kind of girlfriend. I've been trying to call her, but I can't get a signal."

"I have one," I said, pulling out my phone. "Use mine. I'm not even close to using my minutes this month."

Jeb took the phone with a wide smile. As he got up, I noticed just how tall and broad-shouldered he was. If I wasn't so completely devoted to Noah, I would have been deeply smitten. He crossed the few feet, just to a spot by the other side. I watched him try the number, but he clicked the phone shut without ever speaking.

"I couldn't get her," he said, sitting back down and returning my phone.

"So," I said, smiling. "This is, kind of your girlfriend? You still aren't sure if you're dating yet?"

I remembered those times well, when Noah and I first got together, and I wasn't sure if I was his girlfriend. I was so deliciously nervous all the time.

"She cheated on me," he said plainly.

Oh, I'd misread that. Badly. I felt the pang for him, right in the middle of my chest. I really did.

"It's not her fault," he said after a moment. "Not all of it. I…"

I never got to hear what had happened, because the door of the car flew open, and there was a screech, kind of like the sound that Beaker—the horrible, oily cockatoo we had as a fourth-grade pet—used to make. Beaker was the bird Jeremy Rich taught to scream the word *ass*. Beaker loved to screech and scream the word *ass*, and he did it really well. You could hear him all the way down the hall in the girls' room. Beaker eventually got moved to the teachers' lounge, where I guess you're allowed to spread your greasy feathers and scream "ass" all you like.

It wasn't ass-screaming Beaker, though. It was fourteen girls in matching, form-fitting sweats, all of which read RIDGE CHEERLEADING on the butt. (A form of ass-screaming, I suppose.) Each had her name on the back of her sleek warm-up fleece. They clustered around the snack bar, yelling at the top of their lungs. I really hoped and prayed that they wouldn't all say "Oh my God!" at once, but my prayers were not heard, maybe because God was busy listening to all of them.

"There is *no* lean protein," I heard one of them say.

"I *told* you, Madison. You should have had that lettuce wrap when you had the chance."

"I thought they'd at least have *chicken breast*!"

To my enduring dismay, I noticed that both girls having this conversation were named Madison. Worse: three of the others were named Amber. I felt like I was trapped in a social experiment gone wrong—maybe something involving replicants.

A few of the group turned on us. I mean, to us. They turned to me and Jeb. Well, actually they just turned to Jeb.

"Oh my God!" said one of the Ambers. "Is this not the worst trip ever? Did you see the snow?"

She was a sharp one, this Amber. What would she notice next? The train? The moon? The hilarious vagaries of human existence? Her own head?

I didn't say any of that, because death by cheerleader is not really the way I want to go. Amber wasn't addressing this to me, anyway. Amber had no idea I was even there. Her eyes were on Jeb. You could almost see the robotic core in her corneas making all the focusing adjustments and lining him in the crosshairs.

"It's pretty bad," he said politely.

"We're going down to Florida?"

She said it like that, like a question.

"Should be nicer there," he said.

"Yeah. *If* we make it. We're all at cheerleading regionals? Which is rough, because it's the holidays? But we all had Christmas early? We did ours yesterday?"

This is when I noticed that they all seemed to be carrying really new-looking stuff. Shiny phones, conspicuous bracelets and necklaces that they played with, fresh manicures, iPods I'd never even seen before.

Amber One sat down with us—a careful sit, with her knees angled together and her heels turned out. A perky sitting pose of someone used to being the most adorable in the general vicinity.

"This is Julie," Jeb said, kindly introducing me to our new friend. Amber told me her name was Amber, and then rattled off all the Ambers and Madisons. There were other names, but to me, they were all Ambers and Madisons. Seemed safe to think of it that way. I had at least a chance of being right.

Amber began chatting away, telling us all about the competition. She did this amazing thing where she included me in the conversation *and* ignored me at the same time. Plus, she was sending me a mental message—deeply subliminal—that she wanted me to get up and give my seat over to her tribe. They filled every available bit of space in the car as it was. Half of them on the phone, the other half depleting the water, coffee, and Diet Coke supply.

I decided that this was not what I needed to make my life complete.

"I'm going to go back to my seat," I said.

Just as I stood, though, the train slowed dramatically, throwing us all forward in one big splash of hot and cold liquids. The wheels cried out in protest as they dragged down the track for about a minute, and then we stopped, hard. I heard luggage all up and down the train thundering down from racks, and then people falling where they stood. People like me. I landed on a Madison and slammed my chin and cheek on something. I'm not sure what it was, because the lights went out at the same moment, causing a massive yelp of dismay. I felt hands helping me up, and I didn't need to be able to see to know it was Jeb.

"You all right?" he asked.

"Fine. I think."

There was a flicker, and then the lights came back up one by one. Several Ambers were clinging to the snack bar for dear life. There was food all over the floor. Jeb reached down and picked up what was once his phone, now a neatly snapped two-piece affair. He cradled it in his hand like an injured baby bird.

The loudspeaker crackled, and the voice that spoke over it sounded genuinely rattled—not the cool, bossy tone they were using to announce stops along the way.

"Ladies and gentlemen," it said, "please remain calm. A conductor will be checking your cabin to see if anyone has been injured."

I pressed my face against the cold window to see what was going on. We had come to rest next to what looked like a wide road with lots of lanes, something like an interstate. Across the way was a glowing yellow sign, suspended high over the road. It was hard to see through the snow, but I recognized the color and shape. It was for a Waffle House. Just outside of the train, a crew member was stumbling along through the snow, looking under the carriage with a flashlight.

A female conductor threw open the door to our car and started surveying everyone. She was missing her hat.

"What's happening?" I asked when she reached us. "We look really stuck."

She leaned down and had a good look out the window, then gave a low whistle.

"We're not going anywhere, honey," she said in a low voice. "We're just outside of Gracetown. The track dips down below this point, and it's completely covered. Maybe they can send some emergency vehicles to get us by morning. I don't know, though. I wouldn't bet on it. Anyway, you hurt?"

"I'm okay," I assured her.

Amber One was holding her wrist.

"Amber!" another Amber said. "What happened?"

"I twisted it," Amber One moaned. "Bad."

"That's your support wrist on basket toss!"

Six cheerleaders indicated (not subliminally) that they wanted me to move out of the way so that they could get to their wounded member and sit her down. Jeb was trapped in the throng. The lights went dim, the heater audibly cranked down, and the loudspeaker came back on.

"Ladies and gentlemen," the voice said, "we're going to cut a bit of power to conserve energy. If you have blankets or sweaters, you may want to use them now. If any of you require extra warmth, we'll try to provide whatever we can. If you have extra layering, we ask that you share it."

I looked at the yellow sign again, and then back at the cluster of cheerleaders. I had two choices—I could stay here in the cold, dark, stranded train or I could actually *do* something. I could take charge of this day that had run away from me too many times. It wouldn't be hard to get across the road and over to the Waffle House. They probably had heat and lots of food. It was worth a shot, and it was a plan I felt Noah would have approved of. Proactive. I gently pushed my way through the Ambers to get to Jeb.

"There's a Waffle House across the street," I told him. "I'm going to go over and see if it's open."

"A Waffle House?" Jeb replied. "We must be just outside of town, along I-40."

"Don't be crazy," Amber One said. "What if the train leaves?"

"It's not," I said. "The conductor just told me. We're stuck here all night. Over there, they probably have heat and food and a place for people to move around. What else are we going to do?"

"We could practice our enthusiasm rounds," one of the Madisons ventured in a tiny voice.

"You're going by yourself?" Jeb asked. I could tell he wanted to come, but Amber was leaning on him now like her life depended on him.

"I'll be fine," I said. "It's just across the street. Give me your phone number and…"

He held up the broken phone as a grim reminder. I nodded and picked up my backpack.

"I won't be long," I said. "I have to come back, right? Where else am I going to go?"

Chapter Three

Peeking out of the cold vestibule, which was slicked with snow from the open train door, I could just about see the crew members stalking alongside the train with their flashlights. They were a few cars away, so I made my move.

The metal steps were steep, high, and completely covered in frozen snow. Plus, the gap from the train to the ground was about four feet. I sat on the wet bottom step, snow pouring on my head, and pushed myself off as carefully as I could. I fell on all fours into more than a foot of snow, soaking my tights, but it wasn't too painful. I didn't have far to go. We were right next to the road, only twenty feet or so. All I had to do was get down to that, cross, walk under the overpass, and I would be there. It would only take a minute or two.

I've never crossed a six-lane interstate before. The

opportunity had never come up, and if it had, it would have seemed like a bad idea. But there were no cars at all. It felt like the end of the world, a whole new start to life, the old order gone. It took about five minutes to walk across, since the wind was blowing so hard and flakes kept landing in my eyes. Once I got over, I had to cross some other stretch of something. It could have been grass or cement or more road—now it was just white and deep. Whatever it was, there was a curb buried in it, which I tripped over. I was drenched in snow by the time I made it to the door.

It was warm inside the Waffle House. In fact, it was so overheated that the windows had steamed, causing the large plastic holiday decals stuck to them to droop and peel away. Soft jazz Christmas standards blew out through the speakers, joyful as an allergy attack. The predominant smells were floor cleaner and overused cooking oil, but there was a hint of promise. Potatoes and onions had been fried here not long ago—and they had been good.

People-wise, the situation wasn't much better. From deep in the kitchen, I heard two male voices, interspersed with slapping sounds and laughing. There was a woman lingering in a cloud of her own misery in the farthest corner, an empty plate dotted with cigarette butts in front of her. The only employee in sight was a guy, probably about my age, standing guard at the cash register. His regulation Waffle House shirt was long and untucked, and his spiky hair stuck out of the low-hanging visor on his head. His name tag read DON-KEUN. He was reading a graphic novel when I came in. My entrance brought a little light into his eyes.

"Hey," he said. "You look cold."

It was well observed. I nodded in reply.

Boredom had eaten at Don-Keun. You could hear it in his voice, see it in the way he slouched over the register in defeat. "Everything's free tonight," he said. "You can have whatever you want. Orders from the cook and the acting assistant manager. Both of those are me."

"Thanks," I said.

I think he was about to say something else, but then just flinched in embarrassment as the slap fight in the back grew louder. There was a newspaper and several coffee cups in front of one of the counter seats. I went over to take a seat a few spaces down, in an effort to be somewhat social. As I sat, Don-Keun made a sudden lurch in my direction.

"Um, you might not want to—"

He cut himself off and retreated a step as someone emerged from the direction of the restrooms. It was a man, maybe sixty years old, with sandy hair, a little bit of a beer gut, and glasses. Oh, and he was dressed in tinfoil. Head to toe. Even had a little tinfoil hat. Like you do.

Tinfoil Guy took the seat with the newspaper and the cups and gave me a nod of greeting before I could move.

"How are you on this night?" he asked.

"I could be better," I replied honestly. I didn't know where to look—at his face or his shiny, shiny silver body.

"Bad night to be out."

"Yeah," I said, choosing his shiny, shiny abdomen as my point of focus. "Bad."

"You don't happen to need a tow?"

"Not unless you tow trains."

He thought that over for a moment. It's always awkward when someone doesn't realize you're joking and devotes thought time to what you've said. Double that when the person is wearing tinfoil.

"Too big," he finally replied, shaking his head. "Won't work."

Don-Keun shook his head as well and gave me a back-away-while-you-can—it-is-too-late-to-save-me look.

I smiled and tried to develop a sudden and all-consuming interest in the menu. It only seemed right to order something. I scanned it over and over, as if I just couldn't decide between the waffle sandwich or the hash browns covered in cheese.

"Have some coffee," Don-Keun said, coming over and handing me a cup. The coffee was completely burned and had a rank smell, but this was not the time to be picky. I think he was just offering me backup, anyway.

"You said you were on a train?" he asked.

"Yeah," I said, pointing out the window. Both Don-Keun and Tinfoil Guy turned to look, but the storm had picked up. The train was invisible.

"No," Tinfoil Guy said again. "Trains won't work."

He adjusted his tin cuffs to punctuate this remark.

"Does that help?" I asked, finally feeling the need to mention the obvious.

"Does what help?"

"That stuff. Is it like that stuff runners have to wear when they finish marathons?"

"Which stuff?"

"The tinfoil."

"What tinfoil?" he asked.

On that, I abandoned both politeness and Don-Keun and went and sat by the window, watching the pane shudder as the snow and wind hit it.

Far away, the Smorgasbord was at full tilt. All the food would be out by this point: the freakish hams, multiple turkeys, meatballs, potatoes baked in cream, rice pudding, cookies, the four kinds of pickled fish...

In other words, this would be a bad time to call Noah. Except he had told me to call when I got there. This was as far as I was getting.

So I called, and was immediately shuffled off to voice mail. I hadn't planned out what I was going to say or what kind of attitude I was going to adopt. I defaulted into "funny-ha-ha," and left a quick, probably incomprehensible message about being stranded in a strange town, along an interstate, at a Waffle House, with a man dressed in foil. It wasn't until I hung up that I realized he would think I was joking—*weirdly* joking—and calling him when he was busy to boot. The message would probably annoy him.

I was about to call back and use a more sincere and sad voice to clarify that all of the above was not a joke...when there was a rush of wind, a bit of suction as the outside doors were opened, and then another person in our midst. He was tall, and thin, and apparently male. But it was hard to tell much else because he had wet plastic shopping bags on his head, his hands, and his feet. That made two people using non-clothing items for clothes.

I was starting to dislike Gracetown.

"I lost control of my car on Sunrise," the guy said to the room in general. "Had to ditch it."

Don-Keun nodded in understanding.

"Need a tow?" Tinfoil Guy said.

"No, that's okay. It's snowing so hard, I don't even know if I could find it again."

As he peeled off the bags, the guy turned out to be very normal-looking, with damp and dark curly hair, kind of skinny, jeans a little too big for him. He looked at the counter, then headed over to me.

"Is it okay if I sit here?" he asked in a low voice. He nodded slightly in the direction of Tinfoil Guy. Obviously, he didn't want to sit over there, either.

"Sure," I said.

"He's harmless," the guy said, still very quietly. "But he can talk a lot. I got stuck with him for about a half an hour once. He really likes cups. He can talk about cups for a long time."

"Does he always wear tinfoil?"

"I don't think I'd recognize him without it. I'm Stuart, by the way."

"I'm...Julie."

"How did you get here?" he asked.

"My train," I said, pointing to the vista of snow and darkness. "We got stuck."

"Where were you going?" he asked.

"To Florida. To see my grandparents. My parents are in jail."

I decided it was worth a try, just slipping it into the conversation like that. It got the reaction I half expected. Stuart laughed.

"Are you with anyone?" he asked.

"I have a boyfriend," I said.

I'm usually not this stupid, I promise you. My brain was on a Noah track. I was still thinking about my idiotic message.

The corners of Stuart's mouth wrinkled, like he was trying not to laugh. He beat a little rhythm on the table and smiled as if trying to blow my awkward moment away. I *should* have taken the out he was giving me, but I couldn't just leave it. I had to try to cover.

"The only reason I said that," I began, seeing the doomed

conversational path open wide in front of me and getting myself into sprinting position, "is that I'm supposed to be calling him. But I don't have a signal."

Yes. I had stolen Jeb's story. Sadly, though, when I spoke, I didn't take into account that my phone was sitting in front of me, proudly displaying a full range of bars. Stuart looked at it, then at me, but said nothing.

Now I *really* had something to prove. I would never be able to let it go until I showed him just how normal I was.

"I didn't," I said. "Until just now."

"Probably the weather," he said charitably.

"Probably. I'll just try now, really quick."

"Take as long as you like," he said.

Which was fair enough. He'd only sat with me to escape a long conversation about cups with Tinfoil Guy. It wasn't like we were accountable to each other's schedules. Stuart was probably glad that I was breaking off this conversation. He got up and took off his coat as I called. He was wearing a Target uniform underneath, and even more plastic bags. They came tumbling out of the inner folds of his coat, about a dozen of them. He gathered them up, completely unfazed.

When I got Noah's voice mail, I tried to hide my frustration by craning my head to look out the window. I didn't want to leave my pathetic follow-up message in front of Stuart, so I just hung up.

Stuart gave me a little "nothing?" shrug as he sat down.

"They must be busy with the Smorgasbord," I said.

"Smorgasbord?"

"Noah's family is tangentially Swedish, so they put out an amazing Smorgasbord on Christmas Eve."

I saw his eyebrow go up when I said "tangentially." I use that word a lot. It's one of Noah's favorites. I picked it up from him. I wish I'd remembered not to use it around other people, because it was kind of *our word*. Also, when on a campaign to convince a stranger that you aren't a few fries short of a Happy Meal, throwing around phrases like "tangentially Swedish" is not the best way to go.

"Everyone loves a Smorgasbord," he said graciously.

It was time for a change of topic.

"Target," I said, pointing at his shirt. Except I said, "Tarshay," in that French way that really isn't very funny.

"Absolutely," he said. "Now you can see why I had to risk my life getting to work. When your job is important as mine, you have to take some chances; otherwise, society doesn't function. That guy must really want to make a call."

Stuart pointed out the window, and I turned. Jeb was at the phone booth, which was surrounded by about a foot of snow. He was trying to force the door open.

"Poor Jeb," I said. "I should lend him my phone...now that I have a signal."

"Is that Jeb? You're right...Wait...how do you know Jeb?"

"He was on my train. He said he was coming to Gracetown.

 maureen johnson

I guess he plans on walking the rest of the way or something."

"It looks like he really, really wants to make a call," Stuart said, pulling aside the slippery candy cane on the window to get a better look. "Why doesn't he just use his phone?"

"His phone broke when we crashed."

"Crashed?" Stuart repeated. "Your train...crashed?"

"Just into snow."

Stuart was about to press a bit further on the train-crashing subject when the door opened, and in they poured. All fourteen of them, yelping and squealing and trailing snowflakes.

"Oh my God," I said.

* 40 *

Chapter Four

*T*here is nothing about a bad situation that fourteen hyper cheerleaders can't worsen.

It took about three minutes for the unassuming Waffle House to become the new offices of the law firm of Amber, Amber, Amber, and Madison. They set up camp in a clump of booths in the corner opposite from us. A few of them gave me an "oh, good, you are still alive" nod, but for the most part, they had no interest in anyone else.

This did not mean that no one had an interest in *them*, however.

Don-Keun was a new man. The moment they arrived, he vanished for a second. We heard muffled ecstatic screaming coming from somewhere in the back of the Waffle House kitchen, then he reappeared, his face shining with the kind of radiance usually associated with religious epiphany. Looking at him made me tired. Behind him were two more guys, awed acolytes following in his wake.

"What do you need, ladies?" Don-Keun called happily.

"Can we practice handstands in here?" Amber One said. I guess her basket-toss wrist was feeling better. Tough types, these cheerleaders. Tough and crazy. Who treks through a blizzard to practice handstands in a Waffle House? *I* only went there to get away from them.

"Ladies," he said, "you can do *whatever* you want."

Amber One liked this answer.

"Could you, maybe, like mop the floor? Just this bit right here? Just so we don't get stuff on our hands? And could you spot us?"

He almost broke his own ankles trying to get to the mop closet.

Stuart had been watching all of this wordlessly. He didn't have that same glorious look as Don-Keun or his friends, but the matter had clearly made his radar. He cocked his head to the side, like he was trying to figure out a really hard math problem.

"Things around here have deviated from the usual," he said.

"Yeah," I said. "You could say that. Is there anywhere else to go? A Starbucks or something?"

He almost flinched when I mentioned Starbucks. I guessed he was one of those antichain types, which seemed odd for someone who worked at Target.

"It's closed," he said. "Pretty much everything is. There's the Duke and Duchess. That might still be open, but that's just a convenience store. It's Christmas Eve, and with this storm..."

Stuart must have sensed my despair from the way I began lightly banging my forehead on the table.

"I'm going to get back to my house," he said, slipping his hand across the table as cushioning and preventing me from doing myself any more damage. "Why don't you come with me? At least it's out of the snow. My mom would never forgive me if I didn't ask you if you needed somewhere to go."

I thought this over. My cold, dead train was on the other side of the road. My current option was a Waffle House full of cheerleaders and a guy dressed in Reynolds Wrap. My parents were guests of the state, hundreds of miles away. And the biggest snowstorm in fifty years was right on top of us. Yeah, I needed somewhere to go.

Still, it was hard to unwire the "stranger danger" message that ran through my head...even though the stranger was really the one taking the chance. I had *all* the crazy cards tonight. I wouldn't have taken me home.

"Here," he said. "A little proof of identity. This is my official

Target employee card. They don't let just *anyone* work at Target. And here's a driver's license.... Ignore the haircut, please.... Name, address, social, it's all on there."

He pulled the cards out of his wallet to finish the joke. I noticed that there was a picture of him with a girl in the picture flap, obviously from a prom. That reassured me. He was a normal guy with a girlfriend. He even had a last name—Weintraub.

"How far is it?" I asked.

"About a half mile that way," he said, pointing at what appeared to be nothing at all—formless white lumps that could have been houses, could have been trees, could have been life-size models of Godzilla.

"A half mile?"

"Well, it's a half mile if we take the short way. The long way is a little over a mile. It won't be bad. I could have kept going, but this was open, so I just stopped for a warmth break."

"Are you sure your family won't mind?"

"My mom would literally beat me down with a hose if I didn't offer someone help on Christmas Eve."

Don-Keun vaulted the counter with a mop, almost impaling himself in the process. He started cleaning the floor around Amber One's feet. Outside, Jeb had gotten into the booth. He was deeply entrenched in a drama of his own. I was alone.

"Okay," I said. "I'll come."

I don't think anyone noticed our getting up and leaving except for Tinfoil Guy. He had his back turned to the cheerleaders in complete disinterest, and he saluted us as we headed for the door.

"You're going to need a hat," Stuart said, as we stepped into the frigid vestibule.

"I don't have a hat. I was going to Florida."

"I don't have a hat, either. But I have these..."

He held up the plastic bags and demonstrated by putting the bag on his head, wrapping it once around, and tucking it in so that it made a snug but strange-looking turban, puffed up at the top. Wearing a bag on your head seemed like something that Amber and Amber and Amber would have refused to do... and I felt like making a point that *I* wasn't like that. I gamely wound it around my head.

"You should really put them around your hands, too," he said, passing me a few more. "I don't know what to do about your legs. They have to be cold."

They were, but for some reason I didn't want him to think that I couldn't handle that.

"No," I lied. "These tights are really thick. And these boots... they're solid. I'll take them for my hands, though."

He raised an eyebrow. "You sure?"

"Positive." I had no idea why I was saying this. It just seemed like telling the truth would mean admitting some weakness.

Stuart had to push hard to fully open the door against the wind and accumulated snow. I didn't know snow could pour. I've seen flurries and even steady snow that left an inch or two, but this was sticky and heavy and the flakes were the size of quarters. Within seconds, I was drenched. I hesitated at the bottom of the steps, and Stuart turned around to check on me.

"Sure?" he asked again.

I knew that I was either going to turn right there and then, or I was going to have to go all the way.

I gave a quick look back and saw the three Madisons doing a handstand pyramid in the middle of the restaurant.

"Yes," I said. "Let's go."

Chapter Five

$\mathcal{W}$e took a small back road away from the Waffle House, guided only by the traffic warning lights that blinked on and off every other second, cutting a strobing yellow path through the dark. We walked right down the middle of the street, again in that postapocalyptic style. Silence reigned for at least fifteen minutes. Talking took energy we needed just to keep going, and opening our mouths meant that cold air could get in.

Every step was a tiny trial. The snow was so deep and sticky that it took a lot of force to withdraw my foot from my own footprint. My legs, of course, were frozen to the point where they started to feel warm again. The bags on my head and hands were somewhat effective. When we had set our pace, Stuart cracked open the conversation.

"Where is your family really?" he asked.

"In jail."

"Yeah. You said that inside. But when I said *really*—"

"They're *in jail*," I said for the third time.

I tried to make this one stick. He got the point enough not to ask the question again, but he had to wrestle with my answer for a moment.

"For what?" he finally said.

"Uh, they were part of a...riot."

"What, are they protesters?"

"They're shoppers," I said. "They were in a shopping riot."

He stopped dead in his spot.

"Don't even tell me that they were in the Flobie riot in Charlotte."

"That's the one," I said.

"Oh my God! Your parents are in the Flobie Five!"

"The Flobie Five?" I repeated weakly.

"The Flobie Five were *the* topic of the day at work. I think every other customer brought them up. They had footage of the riot playing all day on the news...."

News? Footage? All day? Oh, good. Good, good, good. Famous parents—just what every girl dreams of.

"Everyone loves the Flobie Five," he said. "Well, a lot of people do. Or, at least, people think it's funny."

But then he must have realized it wasn't so funny for me,

and that that was the reason I was wandering through a strange town on Christmas Eve with bags on my head.

"It makes you very cool," he said, taking big, jumping steps to get in front of me. "CNN would interview you, for sure. Daughter of Flobie! But don't worry. I'll keep them back!"

He made a big display of pretending to hold back reporters and punching photographers, which was tricky choreography. It did cheer me up a little. I started playing the part a little myself, throwing my hands up over my face as if flashbulbs were going off. We did this for a while. It was a good distraction from our reality.

"It's ridiculous," I finally said, after I almost fell over as I tried to dodge an imaginary paparazzo. "My parents are in jail. Over a ceramic Santa house."

"Better than for dealing crack," he said, falling back in line beside me. "Right? Must be."

"Are you always this chipper?"

"Always. It's a requirement for working at Target. I'm like Captain Smiley."

"Your girlfriend must love that!"

I only said it to make myself seem clever and observant, expecting him to say, "How did you know that I…?" And I would say, "I saw the photo in your wallet." And he would think I was very Sherlock Holmes and I would seem a little less deranged than I first appeared back at the Waffle House.

(Sometimes, you have to wait a little bit for this kind of gratification, but it's still worth it.)

Instead, he just whipped his head around quickly in my direction, blinked, and then turned back down the road with a very determined stride. The playfulness was gone, and he was all business.

"It's not too much farther. But this is where we have to decide. There are two ways we can go from here. The down-this-road way, which will probably take us another forty-five minutes at the rate we're going. Or the shortcut."

"The shortcut," I answered immediately. "Obviously."

"It *is* way, way shorter, because this road bends around and the shortcut goes straight through. I'd definitely take it if it was just me, which it was up until a half an hour ago...."

"Shortcut," I said again.

Standing in that storm, with the snow and wind burning the skin off my face and my head and hands wrapped in plastic bags—I felt I really didn't need any more information. Whatever this shortcut was, it couldn't be much worse than what we were already doing. And if Stuart had been planning on taking it before, there was no reason why he couldn't take it with me.

"Okay," Stuart said. "Basically, the shortcut takes us behind these houses. My house is just behind there, about two hundred yards. I think. Something like that."

We left the blinking yellow path and cut down a completely

shadowy path between some houses. I pulled my phone out of my pocket to check it as we walked. There was no call from Noah. I tried to be stealthy about this, but Stuart saw me.

"No call?" he asked.

"Not yet. He must still be busy."

"Does he know about your parents?"

"He knows," I said. "I tell him everything."

"Does that go both ways?" he asked.

"Does what go both ways?"

"You said you tell him everything," he replied. "You didn't say *we* tell *each other* everything."

What kind of question was that? "Of course," I said quickly.

"What's he like, aside from being tangentially Swedish?"

"He's smart," I said. "But he's not obnoxious smart, like one of those people who always have to tell you their GPA, or give you subtle hints about their SAT score or class rank or whatever. It's just natural to him. He doesn't work that hard for grades, and he doesn't care that much. But they're good. Really good. Plays soccer. He's in Mathletes. He's really popular."

Yes, I actually said that. Yes, it sounded like some kind of sales pitch. Yes, Stuart got that smirky I'm-trying-not-to-laugh-at-you look again. But how was I supposed to answer that question? Everyone I knew knew Noah. They knew what he was, what he represented. I didn't usually have to explain.

"Good résumé," he said, not sounding all that impressed.

"But what's he like?" Oh, God. This conversation was going to go on.

"He's...like what I just said."

"Personality-wise. Is he secretly a poet or something? Does he dance around his room when he thinks no one is looking? Is he funny, like you? What's his *essence*?"

Stuart had to have been playing with my head with this essence stuff. Although, there was something about how he had asked if Noah was funny, like me. That was kind of nice. And the answer was no. Noah was many things, but funny was not one of them. He usually seemed relatively amused by me, but as you may have noticed by now, sometimes I can't shut up. On those occasions, he just looked tired.

"Intense," I said. "His essence is intense."

"Good intense?"

"Would I date him otherwise? Is it much farther?"

Stuart got the message this time and shut up. We walked on in silence until it was just empty space with a few trees. I could see that far off, at the top of an incline, there were more houses. I could just make out the distant glow of holiday lights. The snow was so thick in the air that everything was blurry. It would have been beautiful, if it didn't sting so much. I realized my hands had gotten so cold that they'd rounded the corner and now almost felt hot. My legs wouldn't last much longer.

Stuart put his arm out and stopped me.

"Okay," he said. "I have to explain something. We're going over a little creek. It's frozen. I saw people sliding on it earlier."

"How deep a creek?"

"Not that deep. Maybe five feet."

"Where is it?"

"It's somewhere right in front of us," he said.

I looked out over the blank horizon. Somewhere under there was a small body of water, hidden under the snow.

"We can go back," he said.

"You were going to go this way, no matter what?" I asked.

"Yeah, but you don't have to prove anything to me."

"It's fine," I said, trying to sound more certain than I felt. "So, we just keep walking?"

"That's the plan."

So that's what we did. We knew we'd hit the creek when the snow got a little less deep, and there was a slight slipperiness underneath us instead of the thick, crunching, solid feeling. This is when Stuart decided to speak again.

"Those guys back at the Waffle House are so lucky. They're about to have the best night of their lives," he said.

There was something in his tone that sounded like a challenge, like he wanted me to take the bait. Which means I shouldn't have. But I did, of course.

"God," I said. "Why are all guys so easy like that?"

"Like what?" he said, giving me a sideways glance, slipping in the process.

"Saying that they're lucky."

"Because…they're trapped in a Waffle House with a dozen cheerleaders?"

"Where does this arrogant fantasy come from?" I said, maybe a little more sharply than I intended. "Do guys really believe that if they are the only male in the area, that girls will suddenly crawl on top of them? Like we scavenge for lone survivors and reward them with group make-out sessions?"

"That *isn't* what happens?" he asked.

I didn't even dignify that remark with a comeback.

"But what's wrong with cheerleaders?" he asked, sounding very pleased that he'd gotten such a rise out of me. "I'm not saying I *only* like cheerleaders. I'm just not prejudiced against them."

"It's not prejudice," I said firmly.

"It's not? What is it then?"

"It's the idea of cheerleaders," I said. "Girls, on the sidelines, in short skirts, telling guys that they're great. Chosen for their looks."

"I don't know," he said tauntingly. "Judging groups of people you don't know, making assumptions, talking about their looks…it *sounds* like prejudice, but—"

"I am *not prejudiced*!" I shot back, unable to control my reaction now. There was so much darkness around us at that moment. Above us, there was a hazy pewter-pink sky. Around us, there were only the outlines of the skinny bare trees, like thin hands bursting out of the earth. Endless white ground below, and swirling flakes, and a lonely whistle of wind, and the shadows of houses.

"Look," Stuart said, refusing to quit this annoying game, "how do you know that in their spare time, they aren't EMTs or something? Maybe they save kittens, or run food banks, or—"

"Because they don't," I said, stepping ahead of him. I slipped a little but jerked myself upright. "In their spare time, they get waxings."

"You don't know that," he called from behind me.

"I wouldn't have to explain this to Noah," I said. "He would just get it."

"You know," Stuart said evenly, "as wonderful as you think this Noah is—I'm not all that impressed with him right now."

I'd had it. I turned around and started walking the way we had come, taking hard, firm steps.

"Where are you going?" he asked. "Oh, come on…"

He tried to make it sound like it was no big deal, but I had simply had it. I stamped down hard to keep my gait steady.

"It's a long way back!" he said, hurrying to catch up with me. "Don't. Seriously."

"I'm sorry," I said, like I didn't really care very much. "I just think it would be better if I…"

There was a noise. A new noise under the whistle and the squeak and shift of ice and snow. It was a snapping noise that sounded kind of like a log on a fire, which was unpleasantly ironic. We both stopped exactly where we stood. Stuart flashed me a look of alarm.

"Don't mov—"

And then the surface beneath us just went away.

Chapter Six

*M*aybe you've never fallen into a frozen stream. Here's what happens.

1. It is cold. So cold that the Department of Temperature Acknowledgment and Regulation in your brain gets the readings and says, "I can't deal with this. I'm out of here." It puts up the OUT TO LUNCH sign and passes all responsibility to the...

2. Department of Pain and the Processing Thereof, which gets all this gobbledygook from the temperature department that it can't understand. "This is so not our job," it says. So it just starts hitting random buttons, filling you with strange and unpleasant sensations, and calls the...

3. Office of Confusion and Panic, where there is always someone ready to hop on the phone the moment it rings. This

office is at least willing to take some action. The Office of
Confusion and Panic *loves* hitting buttons.

So, for a split second, Stuart and I were unable to do anything because of this bureaucratic mess going on in our heads.
When we recovered a little, I was able to take some stock
of what was happening to me. The good news was, we were
only in up to our chests. Well, I was. The water came exactly
breast-high. Stuart was in up to his mid-abdomen. The bad
news was, we were in a hole in the ice, and it's hard to get out
of a hole in the ice when you are pretty much paralyzed with
cold. We both tried to climb out, but the ice just kept breaking
every time we put pressure on it.

As an automatic reaction, we grabbed each other.

"Okay," Stuart said, shivering hard. "This is c-cold. And
kind of bad."

"No? Really?" I screamed. Except there wasn't enough air
in my lungs to allow me to scream, so it came out like a spooky
little hiss.

"We...s-should...b-break it."

This idea had occurred to me, too, but it was reassuring to
hear it said out loud. We both started smashing at the ice with
stiff, robotlike arms, until we reached the thick crust. The
water was a bit shallower, but not by much.

"I'll boost you up with my hand," Stuart said. "Step up."

When I tried to move my leg, it refused to cooperate right

away. My legs were so numb that they didn't really work anymore. Once I got them going, Stuart's hands were too cold to support me. It took some tries, but I eventually got a foothold.

Of course, once I got up, I made the important discovery that *ice is slippery*, and therefore very hard to hold on to, especially when your hands are also covered in wet bags. I reached back and helped pull Stuart, who landed flat on the ice.

We were out. And being out felt a lot worse than being in, weirdly enough.

"Iss...not...tha...far," he said. It was hard to understand him. My lungs felt like they were wobbling. He grabbed my hand and pulled me toward a house just at the top of the rise. If he hadn't dragged me, I would never have made it up the hill.

I have never, ever been so happy to see a house. It was entirely outlined by a faint greenish glow, interspersed with tiny dots of red. The back door was unlocked, and we stepped into a paradise. It wasn't that it was the most amazing house I had ever been in—it was simply a house, with warmth, and a residual smell of cooked turkey and cookies and tree.

Stuart didn't stop pulling me until we reached a door, which turned out to lead to a bathroom with a glass shower stall.

"Here," he said, pressing me in. "Shower. Now. Warm water."

The door slammed and I heard him run off. I stripped off what I was wearing immediately, stumbling as I reached for the shower knob. My clothes were frighteningly heavy, full of water and snow and mud.

I stayed in there a long time, slumped against the wall, filling the little room with steam. The water changed temperature once or twice, probably because Stuart was also taking a shower somewhere else in the house.

I turned off the water only when it started to go cold. When I emerged into the thick steam, I saw that my clothes were gone. Someone had extracted them from the bathroom without my noticing. In their place were two large towels, a pair of sweatpants, a sweatshirt, socks, and slippers. The clothes were for a guy, except for the socks and slippers. The socks were thick and pink, and the slippers were white fluffy booties, very worn.

I grabbed for the nearest item, which was a sweatshirt, and held it up to my naked self, even though I was clearly alone in the bathroom now. *Someone* had come in. *Someone* had been lurking around, removing my clothes and replacing them with new, dry ones. Had Stuart let himself in while I was showering? Had he seen me in my natural state? Did I even care at this point?

I dressed quickly, putting on every single item that had been left for me. I opened the door a crack and peered out. The kitchen appeared empty. I opened the door wider, and suddenly a woman popped out of nowhere. She was mom-aged, with curly blonde hair that looked like it had been fried by using a home coloring kit. She was wearing a sweatshirt with a picture of two hugging koalas in Santa hats. The only thing I really cared about, though, was the fact that she was holding out a steaming mug.

"You poor thing!" she said. She was really loud, one of those people you can easily hear across entire parking lots. "Stuart's upstairs. I'm his mom."

I accepted the mug. It could have been a cup of hot poison, but I would have drunk it anyway.

"Poor thing," she said again. "Don't you worry. We'll get you warm again. Sorry I couldn't find anything to fit you better. Those are Stuart's, and the only clean ones I could find in the laundry. I put your clothes in the washer, and your shoes and coat are drying on the heater. If you need to call anyone, you just go right ahead. Don't worry if it's long distance."

This was my introduction to Stuart's mom ("Call me Debbie"). I'd known her for all of twenty seconds, and already she had seen my underwear and was offering me her son's clothes. She immediately planted me at the kitchen table and started pulling out endless Saran-wrapped plates from the refrigerator.

"We had Christmas Eve dinner while Stuart was at work, but I made plenty! Plenty! Eat up!"

There was a lot of food: turkey and mashed potatoes, gravy,

stuffing, the works. She brought *all* of it out and insisted on making me a big plateful, with a hot cup of chicken-dumpling soup on the side. By this point, I was hungry—maybe hungrier than I'd ever been in my life.

Stuart reappeared in the doorway. Like me, he was dressed for warmth. He was wearing flannel pajama bottoms and a stretched-out cable sweater. I don't know...maybe it was the sense of gratitude, my general happiness at being alive, the absence of a bag on his head...but he was kind of good-looking. And any of my former annoyance with him was gone.

"You'll set Julie up for the night?" she asked. "Make sure to turn off the tree so it doesn't keep her awake."

"I'm sorry..." I said. It was only now that I realized that I had just crashed into their lives on Christmas.

"Don't you apologize! I'm glad you had the sense to come here! We'll take care of you. Make sure she has enough blankets, Stuart."

"There will be blankets," he assured her.

"She needs one now. Look. She's freezing. So do you. Sit here."

She hustled into the living room. Stuart raised his eyebrows as if to say, *This may go on for a while.* She returned with two fleece throws. I was wrapped in a deep blue one. She swaddled me in it, like I was a baby, to the point where it was kind of hard to move my arms.

"You need more hot chocolate," she said. "Or tea? We have all kinds."

"I've got it, Mom," Stuart said.

"More soup? Eat the soup. That's homemade, and chicken soup is like natural penicillin. After the chill you've both had—"

"I've got it, Mom."

Debbie took my half-empty soup cup, refilled it to the top, and put it in the microwave.

"Make sure she knows where everything is, Stuart. If you want anything during the night, you just get it. You make yourself at home. You're one of ours now, Julie."

I appreciated the sentiment, but I thought that was a strange way of putting it.

Chapter Seven

Stuart and I spent several quiet moments contentedly stuffing our faces once Debbie was gone. Except, I got the feeling that she wasn't really gone—I never heard her walk away. I think Stuart felt this, too, because he kept turning around.

"This soup really is amazing," I said, because that sounded like a good remark to have overheard. "I've never had anything like it. It's the dumplings..."

"You're probably not Jewish, that's why," he said, getting up and shutting the accordion kitchen door. "Those are matzo balls."

"You're Jewish?"

Stuart held up a finger, indicating I should wait. He rattled the door a little, and there was a series of rapid, creaking steps, like someone trying to hurry quietly up the stairs.

"Sorry," he said. "I thought we had company. Must have been mice. Yeah, my mom is, so technically, yes. But she has this thing about Christmas. I think she does it to fit in. She goes kind of overboard, though."

The kitchen had been completely converted for the season. The hand towels, the toaster cover, the fridge magnets, the curtains, the tablecloth, the centerpiece…the more I looked, the more Christmasy it got.

"Did you note the fake electric holly on the way in?" Stuart asked. "Our house is never going to be on the cover of *Southern Jew* at this rate."

"So, why…"

He shrugged.

"Because it's what people do," he said, picking up another piece of turkey, folding it, and shoving it in his mouth. "Especially around here. There isn't exactly what you would call a thriving Jewish community. My Hebrew-school class was just me and one other girl."

"Your girlfriend?"

Something passed over his face, a rapid wave of forehead wrinkling and mouth twitching that I suspected was a suppressed laugh.

"Just because there's only two of us doesn't mean we have

to pair-bond," he said. "It's not like someone says, 'Okay—you two Jews! Dance!' No, she's not my girlfriend."

"Sorry," I said quickly. This was the second time I had mentioned his girlfriend—trying to show off my observational skill—and again, he just deflected. That was it. No more mentioning it. He obviously didn't want to talk about her. Which was a little odd…he seemed like the type who would happily rattle on about his girlfriend for about seven hours. He just gave that vibe.

"It's okay." He reached for more turkey, looking like he had already forgotten how dumb I could be sometimes. "I tend to think that people like having us around. Like we add something to the neighborhood. We have a playground, an efficient recycling setup, and two Jewish families."

"But isn't it weird?" I asked, picking up the snowman salt shaker. "All these Christmas decorations?"

"Maybe. But it's just a big holiday, you know? It all feels so fake that it seems okay. My mom just likes to celebrate anything, really. Our relatives in other places think it's strange that we have a tree, but trees are nice. It's not like a tree is religious."

"True," I said. "What does your dad think?"

"No idea. He doesn't live here."

Stuart didn't seem very troubled by this fact. He beat another little rhythm on the table to brush the subject away, and stood.

"I'll get you set up for the night," he said. "Be right back."

I got up to have a look around. There were *two* Christmas trees: a tiny one in the picture window, and a massive one—easily eight feet high—in the corner. It was practically bent over from the weight of all the handmade ornaments, the multiple strings of lights, and what must have been ten boxes of silver tinsel.

There was a piano in the living room that was loaded down with opened pages of music, some with comments written on the pages in pen. I don't play any instruments, so all music looks complicated to me—but this looked even more complicated than normal. Someone here knew what they were doing. This wasn't just "piano as furniture."

What really caught my eye, though, was what was sitting on top of the piano. It was much smaller, much less technically complex than ours, but it was a Flobie Santa Village nonetheless, framed with a little barrier of garland.

"You must know what these are," Stuart said, coming down the stairs with a massive load of blankets and pillows, which he dumped on the sofa.

I did, of course. They had five pieces—the Merry Men Café, the gumdrop shop, Festive Frank's Supply Store, the Elfateria, and the ice-cream parlor.

"I guess you guys have more of these than we do," he said.

"We have fifty-six pieces."

He whistled in appreciation, and reached over to switch

on the power. Unlike us, they didn't have a fancy system for switching all the houses on at once. He had to turn the dimmer dial on each one, clicking it to life.

"My mom thinks they're worth something," he said. "She treats them like they're *the precious*."

"They all think that," I said sympathetically.

I looked the pieces over with an expert eye. I don't usually advertise the fact, but I actually know a lot about the Flobie Santa Village, for obvious reasons. I could hold my own at any dealer's show.

"Well," I said, pointing at the Merry Men Café, "this one is kind of worth something. See how it's brick, with green around the windows? This is a first-generation piece. In the second year, they made the windowsills black."

I picked it up carefully and checked the bottom.

"It's not a numbered piece," I said, examining the base. "But still…any first-generation piece with a noticeable difference is good. And they retired the Merry Men Café five years ago, so that makes it worth a bit more. This would go for about four hundred dollars, except that it looks like your chimney was broken off and glued back on."

"Oh, yeah. My sister did that."

"You have a sister?"

"Rachel," Stuart said. "She's five. Don't worry. You'll meet her. And that was kind of amazing."

"I don't think amazing is the right word for that. Maybe *sad*."

He switched all the houses back off.

"Who plays the piano?" I asked.

"Me. It's my talent. I guess we all have one."

Stuart made a kind of ridiculous face, which made me laugh.

"You shouldn't dismiss it," I said. "Schools love people who have musical skills."

God, I sounded so...well, so like one of those people who do things only because they think it will make colleges like them. I was shocked when I realized that was a Noah quote. I had never thought of it as being so obnoxious before.

"Sorry," I said. "I'm just tired."

He waved this away, as if it required no explanation or apology.

"So do mothers," he said. "And neighbors. I'm sort of the performing monkey of the subdivision. Luckily, I also like to play, so it works out. So...the sheets and pillows are for you, and..."

"I'm fine," I said. "This is great. It's really nice of you to let me stay."

"Like I said, it's no problem."

He turned to go but stopped halfway up the stairs.

"Hey," he said, "I'm sorry if I was kind of a dick earlier, when we were walking. It was just..."

"Walking in the storm," I said. "I know. It was cold; we were grouchy. Don't worry about it. I'm sorry, too. And thanks."

He looked like he was about to say something else but simply nodded and started back up the stairs. I heard him reach the top, then back down a few. He peered through the top rails.

"Merry Christmas," he added, before disappearing.

This is when it really hit me. My eyes filled up. I missed my family. I missed Noah. I missed home. These people had done all they could, but they weren't my family. Stuart wasn't my boyfriend. I lay there for a long time, twisting on the sofa, listening to a dog snoring somewhere upstairs (I think it was the dog), watching two hours burn away on the very loud ticky-ticky clock.

I simply couldn't stand it.

My phone was in my coat pocket, so I went searching for where my clothes had been stashed. I found them in the laundry room. The coat had been hung up over a heating vent. Apparently, my phone hadn't liked being completely submerged in cold water. The screen was blank. No wonder I hadn't heard from him.

There was a phone on the kitchen counter. I quietly crept out and took it from the cradle and dialed Noah's number. It rang four times before he answered. He sounded very confused when he answered. His voice was tired and deep.

"It's me," I whispered.

"Lee?" he croaked. "What time is it?"

"Three in the morning," I said. "You never called back."

Assorted snuffling noises, as he tried to clear his thoughts.

"Sorry. It was busy all night. You know my mom and the Smorgasbord. Can we talk tomorrow? I'll call you as soon as we finish opening gifts."

I fell silent. I had braved the biggest storm of the year—many years—I had fallen into a frozen creek, and my parents were imprisoned...and he *still* couldn't talk to me?

But...he had had a long night, and it seemed a waste to force my story on him when he was half asleep. People can't really sympathize with you properly when you've woken them up, and I needed him at 100 percent for this.

"Sure," I said. "Tomorrow."

I climbed back into my cave of blankets and pillows. They had a strong, unfamiliar smell. Not bad—just a very strong detergent that I'd never smelled before.

Sometimes, I just didn't *get* Noah. Sometimes I even felt like he dated me as part of his plan, like they were going to have a checklist on the application, and one of the things to tick off was going to be, "Do you have a reasonably intelligent girlfriend who shares your aspirations, and who is fully prepared to accept your limited availability? One who likes to listen to you talk about your own accomplishments for hours at a time?"

No. This was fear and cold talking. This was being in a strange place away from my family. This was stress over the fact that my parents had been arrested in a riot for ceramic houses. And if I just slept, my brain would go back to normal.

I closed my eyes and felt the world swirling with snow. I was dizzy for a moment, and slightly nauseous, and then I was fast, fast asleep, dreaming of waffle sandwiches and cheerleaders doing splits on the tables.

Chapter Eight

*M*orning came in the form of a five-year-old leaping onto my stomach. My eyes popped open from the force.

"Who are you?" she said excitedly. "I'm Rachel!"

"Rachel! Stop jumping on her! She's sleeping!"

This was Stuart's mom's voice.

Rachel was a highly freckled mini-Stuart with incredibly bed-messy hair and a huge smile. She smelled vaguely of Cheerios, and she needed a bath. Debbie was right there as well, nursing a cup of coffee while she switched on the Flobie Santa Village. Stuart stepped out from the direction of the kitchen.

I hate it when I wake up to find that people have been creeping around me and have seen me asleep. Unfortunately, it happens to me a lot. I can sleep like a champion. I once slept through a smoke alarm going off. For three hours. *In my bedroom.*

"We're going to put off opening our presents," Debbie said. "So this morning, we can all just have something to eat and have a nice talk!"

This was clearly for my benefit, as there were no gifts for me. Rachel's face looked like it was going to split in two, like a piece of overripe fruit. Stuart looked to his mother, as if asking if this was really a good idea.

"Except for Rachel," she said quickly.

It's amazing how quickly little kids' moods can shift. She went from total despair to elation in the time it normally takes to sneeze.

"No," I said. "No, you guys should, too."

Debbie was shaking her head firmly and smiling.

"Stuart and I can wait. Why don't you go and get yourself ready for some breakfast?"

I slunk off to the bathroom, head down, to try to do some basic morning repair. My hair looked like it was trying out for the comedy circuit, and my skin was raw and chapped. I did my best with cold water and decorative hand soaps, which is to say, I didn't make a lot of progress.

"Do you want to call your family?" Debbie asked when I emerged. "Wish them a happy holiday?"

I found myself looking to Stuart for help with this one.

"That may be hard," he said. "They're in the Flobie Five."

So much for hiding that fact. Debbie didn't seem put out by it, though. Instead, she got a gleam in her eye like she'd just met a celebrity.

"Your parents were in that?" she asked. "Oh, why didn't you say? I love the Flobie Santa Village. And it was so silly to put them in jail. The Flobie Five! Oh, I'm sure they'll let them talk on the phone to their daughter! At Christmas! It's not like they killed somebody."

Stuart looked up at me knowingly, as if to say, *Told you*.

"I don't even know what jail they're in," I said. I felt guilty as soon as I said it. My parents were wasting away in a cell somewhere, and I didn't even know where.

"Well, that's easy enough to find out. Stuart, go online and find out what jail they're in. It has to be on the news."

Stuart was already on his way out of the room, saying he was on it.

"Stuart's a wizard with those kinds of things," she said.

"What kinds of things?"

"Oh, he can find anything online."

Debbie was one of those parents who still hadn't quite grasped that using the Internet was not exactly wizardry, and that we could *all* find anything online. I didn't say this, because you don't want people to feel that they've missed something really obvious, even when they have.

Stuart came back in with the information, and Debbie made the call.

maureen johnson

"I *will* get them to let you talk to your parents," she said, holding her hand over the receiver. "They have no idea how persist— Oh, hello?"

It sounded like they were giving her a bit of trouble, but Debbie beat them down. Sam would have been impressed. She handed me the phone and retreated from the kitchen, all smiles. Stuart picked up a wriggling Rachel and carried her out, as well.

"Jubilee?" my mom said. "Honey! Are you okay? Did you just get to Florida? How are Grandma and Grandpa? Oh, honey..."

"I'm not in Florida. The train never made it. I'm in Gracetown."

"Gracetown?" she repeated. "You only made it that far? Oh, Jubilee...where are you? Are you all right? Are you still on the train?"

I didn't quite feel up to telling the whole story of the last twenty-four hours, so I made it nice and short.

"The train got stuck," I said. "We had to get off. I met some people. I'm staying at their house."

"People?" Her voice hit a high pitch of concern, the kind that said that she suspected drug dealers and molesters. "What kind of *people*?"

"Nice people, Mom. A mom and two kids. They have a Flobie Santa Village. Not as big as ours, but some of the same pieces. They have the gumdrop shop, with the full display. And the gingerbread bakery. They even have a first-generation Merry Men Café."

"Oh," she said, somewhat relieved.

I think my parents think you have to have *some* kind of moral character to be in the Flobie crew. Social deviants don't take the time to lovingly set the tiny gingerbread men displays in the window of the bakery. And yet, lots of people would take that as a sign that someone was unhinged. One person's crazy is another person's sane, I guess. Plus, I thought I was being pretty crafty by describing Stuart as one of "two kids" instead of "some guy I met at a Waffle House with plastic bags on his head."

"Are you still there?" she asked. "What about your train?"

"I think it's still stuck. It got caught in a snowbank last night, and they had to turn down the power and the heat. That's why we got off."

Again, pretty clever to say "we" as opposed to "just me, wandering across a six-lane interstate during a blizzard." It wasn't a lie, either. Jeb and the Ambers and Madisons had made the trek themselves, just after I blazed the trail. Being sixteen means you have to be a genius conversational editor.

"How's..." How do you ask your mom how *jail* is?

"We're fine," she said bravely. "We're... Oh, Julie. Oh, honey. I am so sorry about this. So, so sorry. We didn't mean..."

I could hear that she was about to completely lose it, and that meant that I would soon lose it if I didn't stop her.

"I'm fine," I said. "The people here are taking really good care of me."

"Can I speak to them?"

Them meant Debbie, so I called to her. She got on the phone and had one of those mother-to-mother talks where they express concern for children as a whole and make a lot of scrunched-up faces. Debbie was well up to the task of reassuring my mother, and in listening to her talk, I discovered that she wasn't going to let me go anywhere for at least a day. I heard her shoot down the idea that my train was going anywhere, that there was any chance at all I was going to make it to Florida.

"Don't you worry," she said to my mom. "We're going to take good care of your girl here. We have lots of good food, and we'll keep her nice and snug and warm until things clear up. She'll have a good holiday, I promise you. And we'll send her right back up to you."

A pause while my mother made high-pitched sisterly devotions of gratitude.

"It is no trouble at all!" Debbie went on. "She's an absolute pleasure. And isn't this what the holidays are all about? You just take care of yourselves in there. We Flobie fans are rooting for you."

When she hung up, Debbie was wiping at her eyes and writing a number on her "Elf List" magnetized refrigerator notepad.

"I should call about my train," I said. "If that's okay."

I couldn't get anyone on the phone, probably because it was Christmas, but a recorded voice said that there were "substantial delays." I looked out the window as I listened to it cycle through menu choices. It was still snowing. It wasn't as end-of-the-worldly as last night, but it was pretty steady.

Debbie lingered for a bit but then drifted off. I dialed Noah's number. He picked it up on the seventh ring.

"Noah!" I said, keeping my voice low. "It's me! I'm—"

"Hey!" he said. "Listen, we're all about to sit down and have breakfast."

"I've kind of had a rough night," I said.

"Oh, no. Sorry, Lee. Listen, I'll call you back in a little while, okay? I have the number. Merry Christmas!"

No "I love you." No "My holiday is ruined without you."

Now, I felt myself losing it. I got all choked up, but I didn't want to be one of those girlfriends who sob when their boyfriends can't talk…even if my circumstances were a little beyond normal.

"Sure," I said, holding my voice steady. "Later. Merry Christmas."

And then I ran for the bathroom.

Chapter Nine

*Y*ou can only spend so long in a bathroom without arousing suspicion. Over a half an hour, and people are staring at the door, wondering about you. I was in there at least that long, sitting in the shower stall with the door closed, sobbing into a hand towel that read LET IT SNOW!

Yeah, let it snow. Let it snow and snow and bury me. Very funny, Life.

I was kind of terrified to come out, but when I did, I found that the kitchen was empty. It had been cheered up a bit, though. There was a Christmas candle burning on the middle bit of the stove, the Bing Crosby tunes were rocking out, and a steaming pot of fresh coffee and a cake were waiting on the counter. Debbie appeared from the laundry room next to the stove.

"I had Stuart go next door to borrow a snowsuit for Rachel," she said. "She outgrew her last one, and the people next door have one just her size. He'll be back soon."

She gave me a knowing nod that said, *I know you needed some private time. I have your back.*

"Thanks," I said, sitting down at the table.

"And I spoke to your grandparents," Debbie added. "Your mother gave me their number. They were concerned, but I set their minds at rest. Don't worry, Jubilee. I know holidays can be hard, but we'll try to make this one special for you."

Obviously, my mom had told her my real name. She pronounced it carefully, as if she wanted me to know that she had taken note of it. That she was being sincere.

"They're usually great," I said. "I've never had a bad holiday before."

Debbie got up and poured me some of the coffee, setting the cup down in front of me, along with a gallon of milk and a massive sugar bowl.

"I know that this must be a very rough experience for you," she said, "but I believe in miracles. I know it sounds corny, but I do. And I feel like you coming here has been a little one for us."

I glanced up at her as I poured milk into my coffee and almost flooded the cup. I had noticed a sign in the bathroom that said FREE HUGS GIVEN HERE! There's nothing wrong with that—Debbie was clearly a nice person—but she maybe veered toward the goofy side of soppy.

"Thanks?" I said.

"What I mean is…Stuart looks happier today than he has in…Well, I probably shouldn't be saying this, but…Well, he may already have told you. He tells everyone, and you two already seem to have hit it off, so…"

"Told me what?"

"About Chloe," she said, wide-eyed. "Didn't he tell you?"

"Who's Chloe?"

Debbie had to get up and slice me a thick piece of cake before she could answer. And I do mean thick. Harry Potter volume seven thick. I could have knocked out a burglar with this piece of cake. Once I tasted it, though, it seemed just the right size. Debbie didn't fool around when it came to the butter and sugar.

"Chloe," she said, lowering her voice, "was Stuart's girlfriend. They broke up three months ago, and he…well, he's such a sweet guy…he took it so hard. She was terrible to him. Terrible. Last night was the first night in a long time that I saw a spark of the old Stuart, when you were sitting there with him."

"I…what?"

"Stuart has such a good heart," she went on, oblivious to the fact that I had frozen, a bite of cake halfway to my mouth.

"When his father, and Rachel's father, my ex-husband, left, he was just twelve. But you should have seen how he helped me and how he was with Rachel. He's such a good guy."

I didn't know where to begin. There was something shockingly awkward about discussing Stuart's breakup with his mom. The expression is: a boy's best friend is his mother. It's not: a boy's best *pimp* is his mother. It's that way for a reason.

Even worse, if it could get any worse, which it apparently could...I was the balm that had healed her son's wounds. Her Christmas miracle. She was going to keep me here forever, stuffing me with cake and dressing me in oversize sweatshirts. I would be Bride of Flobie.

"You live in Richmond, right?" she chattered on. "That's, what, a two- or three-hour drive...."

I was thinking about locking myself in the bathroom again, when Rachel came bounding in the doorway and skidding up to me in her slippers. She climbed halfway up onto my lap and studied my eyes up close. She still needed a bath.

"What's the matter?" she said. "Why are you crying?"

"She misses her family," Debbie said. "It's Christmas, and she can't see them because of the snow."

"We'll take care of you," Rachel said, taking my hand and doing that adorable "let me tell you a secret" voice that little kids can get away with. In the light of her mother's recent comments, though, it seemed kind of threatening.

"That's nice, Rachel," Debbie said. "Why don't you go and brush your teeth like a big girl? Jubilee here can brush her teeth."

Can, but hadn't. No toothbrush in my backpack. I was really not at my best when I packed.

I heard the front door open, and a moment later, Stuart arrived in the kitchen with the snowsuit.

"I just had to look at two hundred photos on a digital picture frame," he said. "Two hundred. Mrs. Henderson really wanted me to know just how amazing it was that it could hold two hundred photos. Did I mention that there were *two hundred* of them? Anyway."

He set the snowsuit down, then excused himself to go change his jeans, which were soaked from the snow.

"Don't you worry," Debbie said, as he left. "I'm going to take the little miss to go play outside so you can relax. You and Stuart both got terrible chills last night. You're staying in here and keeping warm at least until we can find out about your train. I promised your mom I would look after you. So you and Stuart stay in here and hang out. Have some nice hot chocolate, something to eat, cuddle up under a blanket..."

Under any other circumstances, I would have assumed that that last sentence meant, "Cuddle up under *two separate* blankets, spaced several feet apart, possibly with a lightly chained wolf between you," because that's what parents always mean. I got a feeling from Debbie that she was fine with the situation, however we wanted to roll. If we felt the need to sit on the sofa and share a blanket to conserve body heat, she was not going to object. In fact, she was likely to turn down the heat and hide all the blankets but one. She took the snowsuit and went off in search of Rachel.

It was so alarming, I temporarily forgot my trauma.

"You look spooked," Stuart said when he returned. "Has my mom been scaring you?"

I laughed a little too hard and coughed on my cake, and Stuart gave me the same look that he'd given me at the Waffle House the night before, when I was rambling on about tangential Swedishness and my bad cell-phone reception. But, like last night, he didn't comment on my behavior. He just got himself a cup of coffee and watched me from the corner of his eye.

"She's taking my sister out for a while," he said. "So it's just going to be us. What do you want to do?"

I put more cake in my mouth and fell silent.

Chapter Ten

Five minutes later, we were in the living room, the tiny Flobie Santa Village twinkling away. Stuart and I sat on the sofa, but not, as Debbie had probably hoped, snuggling under the same blanket. We had two separate ones, and I sat with my legs tucked up, forming a protective knee barrier. Upstairs, I could hear the muffled cries of Rachel as she was shoved into a snowsuit.

I watched Stuart carefully. He still looked handsome. Not in the same way as Noah. Noah wasn't flawless. He had no single amazing feature. Instead, he had a confluence of agreeable aspects that were accepted by one and all to add up to one very attractive whole, perfectly packaged in the right clothes. He wasn't a clothes snob, but Noah had a weird way of predicting what was coming next. Like he'd start wearing his shirts with one side tucked in and one side loose, and then you'd get a catalog, and every guy in it would have his shirt like that. He was always one step ahead.

There was nothing stylish about Stuart. He probably had only a slight interest in his clothes and, I was guessing, absolutely no clue that there were options on how shirts and jeans were worn. He pulled off his sweater, revealing a plain red T-shirt underneath. It would have been too generic for Noah, but there was no self-consciousness in Stuart, so it looked right. And even though it was loose, I could see that he was pretty muscular. Some guys surprise you like that.

If he had any knowledge whatsoever of what his mom was planning, he showed no sign of it. He was making amusing comments about Rachel's gifts, and I was smiling a stiff smile, pretending I was listening.

"Stuart!" Debbie called. "Can you come up here? Rachel's stuck."

"Be right back," he said.

He took the steps two at a time, and I got off the sofa and went over and examined the Flobie pieces. Maybe if I could talk to Debbie about their potential value, she would stop talking to me about Stuart. Of course, that plan could backfire and make her like me *more*.

There was a mumbled family conference going on upstairs. I wasn't sure what had happened with Rachel and the snowsuit, but it sounded pretty complex. Stuart was saying, "Maybe if we turn her upside down..."

Here was another question: Why hadn't he mentioned this Chloe to me? Not that we were best friends or anything, but we did seem to get along, and he had felt comfortable enough to grill me about Noah. Why hadn't he said something when I mentioned his girlfriend, especially, if Debbie was correct on this point, if he told *everyone* about it?

Not that I cared, of course. It was none of my business. Stuart had just wanted to keep his pain to himself—probably because he had no intention of trying to get anywhere with me. We were friends. New friends, but friends. I, more than anyone, could not judge someone because his parent behaved in a strange manner and got him into an awkward situation. Me, with my jailed parents and my midnight run through the blizzard. If his mom had the creepy matchmaker gene, he could not be blamed for it.

When the three of them came down the stairs (Rachel in Stuart's arms, as it didn't appear that she could move in the snowsuit), I felt a lot more relaxed about the whole situation. Stuart and I were both victims of our parents' behaviors. He was like a brother to me in this respect.

By the time Debbie bum-rushed the mummy-wrapped Rachel out into the wild, I had calmed myself. I was going to have a cool and friendly hour or so with Stuart. I liked his company, and there was nothing to worry about. As I turned to commence said cool and friendly hour, I noticed that Stuart was sitting down with a clouded expression on his face. He regarded me cautiously.

"Can I ask you a question?" he said.

"Um..."

He interlaced his fingers nervously. "I don't know how to put this. I need to ask. I was just talking to my mom, and..."

No. No, no, no, no.

"Your name is *Jubilee*?" he said. "Really?"

I crashed onto the sofa in relief, causing him to bounce a little. The conversation I usually dreaded...now it was the most welcome, wonderful thing in the world. Jubilee was jubilant.

"Oh...right. Yeah. She heard that right. I'm named after Jubilee Hall."

"Who's Jubilee Hall?"

"Not who. What. It's one of the Flobie pieces. You don't have it. It's okay. You can laugh. I know it's stupid."

"I'm named after my dad," he said. "Same first and middle name. That's just as stupid."

"It is?" I asked.

"At least you still have your village," he said breezily. "My dad was never around much."

Which was a good point, I had to admit. He didn't sound

particularly bitter about his dad. It sounded like something that was long past and no longer relevant to his life.

"I don't know any Stuarts," I said. "Except for Stuart Little. And you."

"Exactly. Who calls their kid Stuart?"

"Who calls their kid *Jubilee*? It's not even a name. It's not even a thing. What is a jubilee?"

"It's a party, right?" he said. "You're one big traveling party."

"Oh, don't I know it."

"Here," he said, getting up and reaching over for one of Rachel's presents. It was a board game called Mouse Trap. "Let's play."

"It's your little sister's," I said.

"So? I'm going to have to play it with her anyway. Might as well learn. And it looks like it has a lot of pieces. Looks like a good way to kill time."

"I never just get to kill time," I said. "I feel like I should be doing something."

"Like what?"

"Like…"

I had no idea. I was just always on my way somewhere. Noah was not a fooler-arounder. For fun, we'd update the council Web site.

"I realize," Stuart said, holding up the Mouse Trap box and

shaking off the lid, "that you probably lead a fancy life in the big city. Wherever you're from."

"Richmond."

"Fancy Richmond. But here in Gracetown, killing time is an art form. Now…what color do you want?"

I don't know what Debbie and Rachel were doing, but they were out in that snow for a good two hours or more—and Stuart and I played Mouse Trap the entire time. The first time we tried to do it correctly, but Mouse Trap has all these gizmos and things that swing around and drop a marble. It's weirdly complicated for a kids' game.

The second time we played, we made up entirely new rules, which we liked much better. Stuart was really good company—so good that I didn't even notice (that much) that it was taking Noah a while to call me back. When the phone rang, I jumped.

Stuart answered it, because it was his house, and he passed it to me with a kind of strange expression, like he was a little displeased.

"Who was that?" Noah asked, when I got on.

"That's Stuart. I'm staying at his house."

"I thought you said you were going to Florida?"

In the background, I could hear a lot of noise. Music, people talking. Christmas was going on as normal at his house.

"My train got stuck," I said. "We crashed into a drift. I ended up getting off and walking to a Waffle House, and—"

"Why did you get off?"

"Because of the cheerleaders," I said with a sigh.

"Cheerleaders?"

"Anyway, I ended up meeting Stuart, and I'm staying with his family. We fell in a frozen creek on the way. I'm okay, but—"

"Wow," Noah said. "This sounds really complicated."

Finally. He was getting it.

"Listen," he said. "We're about to go over to see our neighbors. Let me call you back in about an hour and you can tell me the whole story."

I had to hold the phone away from my ear, so great was my shock. "Noah," I said, clapping it back into place. "Did you just hear me?"

"I did. You need to tell me all about it. We won't be that long. Maybe an hour or two."

And he was gone, *again*.

"That was quick," Stuart said, coming into the kitchen and going to the stove. He switched on the kettle.

"He had to go somewhere," I said, without much enthusiasm.

"So he just got off? That's kind of stupid."

"Why is that stupid?"

"I'm just saying. I would be worried. I'm a worrier."

"You don't seem like a worrier," I grumbled. "You seem really happy."

"You can be happy and worried. I definitely worry."

"About what?"

"Well, take this storm," he said, pointing at the window. "I kind of worry that my car might get destroyed by a plow."

"That's very deep," I said.

"What was I supposed to say?"

"You're not *supposed* to say anything," I answered. "But what about how this storm might be evidence of climate change? Or what about people who get sick and can't get to the hospital because of the snow?"

"Is that what Noah would say?"

This unexpected pop at my boyfriend was not welcome. Not that Stuart was wrong. Those are exactly the things that Noah would have mentioned. It was kind of creepily accurate.

"You asked me a question," he said, "and I told you the answer. Can I tell you something you really don't want to hear?" he asked.

"No."

"He's going to break up with you."

As soon as he said it, there was a physical bang in my stomach.

"I'm only trying to be helpful, and I'm sorry," he went on,

watching my face. "But he *is* going to break up with you."

Even as he was saying it, something in me knew that Stuart had hit upon something terrible, something…possibly true. Noah was avoiding me like I was a chore—except Noah didn't avoid chores. He embraced them. I was the only thing he was walking away from. Beautiful, popular, fabulous-on-all-levels Noah was pushing me aside. This realization burned. I hated Stuart for saying it, and I needed him to know it.

"Are you just saying this because of *Chloe*?" I asked.

It worked. Stuart's head snapped back a little. He clicked his jaw back and forth a few times, then steadied himself.

"Let me guess," he said. "My mom told you all about it."

"She didn't tell me *all* about it."

"This has nothing to do with Chloe," he said.

"Oh no?" I replied. I had no idea what happened between Stuart and Chloe, but I'd gotten the reaction I wanted.

He stood up, and looked very tall from where I was.

"Chloe has nothing to do with it," he said again. "Do you want to know how I know what's going to happen?"

No, actually. I didn't. But Stuart was going to tell me anyway.

"First, he's avoiding you on Christmas. Want to know who does that? People who are about to break up with someone. You know why? Because big days make them panic. Holidays, birthdays, anniversaries…they feel guilty, and they can't get into it with you."

"He's just busy," I said weakly. "He has a lot to do."

"Yeah, well, if I had a girlfriend, and her parents had been arrested on Christmas Eve, and she had to take a long train ride through a storm...I'd have my phone in my hand all night. And I would answer it. On the first ring. Every time. I'd be calling her to check on her."

I was stunned silent. He was right. That's exactly what Noah *should* have done.

"Plus, you just told him you fell into a frozen creek and you were trapped in a strange town. And he hung up? I'd *do* something. I'd get down here, snow or no snow. Maybe that sounds stupid, but I would. And if you want my advice? If he isn't breaking up with you, you should dump his ass."

Stuart said all of this in a big rush, as if the words were blown up by some emotional windstorm deep inside. But there was a gravity to it, and it was...touching. Because he clearly meant it. He said everything that I had wished Noah would say. I think he felt bad, because he shifted back and forth silently after that, waiting to see what damage he had caused. It was a minute or two before I could speak.

"I need a minute," I finally said. "Is there somewhere...I can go?"

"My room," he offered. "Second on the left. It's kind of a mess, but..."

I got up and left the table.

Chapter Eleven

Stuart's room was messy. He wasn't kidding. This was the opposite of Noah's room. The only thing that was completely upright was a framed copy of the picture I had seen in his wallet sitting on his bureau. I went over and had a look at it. Chloe was a stunner, no kidding. Long, deep brown hair. Eyelashes you could clean a floor with. A big, bright smile, a natural tan, a splash of freckles. She had pretty right down to the bone.

I sat on his unmade bed and tried to think, but there was just a low hum in my head. From downstairs, I heard the sound of a piano being played, really well. Stuart was running through Christmas songs. He had real style—not just like one of those people who play by rote. He could have been playing in a restaurant or a hotel lobby. Probably somewhere better than that, even, but those were the only places I'd seen piano players, really. Outside the window, two little birds huddled together on a branch, shaking snow off themselves.

There was a phone on Stuart's floor. I picked it up and dialed. Noah sounded just the tiniest bit annoyed when he answered.

"Hey," he said. "What's up? We're about to go, and—"

"In the last twenty-four hours," I said, cutting him off, "my parents have been arrested. I got put on a train, which got stuck in a blizzard. I've walked miles in deep snow with bags on my head. I fell into a stream, and I'm stuck in a strange town with people I don't know. And your excuse for not being able to talk is...what, exactly? That it's Christmas?"

That shut him up. Which wasn't really what I was aiming for, but I was glad to see he had some sense of shame.

"Do you still want to go out with me?" I asked. "Be honest with me, Noah."

The other end of the line went silent for a long time. Too long for the answer to be "Yes. You are the love of my life."

"Lee," Noah said, his voice sounding low and strained. "We shouldn't talk about this now."

"Why?" I asked.

"It's Christmas."

"Isn't that really *more* reason to talk?"

"You know how it is here."

"Well," I said, hearing anger spring into my voice. "You have to talk to me, because I am breaking up with you."

I could barely believe what was coming out of my mouth. The words seemed to come from a place deep inside me, far beyond the place where I stored them, past the ideas...from some room in the back that I didn't even know was there.

There was a long silence.

"Okay," he said. It was impossible to tell what tone was in his voice. It may have been sadness. It may have been relief. He didn't beg me to take it back. He didn't cry. He just did nothing.

"Well?" I asked.

"Well, what?"

"Aren't you even going to say anything?"

"I've kind of known for a while," he said. "I was thinking about it, too. And if this is what you want, you know, I guess it's for the best, and..."

"Merry Christmas," I said. I hung up. My hand was shaking. My whole body was, practically. I sat on Stuart's bed and wrapped my arms around myself. Downstairs, the music stopped, and the house filled up with a drowning kind of quiet.

Stuart appeared at the door, pushing it open cautiously. "Just checking to make sure you were okay," he said.

"I did it," I replied. "I just picked up the phone and did it."

Stuart came and sat down. He didn't put his arm around me, just sat next to me, kind of close, but with a little space between us.

"He didn't seem surprised," I said.

"Assholes never are. What did he say?"

"Something about how he's known it for a while, how it's probably for the best."

For some reason, this made me hiccup. We sat in silence for a while. My head was spinning.

"Chloe was like Noah," he finally said. "Really...perfect. Beautiful. Good grades. She sang, she did charity work, and she was a...you'll like this...a cheerleader."

"She sounds like a prize," I said grimly.

"I never knew why she went out with me. I was just some guy, and she was *Chloe Newland*. We dated for fourteen months. We were really happy, as far as I knew. At least, I was. The only problem was that she was always busy, and then she got busier and busier. Too busy to stop by my locker or the house, to call, to e-mail. So I would stop by her house. And call her. And e-mail her."

It was all so horribly familiar.

"One night," he went on, "we were supposed to study together, and she just didn't show up. I drove over to her house, but her mom said she wasn't there. And then I started to get kinda worried, because usually she would at least text me if she needed to cancel. So I started driving around, looking for her car—I mean, there are only so many places you can go in Gracetown. I found it in front of Starbucks, which made sense. We study there a lot because...what other option does society give us, right? It's Starbucks or death, sometimes."

He was wringing his hands furiously now, pulling on his fingers.

"What I *figured*," he said pointedly, "is that I just made a mistake and that I was supposed to be studying with her at Starbucks all along, and I'd just forgotten. Chloe didn't really like coming here to the house very much. Sometimes she got a little freaked out by my mom, if you can believe that."

He looked up, as if waiting for a laugh from me. I managed a little smile.

"I was *so relieved* when I saw her car there. I'd been getting more and more upset driving around. I felt like a moron. *Of course* she was waiting for me at Starbucks. I went inside, but she wasn't at any of the tables. One of my friends, Addie, works the counter. I asked her if she'd seen Chloe, since her car was there."

Stuart ran his hands through his hair until it got kind of huge. I resisted the urge to pat it down. I kind of liked it that way, anyway. Something about his really big hair made me feel better—took away some of the burn I felt in my chest.

"Addie, she just got this very sad look on her face and she said, 'I think she's in the bathroom.' I couldn't figure out what was so incredibly sad about being in the bathroom. So I bought myself a drink, and I got one for Chloe, and I sat down and waited. There's only one bathroom in our Starbucks, so she had to come out eventually. I didn't have my computer or any books with me, so I was just generally staring at the wall mural where the bathroom door is. I was thinking about how stupid I was to get upset with her and how I'd kept her waiting, and then I realized that she'd been in the bathroom for a really long time and that Addie was still looking at me, really sadly. Addie went over and knocked on the door, and Chloe came out. So did Todd, the Cougar."

"Todd, the *Cougar*?"

"It's not a nickname. He's *literally* the Cougar. He's our mascot. He wears the cougar costume and does the cougar dances and everything. For a minute, my brain was trying to put it all together...trying to figure out why Chloe and Todd the Cougar were in a Starbucks bathroom. I guess my first hope was that it couldn't be anything bad because everyone seemed to know they were in there. But from the look on Addie's face, and the look on Chloe's face—I didn't look at Todd—it finally clicked. I still don't know if they went in there because they saw me coming, or if they'd been in there for a while. If you're hiding from your boyfriend in the bathroom with the Cougar...the details kind of don't matter."

I momentarily forgot all about my phone call. I was in that Starbucks with Stuart, seeing a cheerleader I didn't know emerge from a bathroom with Todd the Cougar. Except in my vision, he was wearing the cougar outfit, which probably wasn't how it really went down.

"What did you do?" I asked.

"Nothing."

"Nothing?"

"Nothing. I just stood there, thinking I was going to be sick on the spot. But Chloe got furious. With me."

"How does *that* work?" I said, furious on his behalf.

"I think she was freaked out by the fact that she'd been caught, and it was the only way she could think to react. She accused me of spying on her. She called me possessive. She said I put too much pressure on her. I think she meant emotionally—I guess—but it came out sounding *so bad*. So on top of it all, she made me sound like a letch in front of everyone in Starbucks, which might as well be everyone in town because nothing stays quiet here. I wanted to say, 'You're making out with the Cougar in the Starbucks bathroom. *I am not the villain of this story.*' Only I didn't say that because I literally couldn't talk. So it must have looked like I *agreed* with her. Like I was admitting that I was a possessive, grabby, sex-freak stalker...and not the guy who was in love with her, who had been in love with her for more than a year, who would have done anything she asked...."

There probably was a point after the breakup when Stuart told this story all the time, but he clearly hadn't done it in a while. He was out of practice. His expression didn't change a lot—all of his emotion seemed to come out of his hands. He had stopped wringing them, and now they shook, just ever so slightly.

"Addie finally walked her outside to talk her down," he said. "That's how it all ended. And I got a latte, on the house. So it wasn't a total loss. I became the guy who was famously dumped in public when his girlfriend cheated with the Cougar. Anyway…I had a point in saying all of that. My point is, that guy…"

He pointed accusingly at the phone.

"…is a dick. Although that probably doesn't mean much to you right now."

My memories of the last year were playing back through my mind at super-speed, but I was looking at them all from a different camera angle. There I was, Noah holding my hand, one step ahead of me, pulling me through the hall, talking to everyone else but me along the way. I sat with him in the front row at school basketball games, even though he knew that ever since I'd gotten hit in the face with a wayward ball I was scared of those seats. But still, we sat there, me frozen in terror, watching a game that never interested me to begin with. Yes, I sat with the upper-echelon seniors at lunch, but the conversations were repetitive. All they ever talked about was how busy they all were, how they were building their résumés for their college applications. How they were meeting with recruiters. How they were organizing their calendars online. Who was recommending them.

God...I'd been bored for a year. I hadn't talked about *myself* in ages. Stuart was talking about me. He was paying attention. It felt foreign, a little embarrassingly intimate, but kind of great. My eyes filled up.

Seeing this, Stuart braced himself and opened his arms a little, as if inviting me to give up my efforts to contain myself. We had inched marginally closer together at some point, and there was an expectant energy. Something was about to give. I felt myself gearing up to start bawling. This made me angry. Noah didn't deserve it. I was *not going to start crying*.

So I kissed him.

I mean, really kissed him. I knocked him backward. He kissed me back. A good kiss, too. Not too dry, not too wet. It was a bit on the frantic side, maybe because neither one of us had done the mental preparation, so we were both thinking, *Oh, right! Kissing! Quickly! Quickly! More movement! Deploy tongue!*

It took us about a minute to recover and settle into a slightly slower pattern. I felt myself kind of floating away, when there was a huge stomping and crashing and yelling from downstairs. Apparently, Debbie and Rachel had chosen this moment to tie up the sled dogs and return from their personal Iditarod through the streets of Gracetown. They tromped back inside in that ridiculously loud way you do when you come out of snow or rain. (Why does wet weather make you louder?)

"Stuart! Jubilee! I have special cupcakes from Santa!" Debbie was screaming.

Neither of us moved. I was still leaning on top of Stuart, essentially pinning him down. We heard her come halfway up the stairs, where she must have seen the bedroom light on.

Again, the normal parent reaction would have been to say something like, "You had better come out here this moment or I am releasing the tiger!" But Debbie was not a normal parent, so we heard her giggle and creep away, saying, "Shhh! Rachel! Come with Mommy! Stuart is busy!"

Debbie's sudden appearance in this scene made my stomach turn. Stuart rolled his eyes back in his head in agony. I released him, and he jumped up.

"I should go down," he said. "You okay? Need anything or—"

"I'm great!" I said, with sudden, insane enthusiasm. But Stuart was by now well used to my tactics, my attempts to make myself look sane.

Quite sensibly, he bolted from the room.

Chapter Twelve

*W*ant to know how long it took me to break up with my "perfect" boyfriend and make out with a new guy? It had taken...wait for it...*twenty-three minutes*. (I noticed Stuart's clock when I first picked up the phone. It wasn't like I had a stopwatch.)

Much as I would have liked to, I couldn't hide upstairs forever. Sooner or later, I was going to have to come down and face the world. I sat on the floor in the doorway and listened as closely as I could to what was happening downstairs. Mostly, all I could hear was Rachel banging on some toys, and then I heard someone go outside. That seemed as good a cue as any. I quietly hit the stairs. In the living room, Rachel was noodling around with the Mouse Trap, which still sat out on the table. She gave me a big, toothy smile.

"Were you playing with Stuart?" she asked.

The question was loaded. I was a filthy, filthy woman, and even the five-year-old knew it.

"Yes," I said, trying to keep some dignity. "We were playing Mouse Trap. How was the snow, Rachel?"

"Mommy says that Stuart likes you. I can stick a marble in my nose. Wanna see?"

"No, you probably shouldn't—"

Rachel stuck one of the Mouse Trap marbles right up her nose. She extracted it and held it up for examination. "See?" she said.

Oh, I saw all right.

"Jubilee? Is that you?"

Debbie appeared at the kitchen door, looking flushed and well exercised and very damp.

"Stuart just went across the street to help Mrs. Addler shovel her path," she said. "He saw her struggling. She has a glass eye and a bad back, you see. You two have a...nice afternoon?"

"It was fine," I said stiffly. "We played Mouse Trap."

"Is that what they're calling it these days?" she asked, throwing me a terrible grin. "I have to go give Rachel a quick bath. Feel free to make yourself some cocoa or whatever you like!"

She stopped short of adding "...future child-bride of my only son."

She rounded up Rachel with a pointed, "Come on, we can go upstairs *now*," leaving me to the hot chocolate and my shame and misery. I went to the living room window and looked out. Sure enough, Stuart was out there, lending a glad hand to his neighbor in her moment of need. He was just getting away from me, of course. It only made sense. I would have done the same thing. It was perfectly reasonable to deduce that I was only going to get worse. I would keep spiraling down, sinking deeper and deeper into a mire of rash and largely inexplicable behaviors. Like my jailed parents before me, I was a live wire. Best to go and shovel a few tons of snow for a glass-eyed neighbor and hope I went away.

Which was precisely what I had to do. Go away. Get out of this house and his life while I still had a shred of dignity left. I would go and find my train, which was probably leaving town soon, anyway.

I moved quickly as soon as I made this decision, running to the kitchen. I picked up my phone from the counter, smacked it around a little, and poked at the on/off button. I didn't expect this to work, but there was some mercy. After a moment or two, it struggled back into existence. The screen was off center and the words were scrambled, but there was some life in the thing.

My clothes, coat, shoes, and bag were all in the laundry room off of the kitchen, in various stages of dryness. I threw them on, leaving the sweat clothes on the washer. They had a container of plastic bags in the corner, so I took about ten of them. I felt bad taking something without asking, but plastic bags don't really count as "something." They're like tissues, except less expensive. As a last gesture, I reached over and nabbed one of their holiday return address labels from an organizer on the counter. I would send them a note when I got home. I may have been a complete lunatic, but I was a complete lunatic with *manners*.

Obviously, I had to take the back door, the one we had come in the night before. If I went out the front, Stuart would see me. The snow had piled up against this door, at least two feet of it—and it was no longer the slushy, wet snow of the night before. It had hardened in the cold. But I was fueled by the power of confusion and panic, which, like I said, is always ready and waiting to get to work. I threw all my weight against the door, feeling it wobble and strain. I was worried that I might break it from the force, which would have put an entirely different complexion on my departure. I could envision it all too clearly: Stuart or Debbbie finding the dented door off its hinges, lying in the snow. "She came in, ravaged the boy, stole plastic bags, and ripped off the door in her escape," the police would say in the APB. "Probably making her way to bust her parents out of jail."

I managed to get it open just enough to force myself through, ripping my bags and scraping my arm in the process. Once I was out, it jammed in position, so I had to spend another two or three minutes pushing it shut. That accomplished, I faced another problem. I couldn't return the way we had come, because I didn't want to take another dip in the frozen stream. Not that I could have worked out that path anyway. All of our tracks were gone. I was on a slight rise, facing an unfamiliar cluster of scruffy bare trees and the backs of dozens of identical-looking houses. The only thing I knew for sure was that the stream was below me, probably somewhere in those trees. The safest bet was to stick close to the houses and weave my way through a few backyards. Then I could get back on a road, and from there, I assumed, it would be easy to find my way back to the interstate, the Waffle House, and my train.

See my previous note about me and my assumptions.

Stuart's subdivision didn't follow the lovely, neat logic of the streets of the Flobie Santa Village. These houses had been plunked down with an alarming randomness—unevenly spaced, on crooked lines, like whoever had designed the place had said, "We'll just follow this cat, and wherever he sits down, we'll build something." The disorientation was so bad that I couldn't even figure out where the road was supposed to be. Nothing had been plowed, and the streetlights of the night before were off. The sky was white instead of the crazy pink of the night before. It was the bleakest horizon I've ever seen, and there was no obvious route out.

As I trudged through the development, I had plenty of time to consider what I had just done to my life. How was I going to explain the breakup to my family? They *loved* Noah. Not as much as me, obviously, but a lot. My parents were clearly proud that I had such an impressive boyfriend. Then again, my parents were in jail over a Flobie Elf Hotel, so maybe they needed to get their priorities in order. Besides, if I said I was happier this way, they would accept it.

My friends, people at school…that was a different story. I hadn't dated Noah for the perks—they were just part of the service.

And there was Stuart, of course.

Stuart, who had just witnessed me go through an entire rainbow of emotions and experiences. There was parents-have-just-been-jailed me, stuck-in-a-strange-town me, insane-and-can't-shut-up me, kind-of-snarky-to-the-strange-guy-trying-to-be-helpful me, breakup me, and the extremely popular jump-on-top-of-you-unexpectedly me.

I had messed this up so very, very badly. All of it. The regret and humiliation hurt much more than the cold. It took me a few streets to realize that it wasn't Noah I was really regretting…it was Stuart. Stuart who rescued me. Stuart who actually seemed to want to spend his time with me. Stuart who talked to me straight and told me not to sell myself short.

This was the Stuart who would be so relieved to find me gone, for all of the reasons I just listed. As long as the news stories about my parents' arrest weren't too detailed, I would be untraceable. Well, untraceable-ish. Maybe he could find me online somewhere, but he would never look. Not after the freak show I had just put on.

Unless I just wound up at his door again. Which, after an hour of wandering the development, I realized was a real danger. I was looking at the same stupid houses, getting stuck in cul-de-sacs. I occasionally stopped and asked for directions from people who were shoveling their driveways, but they all seemed really concerned that I was trying to walk that far and didn't want to tell me how to go. At least half of them asked me to come inside and get warm, which sounded good, but I wasn't taking any more chances. I had gone into one house in Gracetown, and look where it had gotten me.

I was slugging along past a group of little girls, giggling in the snow, when the despair really set in. The tears were about to flow forth. I couldn't really feel my feet anymore. My knees were stiffened. And that's when I heard his voice behind me.

"Hold up," Stuart said.

I stopped suddenly. Running away is pretty pathetic, but it's even worse getting caught. I stood there for a moment, unwilling (and partially unable) to turn around and face him. I tried to arrange my expression in the most casual funny-meeting-you-here, isn't-life-hilarious! way I could. From the way my jaw muscles were straining by my ears, I'm pretty sure it was a lot more like my I've-got-lockjaw! face.

"Sorry," I said, through my clenched smile. "I just thought I should get back to the train, and—"

"Yeah," he said, quietly cutting me off. "I kind of figured that."

Stuart wasn't even looking up at me. He pulled a proper, if slightly embarrassing, hat out of his pocket. It looked like one of Rachel's. It had a big pom-pom on top.

"I think you probably need this," he said, holding out the hat. "You can have it. Rachel doesn't need it back."

I took it and pulled it on my head, because it looked like he was prepared to stand there, holding it out, until the snow melted around him. It was a tight fit but still brought a welcome warmth to my ears.

"I followed your footsteps," he said, in answer to the unspoken question. "Snow makes it easy."

I had been tracked, like a bear.

"Sorry to make you go to all that trouble," I said.

"I didn't have to go that far, really. You're about three streets over. You just kept going in loops."

A really inept bear.

"I can't believe you went back out in that outfit," he said. "You should let me walk you. You're not going to get there this way."

"I'm fine," I said quickly. "Someone just told me the way."

"You don't have to go, you know."

I wanted to say something else but couldn't think of anything. He took this to mean that I wanted him to go, so he nodded.

"Be careful, okay? And, can you just let me know that you made it? Call or—"

Just then, my phone started ringing. The ring must have been damaged by the water as well, so now it had a high, keening note—kind of the sound I imagine a mermaid might make if you punched her in the face. Surprised. A little accusatory. Hurt. Gurgley.

It was Noah. On my messed-up screen, it actually said "Mobg" was calling, but I knew what it meant. I didn't answer; I just stared at it. Stuart stared at it. The little girls around us stared at us staring at it. It stopped ringing, then started again. It pulsed in my hand, insistent.

"I'm sorry if I was an idiot," Stuart said, speaking up to talk over the noise. "And you probably don't care what I think, but you shouldn't answer that."

"What do you mean *you* were an idiot?" I asked.

Stuart fell silent. The ringing stopped and started again. Mobg really wanted to talk to me.

"I told Chloe I would wait for her," he finally said. "I told her I would wait as long as it took. She told me not to bother, but I waited anyway. For months, I was determined not to even look at another girl. I even tried not to look at the cheerleaders. Not look, look, I mean."

I knew what he meant.

"But I noticed you," he went on. "And it drove me crazy, from the first minute. Not just that I noticed you, but that

I could see that you were going out with some supposedly perfect guy who clearly didn't deserve you. Which, frankly, was kind of the situation I was in. It sounds like he's kind of realized his mistake, though."

He nodded at the phone, which started ringing again.

"I'm still really glad you came," he added. "And don't give in to that guy, okay? If nothing else? Don't give in to that guy. He doesn't deserve you. Don't let him fool you."

It rang and it rang and it rang. I looked at the screen one last time, then at Stuart, and then I reached my arm back and threw the phone as hard as I could (sadly, not that far), and it vanished into the snow. The eight-year-olds, who were truly fascinated with our every move at this point, chased after it.

"Lost it," I said. "Whoops."

This was the first time in all of this that Stuart actually looked up at me. I had dropped the horrible grimace by this point. He stepped forward, lifted my chin, and kissed me. *Kissed* me, kissed me. And I didn't notice the cold, or care that the girls who now had my phone came up behind us and started going, "OoooOOOoooOOoooh."

"One thing," I said, when we had broken apart and the swirling feeling in my head subsided. "Maybe...don't tell your mom too much about this. I think she has ideas."

"What?" he asked, all innocence, as he put an arm around my shoulders and led me back toward his house. "Don't your parents cheer and stare when you make out with someone? Is that weird where you come from? I guess they don't get to see it much, though. From jail, I mean."

"Shut it, Weintraub. If I knock you down in the snow, these kids will swarm and eat you."

A lone truck puttered past, and Tinfoil Guy gave us a stiff salute as he drove farther into Gracetown. We all moved to make way for him—Stuart, me, the little girls. Stuart zipped open his coat and invited me to tuck myself under his arm, and then we made our way through the snow.

"You want to go back to my house the long way?" he asked. "Or the shortcut? You have to be cold."

"Long way," I replied. "The long way, for sure."

A Cheertastic Christmas Miracle
john green

To Ilene Cooper, who has guided me through so many blizzards

Chapter One

JP and the Duke and I were four movies in to our James Bond marathon when my mother called home for the sixth time in five hours. I didn't even glance at the caller ID. I knew it was Mom. The Duke rolled her eyes and paused the movie. "Does she think you're *going* somewhere? There's a blizzard."

I shrugged and picked up the phone.

"No luck," Mom said. In the background, a loud voice droned on about the importance of securing the homeland.

"Sorry, Mom. That sucks."

"This is ridiculous!" she shouted. "We can't get a flight to *anywhere*, let alone home." They'd been stuck in Boston for three days. Doctors' conference. She was getting kind of despondent about the whole Christmas-in-Boston thing. It was as if Boston were a war zone. Honestly, I felt sort of giddy about it. Something about me has always liked the drama and inconvenience of bad weather. The worse the better, really.

"Yeah, sucks," I said.

"It's supposed to blow through by morning, but everything is so backed up. They can't even guarantee we'll be home *tomorrow*. Your dad is trying to rent a car, but the lines are long. And even *then* it will be eight or nine in the morning, even if we drive all night! But we can't spend Christmas apart!"

"I'll just go over to the Duke's," I said. "Her parents already told me I could stay there. I'll go over there and open all my presents, and talk about how my parents neglect me, and then maybe the Duke will give me some of her presents because she feels so bad about how my mom doesn't love me." I glanced over at the Duke, who smirked at me.

"Tobin," Mom said disapprovingly. She wasn't a particularly funny person. It suited her professionally—I mean, you don't want your cancer surgeon to walk into the examination room and be like, "Guy walks into a bar. Bartender says, 'What'll ya have?' And the guy says, 'Whaddya got?' And the bartender says, 'I don't know what I got, but I know what you got: Stage IV melanoma.'"

"I'm just saying I'll be fine. Are you guys gonna go back to the hotel?"

"I guess, unless your father can get us a car. He's being such a saint about all this."

"Okay," I said. I glanced at JP, and he mouthed, *Hang. Up. The. Phone.* I really wanted to return to the place on the couch between JP and the Duke and go back to watching the new James Bond kill people in fascinating ways.

"Everything's fine there?" Mom asked. Lord.

"Yeah, yeah. I mean, it's snowing. But the Duke and JP are here. And they can't really abandon me, either, because they'd freeze if they tried to walk back to their houses. We're just watching Bond movies. Power's still on and everything."

"Call me if anything happens. *Anything.*"

"Yup, got it," I said.

"Okay," she said. "Okay. God, I'm sorry about this, Tobin. I love you. I'm sorry."

"It's really not a big deal," I said, because it really wasn't. Here I was, in a large house without adult supervision, with my best friends on the couch. Nothing against my parents, who are fine people and everything, but they could have stayed in Boston right through New Year's without my being disappointed.

"I'll call you from the hotel," Mom said.

JP apparently heard her through the phone, because he mumbled, "I'm sure you will," as I said my good-byes.

"I think she has an attachment disorder," JP said when I hung up.

"Well, it's Christmas," I said.

"And why don't you come over to *my* house for Christmas?" JP asked.

"Shitty food," I answered. I walked around the couch and took my place on the middle cushion.

"Racist!" JP exclaimed.

"It's not racism!" I said.

"You just said that Korean food was shitty," he said.

"No, he didn't," said the Duke, lifting the remote to restart the movie. "He said *your mom's* Korean food was shitty."

"Exactly," I said. "I quite like the food at Keun's house."

"You're an asshat," said JP, which is what JP said when he didn't have a comeback. As comebackless comebacks go, it was a pretty good one. The Duke restarted the movie, and then JP said, "We should call Keun."

The Duke paused the movie again and leaned forward, over me, to speak directly to JP. "JP," she said.

"Yes?"

"Can you please stop talking so I can go back to enjoying Daniel Craig's outrageously good body?"

"That's so gay," JP said.

"I'm a *girl*," said the Duke. "It's not gay for me to be attracted to men. Now, if I said *you* had a hot body, *that* would be gay, because you're built like a lady."

"Oh, burn," I said.

The Duke raised her eyes at me and said, "Although JP's a freaking paragon of masculinity compared to you."

I had no response to that. "Keun is at work," I said. "He gets paid double on Christmas Eve."

"Oh, right," said JP. "I forgot that Waffle Houses are like Lindsay Lohan's legs: always open."

I laughed; the Duke just winced and restarted the movie. Daniel Craig walked out of the water, wearing a pair of Euro boxer briefs that passed as a bathing suit. The Duke sighed contentedly while JP retched. After a couple minutes, I heard a soft clicking sound next to me. JP. Using dental floss. He was obsessed with dental floss.

"That is disgusting," I said. The Duke paused the movie and scowled at me. She didn't have much meanness in her scowl; she scrunched up her button nose and squared her lips. But I could always tell in her eyes if she got really pissed at me, and her eyes still seemed pretty smiley.

"What?" JP said, the floss dangling out of his mouth from between molars.

"Flossing in public. It's just…Please put it away."

He did, reluctantly, but insisted on the last word. "My dentist says he has never seen healthier gums. *Never.*"

I rolled my eyes. The Duke brushed a stray curl behind her ear and unpaused Bond. I watched for a minute, but then I found myself looking out the window, a distant streetlight illuminating the snow like a billion falling stars in miniature. And even though I hated to inconvenience my parents or deny them a Christmas at home, I could not help but wish for more snow.

Chapter Two

The phone rang ten minutes after we restarted the movie.

"Jesus Christ," JP said, grabbing the remote to hit pause.

"Your mom calls more than a clingy boyfriend," the Duke added.

I jumped over the back of the couch and grabbed the phone. "Hey," I said, "how's it going?"

"Tobin," replied the voice on the other end of the line. Not my mom. Keun.

"Keun, aren't you su—"

"Is JP with you?"

"He is."

"Do you have speakerphone?"

"Uh, why do you w—"

"DO YOU HAVE SPEAKERPHONE?!" he shouted.

"Hold on." As I looked for the button, I said, "It's Keun. He wants to be put on speaker. He's being weird."

"Fancy that," said the Duke. "Next you'll tell me that the sun is a mass of incandescent gas or that JP has tiny balls."

"Don't go there," JP said.

"Don't go where? Into your pants with a high-powered magnifying glass on a search for your tiny balls?"

I found the speakerphone button and pressed it.

"Keun, can you hear me?"

"Yes," he said. There was a lot of noise in the background. Girl noises. "I need you guys to listen."

JP said to the Duke, "Where does the owner of the world's smallest breasts get off impugning someone else's personal parts?" The Duke threw a pillow at JP.

"YOU MUST LISTEN NOW!" shouted Keun from the phone. Everyone shut up then. Keun was incredibly smart, and he always talked like he had memorized his remarks in advance. "Okay. So my manager didn't come to work today, because his car got stuck in snow. So I am cook and acting assistant manager. There are two other employees here—they are (one) Mitchell Croman, and (two) Billy Talos." Mitchell and Billy both went to our school, although it would not be accurate to say that I knew them, on account of how I rather doubted either could pick me out of a lineup. "Until about twelve minutes ago, it was a quiet night. Our only customers were Tinfoil Guy and Doris, America's oldest living smoker. And then this girl showed up, and then Stuart Weintraub"—another classmate, and a good guy—"arrived covered in Target bags. They distracted Tinfoil Guy a little, and I was just reading *The Dark Knight* and—"

"Keun, is there a *point?*" I asked. He could ramble sometimes.

"Oh, there's a point," he answered. "There are fourteen points. Because about five minutes after Stuart Weintraub showed up, the good and loving Lord Almighty looked kindly upon His servant Keun and saw fit to usher fourteen Pennsylvanian cheerleaders—*wearing their warm-up outfits*—into our lowly Waffle House. Gentlemen, I am not kidding you. Our Waffle House is full of cheerleaders. Their train is stuck in the snow, and they are staying here for the night. They are high on caffeine. They are doing splits on the breakfast counter.

"Let me be perfectly clear: there has been a Cheertastic Christmas Miracle at the Waffle House. I am looking at these girls right now. They are so hot that their hotness could melt the snow. Their hotness could cook the waffles. Their hotness could—no, *will*—warm the places in my heart that have been so cold for so long that I have nearly forgotten they ever existed."

A girl voice—a voice at once cheery and sultry—shouted into the phone then. By now I was standing directly above the speaker, staring at it with a kind of reverence. JP was by my side. "Are those your friends? Oh my God, tell them to bring Twister!"

Keun spoke again. "And now you realize what is at stake! The greatest night of my life has just begun. And I am inviting you to join me, because I am the best friend ever. But here's the catch: after I get off the phone with you, Mitchell and Billy will be calling their friends. And we've agreed in advance that there's only room here for one more carful of guys. I cannot further dilute the cheerleader-to-guy ratio. Now, I am making the first call, because I'm acting assistant manager. So you have a head start. I know you will not fail. I know I can count upon you to deliver the Twister. Gentlemen, may you travel safely and swiftly. But if you die tonight, die in the comfort that you have sacrificed your lives for that noblest of human causes. The pursuit of cheerleaders."

Chapter Three

JP and I did not even bother to hang up the phone. I just said, "I gotta change," and he said, "Me, too," and then I said, "Duke: Twister! In the game closet!"

I dashed upstairs, my socks sliding on the hardwood floor in the kitchen, and stumbled into my bedroom. I tore open the closet door and began feverishly sorting through the shirts piled on the floor in the vain hope that inside that pile there might be some wondrously perfect shirt down there, a nice striped button-down with no wrinkles that said, "I'm strong and tough but I'm also a surprisingly good listener with a true and abiding passion for cheers and those who lead them." Unfortunately, there was no such shirt to be found. I quickly settled on a dirty but cool yellow Threadless T-shirt under a black v-neck sweater. I kicked off my watching-James-Bond-movies-with-the-Duke-and-JP jeans and hurriedly wiggled into my one pair of nice, dark jeans.

I tucked my chin to my chest and sniffed. I ran into the bathroom and frantically swiped some deodorant under my arms anyway. I looked up at myself in the mirror. I looked okay, aside from the somewhat asymmetrical hair. I hustled back to the room, grabbed my winter coat off the floor, stepped into my Pumas, and then ran downstairs with the shoes half on, shouting, "Everybody ready? I'm ready! Let's go!"

When I arrived downstairs, the Duke was sitting in the middle of the couch, watching the Bond movie. "Duke. Twister. Jacket. Car." I turned and called upstairs, "JP, where are you?"

"Do you have an extra coat?" he answered.

"No, wear yours!" I shouted.

"But I only wore a jacket!" he shouted back.

"Just hurry!" For some reason, the Duke still hadn't stopped the movie. "Duke," I repeated. "Twister. Jacket. Car."

She paused the movie and turned around to me. "Tobin, what is your idea of hell?"

"That seems like a question that could be answered in the car!"

"Because my idea of hell is spending eternity in a Waffle House full of cheerleaders."

"Oh, come on," I said. "Don't be an idiot."

The Duke stood up, the couch still between us. "You're saying we should go out in the worst snowstorm in fifty years and drive twenty miles to hang out with a bunch of random chicks whose idea of fun is to play a game that says right on the box that it was designed for six-year-olds, and *I'm* the idiot?"

I turned my head back toward the stairs. "JP! Hurry!"

"I'm trying!" he called back. "But I have to balance the need to hurry with the need to look fabulous!"

I stepped around the couch and put my arm around the Duke. I smiled down at her. We'd been friends for a long time. I knew her well. I knew she hated cheerleaders. I knew she hated cold weather. I knew she hated getting off the couch when James Bond movies were on.

But the Duke loved Waffle House hash browns. "There are two things you cannot resist," I told her. "The first is James Bond."

"True enough," she said. "What's the other thing?"

"Hash browns," I said. "Golden, delicious Waffle House hash browns."

She did not look at me, not quite. She looked through me, and through the walls of the house, and through the snow, her eyes squinting as she stared into the distance. She was thinking about those hash browns.

"You can get 'em scattered on the grill, smothered with onions, and covered with cheese," I said.

She blinked hard and then shook her head. "God, I am always foiled by my love of hash browns! But I don't want to be stuck there all night."

"One hour unless you're having fun," I promised. She nodded. As she got her coat on, I opened the game closet and grabbed a Twister box with crumpled edges.

When I turned around, JP was standing in front of me. "Oh my God," I said. He had found something terrible in some dark corner of my father's closet: he wore a puffy, periwinkle onesie with tapered legs, an ear-flapped hat atop his head. "You look like a lumberjack with an adult-baby fetish," I said.

"Shut up, asshat," answered JP simply. "This is ski-slope sexy. It says, 'I'm just coming off the slopes after a long day saving lives with the Ski Patrol.'"

The Duke laughed. "It actually says, 'Just because I wasn't the first female astronaut doesn't mean I can't wear her flight suit.'"

"Jesus, fine, I'll go change," he says.

"THERE IS NO TIME!" I shouted.

"You should put on boots," the Duke said, looking at my Pumas.

"NO TIME!" I shouted again.

I ushered them both into the garage, and then we were

inside Carla, my parents' white Honda SUV. Eight minutes had passed since Keun hung up. Our head start had probably already evaporated. It was 11:42 P.M. On a normal night, it took about twenty minutes to get to Waffle House.

It would not prove to be a normal night.

Chapter Four

When I pressed the garage-door button, the scope of our challenge began to dawn on me: a wall of snow a couple feet high was pressed against the garage. Since the Duke and JP arrived around lunchtime, it must have snowed at least a foot and a half.

I switched Carla into four-wheel drive. "I'm just gonna, uh...Do you think I should drive through it?"

"JUST GO," JP said from the backseat. The Duke had successfully called shotgun. I took a deep breath and eased Carla back. She lifted a little when we hit the snow but plowed most of it away, and I began to drive in reverse down the driveway. Actually, it was not driving so much as it was ice-skating backward, but it worked. Soon enough, thanks more to luck than skill, the car was out of the driveway, facing approximately toward the Waffle House.

The snow on the streets was a foot deep. Nothing in our subdivision had been salted or plowed.

"This is such a dumb way to die," the Duke noted, and I was starting to agree with her. But from the back, JP shouted, "Spartans! Tonight, we dine in the Waffle House!"

I nodded my head and put the car into drive and pressed the accelerator. The tires spun and spun, and then we shot off, the falling snow alive in the headlights. I couldn't see the curbs of the road, let alone the painted lines dividing the lanes, so I mostly just tried to stay between the mailboxes.

Grove Park is kind of a bowl, so to leave you have to drive up a very modest hill. JP and the Duke and I all grew up in the Grove Park subdivision, and I've driven up the hill in question thousands of times.

And so the potential problem did not even occur to me as we started to climb. But soon, I noticed that the amount of pressure I placed on the accelerator pedal did not in any way affect the speed at which we were going up the hill. I began to feel a tinge of dread.

We began to slow down. I pressed the accelerator, and listened as the tires spun on the snow. JP swore. We were still creeping forward, though, and I could now see the crest of the hill and the black pavement of the plowed highway above us. "Come on, Carla," I mumbled.

"Give it some gas," JP suggested. I did, and the tires spun some more, and then suddenly Carla ceased climbing.

There was a long moment between when Carla stopped moving forward and when she began to slide, tires locked, back down the hill. It was a quiet moment, a time of contemplation. I am generally pretty averse to taking risks. I was not the sort of person who hikes the entire Appalachian Trail or spends the summer studying in Ecuador, or even the kind of person who eats sushi. When I was little and I would get worried about stuff at night and it would keep me up, my mom would always ask, "What's the worst that could happen?" She thought this was very comforting—she thought it would make me realize that the possible mistakes on my second-grade math homework would not have broad repercussions on my quality of life. But that's not what happened. What happened was that I got to thinking about the worst thing that could happen. Say that I am worried that there are mistakes on my second-grade math homework. Maybe my teacher Ms. Chapman will yell at me. She won't *yell*, but maybe she'll gently disapprove. Maybe her gentle disapproval will upset me. And maybe I'll start crying. Everyone will call me a crybaby, which will further my social isolation, and because no one likes me, I'll turn to drugs for comfort, and by the time I'm in fifth grade, I'll be strung out on heroin. And then I'll die. *That's* the worst that can happen. And it *can* happen. And I believed in thinking through these situations, so as to keep myself from becoming strung out on heroin and/or dead. But I had thrown all that out. And for what? For cheerleaders I didn't know? Nothing against cheerleaders, but surely there were better things to sacrifice for.

I felt the Duke looking at me, and I looked back at her, and her eyes were big and round and scared and maybe a little pissed. And only now, in the drawn-out moment of stillness, did I think through to the worst thing that could happen: this. Provided I survived, my parents would kill me for totaling the car. I would be grounded for years—possibly decades. I would work hundreds of hours over the summer to pay for car repairs.

And then the inexorable thing happened. We began to fishtail back toward the house. I pumped the brake. The Duke pulled up the parking brake, but Carla just slalomed backward, only occasionally responding to my frantic spinning of the steering wheel.

I felt a slight bump and figured we'd hopped a curb; we were retreating down the hill now through the yards of our neighbors as we plowed through snow as high as the wheel wells. We rolled backward past houses, so close that I could see the ornaments on the Christmas trees through living-room windows. Carla miraculously dodged a pickup truck parked in a driveway, and as I watched for approaching mailboxes and cars and houses in the rearview, I happened to glance back at JP. He was smiling. The worst thing that could happen had finally happened. And there was a kind of relief in it, maybe. Anyway, something about his smile made me smile.

I glanced over at the Duke, and then threw my hands off the wheel. She shook her head as if she were angry, but she cracked up, too. To demonstrate the extent to which I did not control Carla, I then grabbed the steering wheel and began dramatically turning it back and forth. She laughed some more and said, "We're so screwed."

And then all at once the brakes started to work, and I could feel myself pressed against the seat, and then finally, as the road leveled out, we slowed to a stop. JP was talking too loud, saying, "Holy crap, I cannot believe we're not dead. We are so not dead!"

I looked around to try to get my bearings. About five feet outside the passenger's-side door was the house of these old retirees, Mr. and Mrs. Olney. A light was on, and after a second of looking I could see Mrs. Olney, wearing a white nightgown, her face almost pressed against the glass, staring at us, her mouth agape. The Duke looked over at her and saluted. I put Carla into drive and cautiously made my way out of the Olneys' yard and back onto what I hoped was the street. I put the car into park and took my shaking hands off the wheel.

"Okay," JP said, trying to calm himself. "Okay. Okay. Okay." He took a breath, and then said, "That was *awesome*! Best roller coaster *ever*!"

"I'm trying not to pee myself," I said. I was ready to go

home—back to James Bond movies—stay up half the night, eat popcorn, sleep a few hours, spend Christmas with the Duke and her parents. I'd lived without the companionship of Pennsylvanian cheerleaders for seventeen and a half years. I could manage another day without them.

JP kept talking. "The whole time I was just thinking, *Man, I am going to die in a baby-blue ski suit.* My mom is going to have to identify my body, and she's going to spend the rest of her life thinking that, in his private time, her son liked to dress up like a hypothermic porn star from the 1970s."

"I think I can manage a night without hash browns," the Duke said.

"Yeah," I agreed. "Yeah." JP protested loudly that he wanted to go on the roller coaster again, but I'd had enough. I called Keun, my finger shaking as I hit his speed-dial number.

"Listen, man, we can't even get out of Grove Park. Too much snow."

"Dude," said Keun. "Try harder. Mitchell's friends haven't even left yet, I don't think. And Billy called a couple of college guys he knows and told them to bring a keg of beer, because the only way these lovely ladies would ever stoop to talking to Billy is if they were intoxic— Hey! Sorry, Billy just hit me with his paper hat. I'm the acting assistant manager, Billy! And I will report your behav— Hey! Anyway, please come. I don't want to be stuck here with Billy and a bunch of sloppy drunk people. My restaurant will get trashed, and I'll get fired, and just…please."

In the back, JP chanted, "Roller coaster! Roller coaster! Roller coaster!" I just flipped the phone shut and turned to the Duke. I was about to lobby for going home when my phone rang again. My mom.

"Couldn't get a car. We're back at the hotel," she said. "Only eight minutes to Christmas, and I was going to wait, but your father is tired and wants to go to bed, so we'll just say it now." My father leaned into the phone, and I could hear his lackluster "Merry Christmas" an octave beneath Mom's boisterous one.

"Merry Christmas," I said. "Call if anything comes up; we've still got two more Bond movies to watch." Just before Mom hung up, my call waiting beeped. Keun. I put him on speaker.

"Tell me you're out of Grove Park."

"Dude, you just called. We're still at the base of the hill," I said. "I think we're headed home, man."

"Get. Here. Now. I just found out who Mitchell invited: Timmy and Tommy Reston. They're on their way. You can still beat them. I know you can! You must! My Cheertastic Christmas Miracle will not be ruined by the Reston twins!" He hung up then. Keun had a certain flair for the dramatic, but I could see his point. The Reston Twins could ruin almost anything. Timmy and Tommy Reston were identical twins who bore absolutely no resemblance to each other. Timmy weighed three hundred pounds, but he wasn't fat. He was just strong, and incredibly fast, and thus the best football player on our football team. Tommy, on the other hand, could fit into one leg of Timmy's jeans, but what he lacked in size, he more than made up for in crazed aggression. When we were in middle school, Timmy and Tommy would get into these epic fights with each other on the basketball court. I don't think either of them had any of their original teeth.

The Duke turned to me. "Okay, it's not just about us any-more, or about cheerleaders. This is about protecting Keun from the Reston twins."

"If they get snowed in at the Waffle House for a few days, and run low on food, you know what's gonna happen," JP said.

The Duke picked up the joke. She was good at that. "They'll have to turn to cannibalism. And Keun will be the first to go."

I just shook my head. "But the car," I said.

"Think of the cheerleaders," JP implored. But I wasn't thinking of the cheerleaders when I nodded. I was thinking of cresting the hill, of the plowed streets that could take us anywhere.

Chapter Five

The Duke, as usual, had a plan. We were still parked in the middle of the road when she shared it with us. "So the problem was that we ran out of speed on the way up the hill. Why? Because we didn't carry enough speed *to* the hill. So back up as far as you can in a straight line, and then gun it. We'll hit the hill going much faster, and the momentum will take us to the top."

It did not strike me as a particularly compelling plan, but I couldn't think of a better one, so I drove backward as far as I could, the hill directly in front of us, barely visible through the fast-falling snow in the headlights. I didn't stop until I was in somebody's front yard, a towering oak tree a few feet behind Carla's back bumper. I spun the tires a little to get down to the hard-packed snow.

"Seat belts buckled?" I asked.

"Yes," they answered together.

"Air bags all on?"

"Affirmative," the Duke said. I glanced over at her. She smiled and raised her eyebrows. I nodded to her.

"I need a countdown, people."

"Five," they said in unison. "Four. Three." I put the gearshift in neutral and began revving the engine. "Two. One." I slammed Carla into drive and we shot off, accelerating in fits and starts between moments of hydroplaning on the snow pack. We hit the hill at forty miles per hour, twenty-five over the Grove Park speed limit. I stood up out of the seat, pressed against the belt, all my weight on the accelerator, but the tires were spinning and we began to slow, so I tapered off.

"Come on!" the Duke said.

"You can do this, Carla," JP mumbled quietly from the back, and she continued forward, slowing incrementally with each passing moment.

"Carla, get your fat gas-guzzling ass to the top of the hill!" I shouted, hitting the steering wheel.

"Don't make fun of her," the Duke said. "She needs gentle encouragement. Carla, baby, we love you. You are such a good car. And we believe in you. We believe in you one hundred percent."

JP began to panic. "We're not gonna make it."

The Duke answered soothingly, "Don't listen to him, Carla.

You're gonna do this." I could see the crest of the hill again, and the newly plowed blacktop of the highway. And Carla was like, *I think I can, I think I can,* and the Duke just kept petting the dashboard, saying, "I love you, Carla. You know that, don't you? I wake up every morning and the first thing I think is that I love Tobin's mom's car. I know that's weird, baby, but I do. I love you. And I know you can do this."

I kept tapping the accelerator, and the wheels kept spinning. Down to eight miles per hour. We were approaching a snow-drift three feet tall where the snowplow had dumped all the snow, blocking our path. We were so close. The speedometer shuttering around five miles per hour.

"Oh God, it's a long way down," JP said, his voice cracking. I glanced in the rearview. It sure was.

We were still inching forward, but only just. The hill was starting to level out, but we were going to come up just short. I kept tapping the accelerator to no avail. "Carla," the Duke said, "it's time to tell you the truth. I'm in love with you. I want to be with you, Carla. I've never felt this way about a c—"

The tires caught on the snow as I had the accelerator near the floor and we blew forward through the snowdrift, the snow as high as the base of the windshield, but we barreled past, half over the snowdrift and half through it. Carla bottomed out on the other side of the drift, and then I slammed on the brakes as we approached the stop sign. Carla's back end fishtailed, and all of a sudden instead of being at the stop sign we were on the highway, facing in the proper direction. I let off the brake and started off down the highway.

"YESSSSSS!" shouted JP from the back. He leaned forward and rubbed the Duke's mess of curly hair. "WE JUST DID SUCH AN AWESOME JOB OF NOT DYING!"

"You sure know how to talk to a car," I told the Duke. I could feel my blood pressure in my entire body. She looked outstandingly calm as she finger-combed her hair back into place.

"Desperate times call for desperate measures," she answered.

It was a blissful first five miles—the highway winds up and down some mountains, which makes for treacherous driving, but we were the only car on the road, and while the road was wet, the salt kept it from being icy. Plus, I was driving a cautious twenty miles an hour, which made the curves seem less terrifying. We were all quiet for a long time—thinking about the hill-topping, I guess—although periodically JP would exhale loudly through his mouth and say, "I can't believe how not dead we are," or some variant on that theme. The snow was too thick and the road too wet for music, so we just sat in silence.

And then after a while the Duke said, "What is it with you and cheerleaders anyway?" She was saying this to me; I knew because for a few months I'd gone out with a girl named

Brittany, who happened to be a cheerleader. Our cheerleading team was actually quite good; they were, on average, far better athletes than the football team they rooted for. They were also notorious for leaving a trail of broken hearts—Stuart Weintraub, the guy Keun had seen in the Waffle House, had been absolutely annihilated by this cheerleader Chloe.

"Um, could it be how hot they are?" JP suggested.

"No," I said, trying to be serious. "It was a coincidence. I didn't like her *because* she was a cheerleader. I mean, she's nice, right?"

The Duke scoffed. "Yeah, in that Joseph-Stalin-I-will-crush-my-enemies kind of way."

JP said to the Duke, "Brittany was cool. She just didn't like *you*, because she didn't get it."

"Didn't get what?" asked the Duke.

"You know, that you're not, like, a threat. Like, most girls, if they have a boyfriend, they don't want their boyfriend hanging out all the time with another girl. And Brittany didn't get that you, like, aren't really a girl."

"If by that you mean that I dislike celebrity magazines, prefer food to anorexia, refuse to watch TV shows about models, and hate the color pink, then yes. I am proud to be not really a girl."

It was true that Brittany didn't like the Duke, but she also didn't like JP. She didn't even like me that much, really. The more we hung out, the more Brittany would get annoyed with my sense of humor and my table manners and everything, which was why we broke up. The truth is that it never mattered that much to me. I was bummed when she dumped me, but it wasn't a Weintraub-style catastrophe. I didn't ever love Brittany, I guess. That was the difference. She was cute and smart and not uninteresting to talk to, but we never actually *did* talk about much. I never felt like everything was at stake with her, because I always knew how it would end. She never seemed worth the risk.

God, I hated talking about Brittany, but the Duke brought her up all the time, probably just for the unadulterated pleasure of annoying me. Or else because she never had any drama of her own to discuss. Lots of guys liked the Duke, but she never seemed interested in anybody. She didn't want to talk your ear off about some guy and how cute he was, and how he sometimes paid her attention and sometimes didn't and all that crap. I liked that about her. The Duke was just normal: she liked to joke around and talk about movies, and she didn't mind yelling or getting yelled at. She was much more like a person than other girls were.

"I don't have a thing for cheerleaders," I repeated.

"But," JP said, "we both have a thing for hot girls who love Twister. That's not about loving cheerleaders, Duke: that's about loving freedom and hope and the indomitable American spirit."

"Yeah, well, call me unpatriotic, but I don't see the cheer-leader thing. Cheer isn't sexy. Dark is sexy. Ambivalent is sexy. Deeper-than-it-looks-at-first-glance is sexy."

"Right," JP said. "That's why you're going out with Billy Talos. Nothing says dark and brooding like a Waffle House waiter."

I glanced in the rearview mirror to see if JP was kidding, but he didn't seem to be. She reached around and punched him on the knee and said, "It's just a job."

"Wait, you're going out with Billy Talos?" I asked. I was surprised mostly because it didn't seem like the Duke would ever go out with anybody, but also because Billy Talos was a beer-and-football kind of guy, whereas the Duke was more of a Shirley-Temple-and-live-theater kind of girl.

The Duke didn't say anything for a second. "No. He just asked me to Winter Formal."

I didn't say anything. It seemed weird the Duke would tell JP about something but not me. JP said, "No offense, but Billy Talos is a little bit *greasy*, isn't he? I feel like if you wrung out his hair every day or two, you could potentially end America's dependence on foreign oil."

"No offense taken," the Duke said, laughing. Clearly she wasn't *that* keen on him. But still, I couldn't picture the Duke with Billy Talos—oily hair aside, he just didn't seem very, like, funny or interesting. But whatever. The Duke and JP moved on to an impassioned discussion of the Waffle House's menu, and whether its raisin toast was superior to its regular toast. It was fun background noise for the drive. The snowflakes hit the windshield and instantly melted. The wipers shoved them aside. The high-beam headlights lit up the snow and the wet road, and I could see just enough of the asphalt to know where my lane was, and where I was going.

I could have driven down that road for a long time before I got tired, but it was almost time to turn onto Sunrise Avenue and head through downtown toward the interstate and Waffle House. It was 12:26. In the morning.

"Hey," I said, interrupting them.

"What?" asked the Duke.

I stole a glance away from the road to talk directly to her. "Merry Christmas."

"Merry Christmas," she said back. "Merry Christmas, JP."

"Merry Christmas, asshats."

Chapter Six

The banks of snow on either side of Sunrise Avenue were huge, as tall as the car, and I felt like we were driving at the bottom of an endless snowboard half-pipe. JP and the Duke were being quiet, all of us concentrating on the road. We had a couple miles to go before we got downtown, and then the Waffle House was a mile east, just off the interstate. Our silence was interrupted by a nineties rap song playing on JP's phone. "Keun," he said. He turned the speaker on.

"WHERE THE HELL ARE YOU GUYS?"

The Duke leaned around so she could be heard. "Keun, look out the window and tell me what you see."

"I'll tell you what I don't see! I don't see you and JP and Tobin in the parking lot of the Waffle House! No word on

Mitchell's college friends, but Billy just heard from the twins: they're about to turn onto Sunrise."

"Then we're fine, because we're *already* on Sunrise," I said.

"HURRY. The cheerleaders want their Twister! Wait, hold on...They're practicing a pyramid, and they need me to spot them. *Spot* them. You know what that means? If they fall, they fall *into my arms*. So I gotta go." I heard the click of Keun hanging up.

"Floor it," JP said. I laughed and kept my speed steady. We just needed to maintain our lead.

As far as skiing down a road in an SUV goes, Sunrise Avenue isn't bad, because unlike most streets in Gracetown, it's pretty straight. With the tire tracks to guide me, my speed crept up to twenty-five. I figured we'd be downtown in two minutes, and eating Keun's special off-menu cheesy waffles in ten. I thought about those waffles topped with melted Kraft singles, about how they tasted both savory and sweet, a taste so profound and complex that it can't even be compared to other tastes, only to emotions. Cheesy waffles, I was thinking, taste like love without the fear of love's dissolution, and as we came to the 90-degree curve Sunrise Avenue takes before heading straight downtown, I could almost taste them.

I approached the curve exactly as I was taught in drivers' ed: with my hands at two and ten o'clock, I turned the steering wheel slightly to the right while gently applying the brakes.

But Carla did not respond appropriately. She kept going straight.

"Tobin," the Duke said. And then, "Turn turn Tobin turn."

I didn't say anything; I just kept turning the steering wheel to the right and pressing the brake. We began to slow as we approached the snowdrift, but we never gave even the slightest hint of turning. Instead, we barreled into a wall of snow with a noise like a sonic boom.

Damn it. Carla tilting to the left. The windshield a wall of tar-speckled white.

Once we stopped, I spun my head around in time to see chunks of icy snow falling behind the car, beginning to cover us up. I responded to this development with the kind of sophisticated language for which I am famous. "Crap crap crap crap crap crap crap stupid stupid stupid stupid stupid crap."

Chapter Seven

The Duke reached over and turned the car off. "Risk of carbon-monoxide poisoning," she said matter-of-factly, as if we were not stone-cold screwed ten miles from home.

"Out through the back!" she ordered, and the authority in her voice calmed me. JP scrambled into the way-back and then opened the top hatch. He bolted out. The Duke followed, and then me, feetfirst. Having now gathered my thoughts, I was finally able to eloquently articulate my feelings about the matter. "Crap crap crap!" I kicked Carla's back bumper, as the snow fell wet onto my face. "Stupid idea God stupid God my parents crap crap crap."

JP put a hand on my shoulder. "It'll be fine."

"No," I said. "It won't. And you know it won't."

"Yes, it will," JP insisted. "You know what? It will *totally* be fine, because I'm going to dig the car out of the snow, and someone will come by, and we'll get help from them—even if it's the twins. I mean, it's not like the twins are going to leave us out here to *freeze* to death."

The Duke looked me over and smirked. "May I point out," she said, "how much you will soon regret not listening to my footwear advice back at the house?" I glanced down at the snow falling on my Pumas and winced.

JP remained upbeat. "Yes! This is going to be fine! There's a reason that God gave me ripped arms and pecs, dude. It's so that I can dig your car out of the snow. I don't even need your help. You just chat among yourselves, and let the Hulk work his magic."

I looked at JP. He weighed perhaps 145 pounds. Squirrels have more impressive musculature. But JP was unfazed. He tied down the earflaps of his hat. He reached into his oh-so-tight snowsuit, pulled out wool gloves, and turned back to the car.

I wasn't interested in helping, because I knew it was hopeless. Carla was six feet into a snowdrift almost as tall as my head, and we didn't even have a shovel. I just stood in the road next to the Duke, wiping the wisp of wet hair sticking out under my hat. "Sorry," I said to the Duke.

"Eh, it's not your fault. It's Carla's fault. You were turning the wheel. Carla just wasn't listening. I knew I shouldn't have loved her. She's like all the others, Tobin: as soon as I confess my love, she abandons me."

I laughed. "I never abandoned you," I said, patting her on the back.

"Yeah, well, (a.) I never confessed my love to you, and (b.) I'm not even female to you."

"We're so screwed," I said absentmindedly as I looked back to see JP tunneling his way around the passenger side of the car. He was like a little mole, and surprisingly effective.

"Yeah, I'm already kind of cold," she said, and then stood next to me, her side against mine. I couldn't imagine how she could be cold beneath that gigantic ski coat, but it didn't matter. It reminded me that at least I wasn't alone out here. I reached up and mussed her hat as I put my arm around her. "Duke, what are we gonna do?"

"This is probably more fun than Waffle House would be, anyway," she said.

"But the Waffle House has *Billy Talos*," I said mockingly. "Now I know why you wanted to go. It had nothing to do with hash browns!"

"Everything has to do with hash browns," she said. "As the poet wrote: So much depends upon the golden hash browns, glazed with oil, beside the scrambled eggs."

I didn't know what she was talking about. I just nodded and stared up the road, wondering when a car would come to rescue us.

"I know it sucks, but it's certainly the most adventurous Christmas ever."

"Yeah, which is actually a good reminder of why I am generally opposed to adventure."

"Nothing wrong with a little risk-taking here and there," the Duke said, looking up at me.

"I couldn't disagree more, and this just proves my point. I took a risk, and now Carla is stuck in a snowbank, and I will soon be disowned."

"I promise you that it will be okay," the Duke said, her voice measured, quiet.

"You're good at that," I said. "At, like, saying crazy things in a way that makes me believe them."

She stood up on her toes, grabbed me by the shoulders, and looked at me, her nose red and snow-wet, her face close to mine. "You do not like cheerleaders. You think they are lame. You like cute, funny, emo girls who I will enjoy hanging out with."

I shrugged my shoulders. "Yeah, that didn't work," I said.

"Damn it." She smiled.

JP emerged from his snow tunnel, shook snow off his periwinkle onesie, and announced, "Tobin, I have a small piece of bad news, but I don't want you to overreact."

"Okay," I said, nervous.

"I can't really think of an easy way to say this. Um, in your opinion, what would be the ideal number of wheels for Carla to currently possess?"

I closed my eyes and let my head swivel up, the streetlight bright through my eyelids, the snow on my lips.

JP continued, "Because to be totally honest, I think the best possible number of wheels for Carla would be four. And right now there are three wheels physically connected to Carla herself, a nonideal number. Fortunately, the fourth is just a very slight distance away, but unfortunately I am not an expert in wheel reattachment."

I pulled my hat down over my face. The depth of my screwedness washed over me, and for the first time I felt cold—cold at my wrists, where my gloves did not quite meet my jacket, cold on my face, and cold in my feet, where the melted snow was already soaking into my socks. My parents wouldn't beat me or brand me with a hot coat hanger or anything. They were too nice for cruelty. And *that*, ultimately, is why I felt so bad: they didn't deserve to have a kid who broke a wheel off their beloved Carla on the way to spend the small hours of Christmas morning with fourteen cheerleaders.

Someone pulled my hat up. JP. "I hope you're not going to let a little hurdle like not having a car keep us from the Waffle House," he said.

The Duke, who was leaning against the half-exposed back end of Carla, laughed, but I didn't.

"JP, now is not the time for funny ha-ha," I said.

He stood up straighter, as if to remind me he was just a little bit taller than I, and then took two steps into the middle of the road, so that he stood directly beneath the streetlight's beam. "I'm not being funny ha-ha," he said. "Is it funny ha-ha to believe in your dreams? Is it funny ha-ha to overcome adversity in order to make those dreams come true? Was it funny ha-ha when Huckleberry Finn rafted hundreds of miles on the Mississippi River in order to make out with nineteenth-century cheerleaders? Was it funny ha-ha when thousands of men and women devoted their lives to space exploration so that Neal Armstrong could hook up with cheerleaders on the moon? *No!* And it's not funny ha-ha to believe that on this great night of miracles, we three wise men must trudge onward toward the great yellow light of the Waffle House sign!"

"Wise *people*," the Duke said dispassionately.

"Oh, come on!" JP said. "I get nothing for that? Nothing?!" He was shouting now over the sound-muffling snow, and JP's voice seemed to me the only sound in the world. "Do you want more? I've got more. Lady and gentleman, when my parents left Korea with nothing but the clothes on their backs and the considerable wealth they had amassed in the shipping business, they had a dream. They had a dream that one day amid the snowy hilltops of western North Carolina, their son would lose his virginity to a cheerleader in the women's bathroom of a Waffle House just off the interstate. My parents have sacrificed so much for this dream! And that is why we must journey on, despite all trials and tribulations! Not for me and least of all for the poor cheerleader in question, but for my parents, and indeed for all immigrants who came to this great nation in the hopes that somehow, some way, their children might have what they themselves could never have: cheerleader sex."

The Duke applauded. I was laughing, but I nodded to JP. The more I thought about it, the stupider it seemed to go hang out with a bunch of cheerleaders I didn't even know, who would only be in town for one night, anyway. Nothing against making out with cheerleaders, but I had some experience in the field, and while it was good fun, it was hardly worth trudging through the snow for. But what could I lose by continuing that had not already been lost? Only my life, and I was more likely to survive by walking the three miles to the Waffle House than the ten miles home. I crawled into the back of the SUV, grabbed some blankets, made sure all the doors were closed, then locked Carla. I put a hand on her bumper and said, "We'll come back for you."

"That's right," the Duke said soothingly to Carla. "We never leave our fallen behind."

We had trudged no more than a hundred feet past the curve when I heard an engine rumbling.

The twins.

Chapter Eight

The twins drove an old, muscled-up, low-riding, cherry-red Ford Mustang—not the kind of car celebrated for its handling in inclement weather. So I felt sure that they, too, would miss the curve, probably rear-ending Carla. But as the engine noise grew to a roar, the Duke pushed JP and me to the side of the road anyway.

They came roaring around the corner—the Mustang kicking up powder behind it, the back end fishtailing but somehow staying on the road—tiny Tommy Reston maniacally turning the steering wheel back and forth. He was some kind of snow-driving savant, the little creep.

So great was the size difference between them that the Mustang tilted visibly to the left, where Timmy Reston's gigantic body had somehow been inserted into the passenger seat. I could see Timmy smiling, the dimples an inch deep on his huge and meaty cheeks. Tommy brought the Mustang to a quick stop maybe thirty feet in front of us, rolled down the window, and leaned his head out.

"Y'all run into some car trouble?" he asked.

I started to walk toward the car. "Yeah, yeah," I said. "We ran into a snowbank. I'm glad to see you guys. Could you give us a ride, at least to downtown?"

"Sure," he said. "Get in." Tommy looked past me then and, with a certain lilt in his voice, said, "Hey there, Angie." Which is technically the Duke's name.

"Hi," she said. I turned back to them and waved for JP and the Duke to come over. I was almost to the car now. I stayed on the driver's side, figuring that it would be impossible to slip into the backseat behind Timmy.

I was even with the hood when Tommy said, "Y'know what? I got room in the back for two losers." And then louder, so JP and the Duke could hear him as they approached, he said, "But I don't got room for two losers *and* a slut." He hit the accelerator, and for just a second the tires spun on the Mustang and nothing happened. I lunged for the door handle, but by the time my fingers got to where it was, the Mustang had taken off. I lost my balance and fell down into the snow. The passing Mustang kicked snow into my face and on my neck and down my chest. I spit some of it out and then watched as Timmy and Tommy sped toward JP and the Duke.

They stood together on the side of the road, the Duke flipping Timmy and Tommy off with both hands. As the Mustang approached, JP took a small step into the road and lifted one of his legs off the ground. Just as the Mustang passed, he kicked its rear quarter panel. It was a small kick, kind of girlish. I couldn't even hear his foot making contact with the car. And yet, somehow it upset the delicate balance of the vehicle just enough—and all at once, the Mustang turned sideways. Tommy must have tried to gun the engine while turning into the skid, but it didn't work. The Mustang shot off the road and into a pile of plowed snow, disappearing entirely except for the brake lights.

I scrambled to my feet and ran toward JP and the Duke.

"Holy crap!" JP said, looking at his foot. "I am so frakkin' strong!"

The Duke walked purposefully toward the Mustang. "We gotta dig them out," she said. "They could die in there."

"Screw that," I said. "I mean, after what they just did? And plus they called you a slut!" But for a moment, I could see her blushing even over the windburn on her cheeks. I always hated that word, and it particularly pissed me off to hear it applied to the Duke, because even though it was a ridiculous and patently untrue thing to say about her, she was still embarrassed, and she knew that we knew that she was embarrassed, and...whatever. It just pissed me off. But I didn't want to call more attention to it by saying anything.

Regardless, the Duke rallied almost instantaneously. "Oh, yeah," she said, rolling her eyes. "Tommy Reston called me a slut. *Wah-wah*. It's an attack on my very womanhood. Whatever. I'm just happy that someone's acknowledging the possibility that I might be a sexual being!"

I looked at her quizzically. I kept walking toward the Mustang with her, and finally I said, "Nothing personal, but I don't want to picture *anyone* who's into Billy Talos as a sexual being."

She stopped, turned, and looked up at me. Very seriously, she said, "Will you just shut up about him? I don't even really like him."

I didn't understand why she was so upset about *that* of all things. We always ragged on each other. "What?" I said defensively.

And she said, "Oh, Christ, forget it. Just come help me save these retarded misogynists from carbon-monoxide poisoning."

And we would have, I'm sure. If necessary, we would have spent hours tunneling out the Reston boys. But our efforts, as it happened, were not needed, because Timmy Reston, being the world's strongest man, just pushed aside thousands of pounds of snow and successfully opened his door. He stood up, only his shoulders and head above the snow, and shouted, "You. Gonna. Die."

It wasn't entirely clear to me whether Timmy meant "you" singular, as in JP, who had already started running, or "you" plural, as in a group of people that included me. But regardless, I took off, urging on the Duke. I kept behind the Duke because I didn't want her to slip without my knowing or anything. I turned around to check the twins' progress and saw Timmy Reston's shoulders and head make their way through the mass of snow. I saw Tommy's head pop up in the space where Timmy had initially exited the car, and he was shouting an angry, incomprehensible flurry of words, the words so smushed in on each other that all I could really hear was his rage. We got past them while they were still trying to get all the way out of the snowbank, and then kept running.

"Come on, Duke," I said.

"I'm...trying," she answered, breathing between words. I could hear them shouting now, and when I glanced back, I could see that they were out of the snow and running toward us, gaining with every stride. There was too much snow on both sides of us to run anywhere but on the street. But if we continued much longer, the twins would catch us and, pre-sumably, proceed to feast upon our kidneys.

I have heard it said that sometimes in moments of intense crisis, a person's adrenaline can surge so much that for a brief period of time he experiences superhuman strength. And per-haps this explains how I managed to grab the Duke, throw her over my right shoulder, and then run like an Olympic sprinter across the slippery snow.

I carried the Duke for several minutes before I even started to get tired, never looking back and never needing to, because the Duke was looking back for me, saying, "Keep going keep going you're faster than they are you are you are," and even if she was talking to me like she talked to Carla on the way up the hill, I didn't care—it worked. It kept my feet pumping beneath me, my arm wrapped around her waist and the small of her back, and I just ran until we reached a small bridge over a two-lane road. I saw JP lying flat on his stomach on the side of the bridge. I figured he'd slipped, and slowed down to help him up, but he just shouted, "No, no, keep going keep going!" And so I kept going. My breathing was quite labored now as the Duke's weight bore down on my shoulder. "Listen, can I put you down?" I asked.

"Yeah, I'm getting kinda queasy anyway."

I stopped and let her down, and said, "You go ahead." She took off without me, and I just slumped down, hands on knees, and watched JP running toward me. In the distance, I could see the twins—well, I could see Timmy, anyway; I suspected Tommy was hiding behind his brother's endless girth. I knew the situation was hopeless now—the twins would inevitably catch us, but I believed we had to fight on, anyway. I took a series of quick, deep breaths as JP reached me, and then I started to run, but he grabbed my coat and said, "No. No. Watch."

So we stood there in the road, the wet air burning my lungs, Tommy bearing down on us, his fat face dominated by a broad scowl. And then, with no warning, Tommy fell face-first into the ground, like he'd been shot in the back. He barely even had time to reach his hands out to break the fall. Timmy tripped over Tommy's body and sprawled out on the snow, too.

"What the hell did you do?" I asked as we took off running toward the Duke.

"I used all my remaining floss to tie a trip line between the sides of the bridge. I raised it right after you carried the Duke past," he said.

"That's rather awesome," I said.

"My gums are already disappointed with me," he mumbled in response. We kept jogging, but I couldn't hear the twins anymore, and when I glanced over my shoulder, I could see only the still-driving snow.

By the time we caught up with the Duke, the brick buildings of downtown surrounded us, and we finally made our way off Sunrise onto the recently plowed Main Street. We were still jogging, although I could barely feel my feet anymore from the cold and the exhaustion. I couldn't hear the twins, but I was still afraid of them. Just one mile to go. We could be there in twenty minutes if we jogged.

The Duke said, "Call Keun, find out if those college guys have already beaten us."

Still keeping pace, I reached into my jeans, pulled out my phone, and called Keun's cell. Someone—not Keun—answered on the first ring.

"Is Keun there?"

"This Tobin?" I recognized the voice now. Billy Talos.

"Yeah," I said. "Hey, Billy."

"Hey, do you got Angie with you?"

"Uh, yeah," I said.

"Y'all close?"

I hedged my bets, not knowing if he would use the information to help his friends. "Reasonably," I said.

"Okay, here's Keun," he said. Keun's boisterous voice came on the line then. "What's up! Where are you! Dude, I think Billy is in love. Like, right now, he is sitting down next to a Madison. One of the Madisons. There are several of them. The world is full of Magical Madisons!"

I glanced over at the Duke to see if she had heard anything through the phone, but she was just looking straight ahead, still jogging. I thought Billy had asked about the Duke because he wanted to see her, not because he didn't want her to catch him trying to hook up with someone else. Lame.

"TOBIN!" Keun shouted into my ear.

"Yeah, what's up?"

"Uh, you called me," he pointed out.

"Right, yeah. We're close. We're at the corner of Main and Third. We should be there in half an hour."

"Excellent, I think you'll still get here first. The college guys are stuck on the side of the road somewhere, apparently."

"Great. Okay, I'll call when we're close."

"Awesome. Oh, hey, you guys have Twister, right?"

I looked over at JP, and then to the Duke. I put a finger over the mic and said, "Did we bring the Twister?"

JP stopped running. The Duke followed suit. JP said, "Crap, we forgot it in Carla."

I uncovered the mic and said, "Keun, I'm sorry, man, but we left Twister in the car."

"Not good," he said with a hint of menace in his voice.

"I know, it sucks. Sorry."

"I'll call you back," he said, and hung up the phone.

We walked for another minute before Keun called me back. "Listen," he said, "we took a vote, and unfortunately, you're gonna need to go back and get the Twister. The majority agreed that no one will be allowed in without Twister."

"What? Who took the vote?"

"Billy, Mitchell, and myself."

"Well, come on, Keun. Lobby them or something! Carla is a twenty-minute walk into the wind and plus the Reston twins are back there somewhere. Get one of them to change their votes!"

"Unfortunately, the vote was three to zero."

"What? Keun? You voted *against us*?"

"I don't see it as a vote against you," he explained. "I see it as a vote in favor of Twister."

"Surely you're kidding," I said. The Duke and JP couldn't hear Keun's end of the conversation, but they were now looking on nervously.

"I don't kid about Twister," Keun said. "You can still get here first! Just hurry!"

I flipped the phone shut and pulled my hat down over my face. "Keun says he won't let us in without Twister," I mumbled.

I stood under the awning of a café and tried to kick the snow off my frozen Pumas. JP was pacing back and forth on the street, looking generally agitated. No one said anything for a while. I kept looking up the street for the Reston twins, but they didn't appear.

"We're going to the Waffle House," JP said.

"Yeah, right," I answered.

"We're going," he said. "We're gonna take a different route back so we don't run into the Reston twins, and we're gonna get Twister, and we're gonna go to the Waffle House. It'll only take an hour if we hurry."

I turned to the Duke, who was standing beside me under the awning. She would tell JP. She would tell him that we just needed to give up and call 911 and see if someone somewhere could pick us up. "I want hash browns," the Duke said from behind me. "I want them scattered and smothered and covered. I want them chunked, topped, and diced."

"What you want is Billy Talos," I said.

She elbowed me in the side. "I said to *shut up* about that, Jesus. And I don't. I want hash browns. That's it. That's the whole thing. I am hungry, and I am the kind of hungry that only hash browns will fix, and so we are going back and we are getting Twister." She just marched off, and JP followed her. I stood under the awning for a moment, but finally I decided that being in a bad mood with your friends beats being in a bad mood without them.

When I caught up to them, all of our hoods were scrunched shut against the oncoming wind as we walked up a street parallel to Sunrise. We had to shout to be heard, and the Duke said, "I'm glad you're here," and I shouted back, "Thanks," and she shouted, "Honestly, hash browns mean nothing without you."

I laughed and pointed out that "Hash Browns Mean Nothing Without You" was a pretty good name for a band.

"Or a song," the Duke said, and then she started singing all glam rock, a glove up to her face holding an imaginary mic as she rocked out an a cappella power ballad. "Oh, I deep fried for you / But now I weep 'n' cry for you / Oh, babe, this meal was made for two / And these hash browns mean nothing, oh these hash browns mean nothing, yeah these HASH BROWNS MEAN NOTHIN' without you."

Chapter Nine

The Duke and JP made great time up the street—they weren't running, but they were sure walking fast. My feet felt frozen, and I was tired from carrying the Duke, so I lagged behind a little, and the onrushing wind meant that I could hear their conversation, but they couldn't hear anything I said.

The Duke was saying (again) that cheerleading wasn't a sport, and then JP pointed at her and gave her a stern shake of the head. "I don't want to hear another negative word about cheerleaders. If it weren't for cheerleaders, who would tell us when and how to be happy during athletic events? If it weren't for cheerleaders, how would America's prettiest girls get the exercise that's so vital to a healthy life?"

I scrambled to catch up with them so I could get off a

line. "Also, without cheerleading, what would become of the polyester miniskirt industry?" I asked. Just talking made the walking better, the wind less bitter.

"Exactly," JP said, wiping his nose on the sleeve of my dad's onesie. "Not even to mention the pom-pom industry. Do you realize how many people around the world are employed in the manufacture, distribution, and sale of pom-poms?"

"Twenty?" guessed the Duke.

"Thousands!" JP answered. "The world must contain millions of pom-poms, attached to millions of cheerleaders! And if it's wrong to want all of those millions of cheerleaders to rub all of their millions of pom-poms on my naked chest, well, then I don't want to be right, Duke. I don't want to be right."

"You're such a clown," she said. "And such a genius."

I fell behind them again but trudged along, not much of a clown and not much of a genius. It was always a pleasure to watch JP show off his wit and see the Duke rise to the occasion. It took us fifteen minutes to circle back to Carla using a route that avoided Sunrise (and, hopefully, the twins). I climbed in through the trunk and grabbed the Twister, and we took off over a chain-link fence and through someone's backyard so as to head straight west, toward the highway. We figured the twins would take the route we had initially taken. That route was quicker, but we all agreed that we hadn't seen a game of Twister in the hands of either Timmy or Tommy, so we didn't think it mattered if they beat us.

* * * *

We walked in silence for a long time past dark wood-frame houses, and I held the Twister over my head to keep some of the snow out of my face. The snow had accumulated in drifts up to the doorknobs on one side of the street, and I thought about how much snow can change a place. I'd never lived anywhere but here. I'd walked or driven on this block a thousand times. I could remember when all the trees died in the blight, and when they planted new ones in all these yards. And over the fences I could see a block over to Main Street, which I knew even better: I knew each gallery selling folk art to tourists, each outdoor shop selling the kind of hiking boots I wished I was wearing.

But it was new now, all of it—cloaked in a white so pure as to be vaguely menacing. No street or sidewalk beneath me, no fire hydrants. Nothing but the white everywhere, like the place itself was gift-wrapped in snow. And it didn't just look different, either; it smelled different, the air now sharp with cold and the wet acidity of snow. And the eerie silence, just the steady rhythm of our shoes crunching underfoot. I couldn't even hear what JP and the Duke were talking about a few feet in front of me as I got lost in the whited-out world.

And I might have convinced myself that we were the only people left awake in all of western North Carolina had we not seen the bright lights of the Duke and Duchess convenience store when we turned off Third Street and onto Maple.

* * * *

The reason we call the Duke "the Duke" is because when we were in eighth grade, we went one time to the Duke and Duchess. And the thing about the Duke and Duchess convenience store is that instead of calling you "sir" or "ma'am" or "you there" or whatever, the employees of the D and D convenience store are supposed to call you either "Duke" or "Duchess."

Now, the Duke arrived a little late to the puberty party, and on top of that, she also always wore jeans and baseball caps, particularly in middle school. So the predictable thing happened: one day we went into the Duke and Duchess to buy Big League Chew or Mountain Dew Code Red or whatever we were using to rot our teeth on that particular week, and after the Duke had made her purchase, the guy behind the counter said, "Thank you, Duke."

It stuck. At one point, I think in ninth grade, we were all at lunch and JP and Keun and I all offered to start calling her Angie, but she said she hated being called Angie, anyway. So we kept with the Duke. It suited her. She had excellent posture, and she was kind of a born leader and everything, and even though she certainly no longer looked even vaguely boyish, she still mostly acted like one of us.

As we walked up Maple, I noticed JP slowing to walk next to me.

"What's up?" I asked.

"Listen, are you okay?" he asked. He reached up and took the Twister from me and tucked it under his arm.

"Um, yeah?"

"Because you're walking, like, I don't know. Like you don't have ankles or knees?" I looked down and saw that I was indeed walking very strangely, my legs far apart and swiveling, my knees barely bending. I looked a bit like a cowboy after a long ride. "Huh," I said, watching my weird gait. "Hmm. I think my feet are just really cold."

"VERY FAST EMERGENCY STOP!" JP yelled. "We've got some potential frostbite back here!"

I shook my head; I was fine, really, but the Duke turned around and saw me walking and said, "To the D and D!"

So they jogged and I waddled. They beat me into the D and D by a long shot, and by the time I got inside, the Duke was already at the counter, purchasing a four-pack of white cotton socks.

We weren't the only customers. As I sat down in a booth at the D and D's miniature "café," I glanced down to the far booth: there, with a steaming cup in front of him, sat the Tinfoil Guy.

Chapter Ten

"What's up?" JP said to the Tinfoil Guy as I pulled off my soaked shoes. It's sort of hard to describe Tinfoil Guy, because he looks like a somewhat grizzled but generally normal older guy except for the fact that he never, under any circumstances, leaves the house unless his entire body from neck to toes is wrapped in tinfoil. I peeled off my nearly frozen socks. My feet were a pale blue. JP offered me a napkin to wipe them off as Tinfoil Guy spoke.

"How are you three, on this night?" The Tinfoil Guy always talked like that, like life was a horror movie and he was the knife-wielding maniac. But he was generally agreed to be harmless. He'd asked all three of us the question, but he was looking only at me.

"Let's see," I answered. "Our car lost a wheel and I can't feel my feet."

"You looked very lonesome out there," he said. "An epic hero against the elements."

"Yeah. Okay. How are you?" I asked, to be polite. *Why did you ask him a question!* I chastised myself. Stupid Southern manners.

"I'm enjoying a most filling cup of noodles," he said. "I do love a good cup. And then I believe I'll go for another walk."

"You don't get cold, with the foil?" I couldn't stop asking questions!

"What foil?" he asked.

"Uh," I said, "right." The Duke brought me the socks. I put on one pair, and then another, and then a third. I saved the fourth in case I needed dry ones later. I could barely squeeze into my Pumas, but nonetheless, I felt like a new man as I stood up to leave.

"Always a pleasure," Tinfoil Guy said to me.

"Oh, yeah," I said. "Merry Christmas."

"May the pigs of fate fly you safely home," he responded. Right. I felt awful for the lady behind the counter, being stuck with him. As I was on my way out, the woman behind the counter said to me, "Duke?"

I turned. "Yes?"

"I couldn't help but overhear," she said. "About your car."

"Yeah," I said. "Sucks."

"Listen," she said. "We can tow it. We got a truck."

"Really?" I asked.

"Yeah, here, give me something I can write down the number on." I fished around in my coat pocket and found a receipt. She wrote down her number and name, Rachel, in loop-heavy script. "Wow, thanks, Rachel."

"Yeah. A hundred fifty bucks plus five bucks a mile, being a holiday and the weather and everything."

I grimaced but nodded. An expensive tow was a hell of a lot better than no tow at all.

We were barely back out on the road—me walking with a newfound awareness of, and appreciation for, my toes—when JP sidled up to me and said, "Honestly, the fact that Tinfoil Guy is, like, forty and still alive gives me hope that I can have a reasonably successful adulthood."

"Yeah." The Duke was walking ahead of us, munching on Cheetos. "Dude," JP said. "Are you looking at the Duke's butt?"

"What? No." And only in telling the lie did I realize that actually I had been looking at her back, although not specifically her butt.

The Duke turned around. "What are you talking about?"

"Your butt!" JP shouted into the wind.

She laughed. "I know it's what you dream about when you're alone at night, JP."

She slowed and we caught up with her. "Honestly, Duke?" JP said, putting his arm around her. "I hope this doesn't hurt your feelings, but if I ever had a sex dream about you, I would have to locate my subconscious, remove it from my body, and beat it to death with a stick."

She shot him down with her usual aplomb. "That doesn't offend me in the least," she said to him. "If you didn't, I'd have to do it for you." And then she turned and looked over at me. I figured she wanted to see if I was laughing—I was, quietly.

We were walking past Governor's Park, home to the biggest playground in town, when in the distance, I heard an engine, loud and powerful. I thought for a second it might be the twins, but then I looked back, and as it drove under a streetlight, I could see the lights above the roof. "Cop," I said quickly, dashing off into the park. JP and the Duke hurried off the road, too. We hunkered down, half behind a snowdrift and half in it, as the cop drove slowly by, a searchlight arcing across the park.

Only after he passed did it occur to me to say, "He might have given us a ride."

"Yeah, to *jail*," JP said.

"Well, but we aren't doing anything criminal," I said.

JP mulled this over for a moment. Being outside at two thirty in the morning on Christmas certainly *felt* wrong, but that didn't mean it *was* wrong. "Don't be an asshat," JP said.

Fair enough. I did the least asshatty thing I could think of, which was to take a few steps through the calf-high snow away from the road and into Governor's Park. Then I let myself fall backward, my arms out, knowing the snow would meet me thick and soft. I lay there for a moment and then made a snow angel. The Duke dove down onto her belly. "Snow angel with boobs!" she said. JP got a running start and then jumped into the snow, landing sprawled out on his side, the Twister wrapped in his arms. He stood up carefully next to the imprint of his body and said, "Outline of body at homicide investigation!"

"What happened to him?" I asked.

"Someone tried to take his Twister, and he died in heroic defense of it," he explained.

I scampered out of my angel and made another, but this time I used my gloves to give my angel horns. "Snow devil!" the Duke shouted, gleeful. With the snow all around us I felt like a little kid in one of those inflatable moon walks—I couldn't get hurt by falling. I couldn't get hurt by anything. The Duke ran toward me, her shoulder low, her head down, and barreled into my chest, tackling me. We hit the ground together and then my momentum rolled me over her, and her face was close enough to mine that our freezing breath intermingled between us. I felt her weight beneath me and something dropped in my stomach as she smiled at me. There was a fraction of a second when I could have slid off of her but didn't, and then she pushed me off and stood up, brushing the snow off her coat and onto my still-prone body.

We got up and stomped back to the road and continued on. I was wetter and colder than I'd been all night, but we were only a mile from the highway, and from there it was just a quick jog down to the Waffle House.

We started off walking together, the Duke talking about how careful I needed to be about frostbite, and me talking about the lengths I would go to in order to reunite the Duke with her greasy boyfriend, and the Duke kicking me in the calves, and JP calling us both asshats. But after a while, the road started to get snowy again, so I found myself walking on the fairly fresh tire track of what I assumed was that cop car. JP was walking in one of the trails, and me in the other, the Duke a few steps in front of us. "Tobin," he said out of nowhere. I looked up and he was right next to me, high-stepping through the snow. "Not that I'm necessarily in favor of the idea," he said, "but I think maybe you like the Duke."

Chapter Eleven

She was just walking in front of us in her shin-high boots, her hood pulled up, her head down. There's a certain something to the way girls walk—particularly when they aren't wearing fancy shoes or anything, when they're just wearing sneakers or whatever—something about the way their legs connect to their hips. Anyway, the Duke was walking, and there was a certain something to it, and I was kind of disgusted with myself for thinking about that certain something. I mean, my girl cousins probably walked with the same certain something, but the point is that sometimes you notice it and sometimes you don't. When Brittany the cheerleader walks, you notice it. When the Duke walks, you don't. Usually.

I spent so long thinking about the Duke and her walk and the lazy wet curls down her back, and the way the thickness of her coat made her arms stick out from her body a little, and all of that, that I took way too long to respond to JP. But finally I said, "Don't be an asshat."

And he said, "You just spent a hell of a long time thinking up that quality comeback."

"No," I said finally. "I don't like the Duke, not like that. I'd tell you if I did, but it's like liking your cousin."

"It's funny you should mention that, because I have a really hot cousin, actually."

"That's disgusting."

"Duke," JP called. "What were you telling me about cousin-screwing the other day? It's, like, totally safe?"

She turned around to us and continued walking, her back to the wind, the snow blowing around her and toward us. "No, it's not totally safe. It raises the risk of birth defects slightly. But I was reading in a book for history that there's, like, a 99.9999 percent chance that at least one of your great-great-great-grandparents married a first cousin."

"So what you're saying is that there's nothing wrong with hooking up with your cousin."

The Duke paused and turned to walk with us. She sighed loudly. "That is not what I'm saying. Also I'm a little tired of talking about cousin hookups and hot cheerleaders."

"What should we talk about instead? The weather? It looks like we're getting some snow," JP said.

"Honestly, I would rather talk about the weather."

I said, "You know, Duke, there are male cheerleaders. You could always just hook up with them."

The Duke stopped talking and totally snapped. Her face was scrunched up as she yelled at me. "You know what? It's sexist. Okay? I hate to be, like, the watchdog for the ladies or whatever, but when you spend a whole night talking about doing girls because they've got short skirts on, or how hot pom-poms are, or whatever. It's sexist, okay? Female cheerleaders wearing dainty little male-fantasy outfits—sexist! Just *assuming* they're dying to make out with you—sexist! I realize that you are, like, bursting with a constant need to rub yourself against girl flesh or whatever, but can you just try to talk about it a little less in front of me?!"

I looked down at the snow falling on snow. I felt like I'd just gotten caught cheating on a test or something. I wanted to say that I didn't even *care* if we went to the Waffle House anymore, but I just shut up. The three of us kept walking in a line. The swirling wind was at our backs now, and I stared down and tried to let it push me on to the Waffle House.

"I'm sorry," I heard the Duke say to JP.

"Nah, it's our fault," he responded without looking over. "I was being an asshat. We just need to…I don't know, sometimes it's hard to remember."

"Yeah, maybe I should thrust my boobs out more or something." The Duke said that loud, like I was supposed to hear it.

There is always the risk: something is good and good and good and good, and then all at once it gets awkward. All at once, she sees you looking at her, and then she doesn't want to joke around with you anymore, because she doesn't want to seem flirty, because she doesn't want you to think she likes you. It's such a disaster, whenever, in the course of human relationships, someone begins to chisel away at the wall of separation between friendship and kissing. Breaking down that wall is the kind of story that might have a happy middle—oh, look, we broke down this wall, I'm going to look at you like a girl and you're going to look at me like a boy and we're going to play a fun game called Can I Put My Hand There What About There What About There. And sometimes that happy middle looks so great that you can convince yourself that it's not the middle but will last forever.

That middle is never the end, though. It wasn't the end with Brittany, God knows. And Brittany and I hadn't even been close friends, not really. Not like the Duke. The Duke was my *best* friend, if I had to pick. I mean, the one person I'd take to a desert island? The Duke. The one CD I'd take? A mix, called "The Earth Is Blue Like an Orange," that she made for me last Christmas. The one book I'd take? The longest book I've ever liked, *The Book Thief*, which the Duke recommended to me. And I did not want to have a happy middle with the Duke at the expense of an Inevitably Disastrous Forever.

But then again (and here is one of my main complaints

about human consciousness): once you think a thought, it is extremely difficult to unthink it. And I had thought *the thought*. We whined about the cold. The Duke kept sniffling, because we didn't have any tissue and she didn't want to blow her nose on the ground. JP, having agreed not to talk about cheerleaders, kept talking about hash browns instead.

JP meant "hash browns" only as a symbol for cheerleaders—it was clear because he was, like, "My favorite thing about the hash browns at the Waffle House is that they wear the cutest little skirts." "Hash browns are always in a great mood. And that rubs off. Seeing hash browns happy makes me happy."

It seemed like as long as it was JP talking, the Duke didn't find it annoying. She was just laughing and responding by *actually* talking about hash browns. "They're going to be so warm," she said. "So crispy and golden and delicious. I want four large orders. Also some raisin toast. God, I love that raisin toast. Mmm, it's going to be carbtastic." I could see the interstate overpass in the distance, the snow piled high on the sides of the bridge. The Waffle House was still probably a half mile away, but it was a straight shot now. The black letters in their yellow boxes promising cheesy waffles, and Keun's impish smile, and the kind of girls who make unthinking easier.

And then as we kept walking, I began to see the light emerge through the thick veil of snow. Not the sign itself at first, but the light it produced. And then finally the sign itself, towering above the tiny restaurant, the sign bigger and brighter than

the little shack of a restaurant could ever be, those black letters in their yellow squares promising warmth and sustenance:
WAFFLE HOUSE. I fell to my knees in the middle of the street
and shouted, "Not in a castle nor in a mansion but in a Waffle
House shall we find our salvation!"

The Duke laughed, pulling me up by the armpits. Her ice-
matted hat was pulled down low over her forehead. I looked
at her and she looked at me and we weren't walking. We were
just standing there, and her eyes were so *interesting*. Not in the
usual way of being interesting, like being extremely blue or
extremely big or flanked by obscenely long lashes or anything.
What interested me about the Duke's eyes was the complexity
of the color—she always said they looked like the bottom of
trash-can bins, a swirl of green and brown and yellow. But she
was underselling herself. She always undersold herself.

Christ. It was a hard thing to unthink.

I might have kept gawking at her forever while she looked
quizzically back at me had I not heard the engine in the
distance and then turned around to see a red Ford Mustang
taking a corner at considerable speed. I grabbed the Duke by
the arm and we ran for a snowbank. I looked up the road for
JP, who'd gotten quite a bit ahead of us now. "JP!" I shouted.
"TWINS!"

Chapter Twelve

*J*P swiveled around. He looked at us, piled in the snow together. He looked at the car. His body froze for a moment. And then he turned up the road and began running, his legs a blur of energy. He was making a break for the Waffle House. The twins' Mustang roared past the Duke and me. Little Tommy Reston leaned out the rolled-down window holding a game of Twister and announced, "We gonna kill you later."

But for the moment they seemed content on killing JP, and as they bore down on him, I shouted, "Run, JP! Run!" I'm sure he couldn't hear me over the rumbling of the Mustang, but I shouted it anyway, one last desperate and furtive cry into the wilderness. From thence forth, the Duke and I were mere witnesses.

JP's head start dissipated quickly—he was running very fast, but he didn't have a chance in hell of beating a brilliantly driven Ford Mustang to the WH.

"I was really looking forward to hash browns," the Duke said morosely.

"Yeah," I answered. The Mustang reached the point where it could overtake JP, but JP just refused to stop running or to get out of the road. The horn honked as I saw the Mustang's brake lights flash on, but JP just kept running. And now I realized JP's insane strategy: he'd calculated that the road was not wide enough with the drifts for the Mustang to pass him on either side, and he believed that the twins would not run him over. This seemed to me a very generous assessment of the twins' benevolence, but for the moment, at least, it was working. The Mustang honked furiously but impotently as JP ran in front of it.

Something changed in my peripheral vision. I looked up at the highway overpass and saw the outlines of two heavyset men slowly waddling toward the exit ramp, carrying a barrel that seemed to be very heavy. The keg. The college guys. I pointed up to the Duke, and she looked at me, and her eyes got wide.

"Shortcut!" she shouted, and then she took off toward the highway, blazing through the snowbank. I'd never seen her run so fast, and I didn't know what she was thinking, but she was thinking something, so I followed. We scampered up the interstate embankment together, the snow thick enough that we could climb with ease. As I jumped the guard rail, I could see JP on the other side of the underpass, still running. But the Mustang had stopped; instead, Timmy and Tommy Reston were chasing him on foot.

The Duke and I were running toward the college guys, and finally one of them looked up and said, "Hey, are you—" but he didn't even finish the sentence. We just ran past them, and the Duke shouted to me, "Take out the mat! Take out the mat!" I opened the Twister box and threw it in the middle of the highway. I held the spinner between clenched teeth and the mat in my hands, and now, finally, I knew what she wanted us to do. Maybe the twins were faster. But with the Duke's brilliant idea, I realized we might have a chance.

When we reached the beginning of the downhill slope of the exit ramp, I flipped out the Twister mat in a single motion. She jumped down onto it butt first, and I followed suit, placing the spinner beneath me. And she shouted, "You're gonna have to dig your right hand into the snow to keep us turning right," and I said, "Okay, okay." We started to slide down, gaining speed, and then as the ramp curved, I dug my hand in, and we turned, still accelerating. I could see JP now on Timmy Reston's back, trying in vain to slow his gargantuan body as it marched toward the Waffle House.

"We can still do it," I said, but I was having doubts. And then I heard a deep rumble above us, and turned around to see a keg of beer rolling down the exit ramp with considerable speed. They were trying to *kill* us. That didn't seem like good sportsmanship at all!

"KEG!" I shouted, and the Duke swiveled her head around. It bounced toward us with menace. I didn't know how much beer kegs weigh, but given the struggle of those guys to carry it, I imagined it weighed plenty enough to kill two promising young high-school students on a Christmas-morning outing with a Twister sled. The Duke stayed turned around, watching the keg as it approached, but I was too scared. And then she shouted, "Now now turn turn turn," and I dug my arm into the snow and she rolled toward me, almost pushing me off the mat, and then things slowed down and I watched as the keg barreled past us, rolling right over the red dots, where the Duke had been. But it shot past us, hit the guard rail, and bounced over. I did not see what came next, but I heard it: a very foamy keg of beer hit something sharp and exploded like a huge beer bomb.

The explosion was so loud that Tommy and Timmy and JP all stopped dead in their tracks for at least five seconds. When they began running again, Tommy hit a patch of ice and fell on his face. When he saw his brother fall, the gargantuan Timmy suddenly changed tacks: rather than chasing JP, he hurdled through the roadside snowdrift and started toward the Waffle House itself. JP, a few steps forward, immediately made the same move so that they were headed toward the same door at slightly different angles. The Duke and I were close now—close enough to the bottom of the ramp to feel the deceleration, and close enough to the twins to hear them shouting at JP and at each other. I could see into the half-fogged windows of the Waffle House. Cheerleaders in green warm-up suits. Ponytails.

But as we stood up and I gathered the Twister mat, I knew we were not close enough. Timmy had the inside track to the front door as he pumped his arms, the Twister box looking comically small in his meaty hand. JP was approaching from a slightly different angle, running his guts out through shin-deep powder. The Duke and I were running as fast as we could, but we were well behind. I held out hope for JP, though, until Timmy got a few strides from the door and I realized that he was plainly going to be first to the door. My stomach sank. JP had come so close. His immigrant parents had sacrificed so much. The Duke would be denied her hash browns, and I my cheesy waffles.

And then, as Timmy started to extend his hand for the door, JP pounced. He leaped into the air, his body stretched out like a receiver reaching for an overthrown pass, and he got so much air that it seemed as if he'd jumped from a trampoline. His shoulder nailed Timmy Reston in the chest, and together they fell into a row of snow-draped shrubs next to the door. JP came up first, dashed for the door, pulled it open, and locked it behind him. The Duke and I were within spitting distance now, close enough to hear the shout of jubilation through the glass. JP raised his hands above his head, fists clenched, and the joyful scream continued for what seemed like several minutes.

As JP stared out into the darkness toward us with his hands raised, I watched as Keun—wearing a black "WH" visor, a white-and-yellow-striped shirt, and a brown apron—mobbed JP from behind. Keun grabbed him by the waist and lifted him up, and JP just kept his arms raised. The cheerleaders, crowded together at a bank of booths, looked on. I glanced down at the Duke, who was looking not at the scene but at me, and I laughed, and she laughed.

Tommy and Timmy banged on the windows for a while, but Keun just raised his hands as if to say, *What can I do?* and eventually they walked back toward the Mustang. As we approached the Waffle House, we walked past them, and Timmy lunged menacingly at me, but that was it. When I turned to watch them go, I saw the three college guys trying to scoot down the exit ramp.

The Duke and I reached the door finally, and I pulled on it; Keun unlocked it, saying, "Technically, I shouldn't let you in, since only JP beat the Restons. But you have the Twister." We pushed past him, and the warm air rushed onto my face. I hadn't even noticed until then how numb my body had gotten, but it tingled as it warmed, coming back to life. I threw the soaking-wet Twister mat and spinner down onto the tiled floor, and shouted, *"The Twister has arrived!"*

Keun shouted, *"Hooray!"* but the news barely even warranted a glance from the gaggle of green across the dining room.

I grabbed Keun and hugged him with one arm and with the other mussed up the hair sticking through his visor. "I need some cheesy waffles in the worst way," I told him. The Duke asked for hash browns and then collapsed into a booth next to the jukebox. JP and I sidled up to the breakfast counter and talked to Keun while he cooked.

"I can't help but notice that the cheerleaders are not, you know, hanging all over you."

"Yeah," he said, his back to us as he worked the waffle irons. "Yeah. I'm hoping Twister will change that. They did try to flirt with Mr. I-Have-a-Ponytail-but-I'm-Still-Macho," Keun said, gesturing with his head toward a guy passed out at a booth, "but apparently he is obsessed with his girlfriend."

"Yeah, the Twister seems to be working really well," I said. The wet mat lay crumpled on the floor, utterly ignored by the cheerleaders.

JP leaned over me to look at the cheerleaders and then shook his head. "It only occurs to me now that I can awkwardly glance at cheerleaders while eating pretty much every day during lunch."

"Yeah," I said.

"I mean, they obviously don't want to talk."

"Indeed," I said. They were crowded around three booths in a kind of oblong huddle. They were talking very fast, and very intently, with one another. I could hear some of the words, but they made no sense to me—herkies and kewpies and extensions. They were talking about a cheerleading competition. There are discussion topics I find less interesting than cheerleading competitions. But not many.

"Hey, the sleepy guy awakes," JP said.

I looked over at the booth and saw a guy with dark eyes and a ponytail squinting at me. I recognized him after a second. "That guy goes to Gracetown," I said.

"Yeah," Keun answered. "Jeb."

"Right," I said. Jeb was a junior. Didn't know him well, but I'd seen him around. He apparently recognized me, too, because he rose from the booth and walked up to me.

"Tobin?" he said.

I nodded and shook his hand.

"Do you know Addie?" he asked.

I looked at him blankly.

"A junior? Beautiful?" he said.

I scrunched up my eyes. "Um, no?"

"Long blonde hair, kind of dramatic?" he said, sounding both desperate and also like he couldn't get his head around the fact that I wouldn't know this girl he was rambling on about.

"Um, sorry, dude. Not ringing any bells."

His eyes closed. I saw his whole body deflate.

"We started dating on Christmas Eve," he said, staring into the middle distance.

"Yesterday?" I said, thinking, *You've been dating for a day and you're this worked up? One more reason to avoid the happy middle.*

"Not yesterday," Jeb said wearily. "A year from yesterday."

I turned to Keun. "Dude," I said. "This guy is in bad shape."

Keun nodded while scattering the Duke's hash browns on the grill. "I'm gonna give him a ride into town in the morning," Keun said. "Although what's the rule, Jeb?"

Jeb said it like Keun had told him the rule a thousand times before. "We don't leave until the last cheerleader leaves."

"That's right, buddy. Maybe you should go back to bed."

"Just," Jeb said, "just if you happen to see her or something, will you just tell her I got, um, delayed?"

"I guess," I said. I must not have been convincing enough, because he turned around and made eye contact with the Duke.

"Tell her I'm coming," he said, and what's weird was that she got it. Or seemed to. Or anyway, she nodded in a way that said, *Yeah, I'll tell her, if for some reason I see this girl I don't know out in a snowdrift at four A.M.* And as she smiled sympathetically to him, again I had the untakebackable thought.

Her smile seemed to please him. He slouched back to his booth.

I talked to Keun until he finished my waffle and delivered it to me steaming hot. "God, that looks good, Keun," I said, but he'd already turned around to plate the Duke's hash browns. He was picking the plate up when Billy Talos appeared, grabbed the plate, delivered it to the Duke, and sat down next to her.

I glanced back at them a couple times, leaning across the table and talking intently to each other. I wanted to cut in and let her know that he'd been flirting with one of several Madisons as we'd been trudging through the snow, but I figured it was none of my business.

"I'm going to talk to one of them," I announced to JP and Keun.

JP was incredulous. "One of who? The cheerleaders?"

I nodded.

"Dude," Keun said. "I've been trying all night. They're packed too tightly to talk to just one of them. And when you try to talk to all of them, they just kind of ignore you."

But I had to talk to one of them, or at least appear to. "It's like lions hunting gazelles," I said as we watched the gaggle intently. "You just find a straggler, and"—a tiny blonde girl turned away from the pack—"pounce," I said, as I jumped up off the stool.

I walked up to her with purpose. "I'm Tobin," I said, extending my hand.

"Amber," she said.

"Beautiful name," I said.

She nodded, and her eyes darted around. She wanted a way out, but I couldn't give her one yet. I fumbled for a question. "Um, any word on the status of your train?" I asked.

"Our train might not even leave *tomorrow*," she informed me.

"Yeah, that's too bad," I said, smiling. I glanced over my shoulder toward Billy and the Duke, only she was gone. The hash browns still steamed off the plate; she'd poured the ketchup on a side plate to dip them into like she always did, but then left. I left Amber and walked over to Billy.

"She went outside," he said simply.

Who in their right mind would go *outside* when the hash browns and the warmth and the fourteen cheerleaders were all *inside*?

I grabbed my hat from the counter and pulled it down low over my ears, and then I put my gloves back on and ventured back into the wind. The Duke was sitting on the curb of the parking lot, just barely underneath the awning, half protected from the still-falling snow.

I sat down next to her. "You missed the postnasal drip?"

She sniffled and didn't look up at me. "Just go back inside," she said. "It's not a big deal."

"What's not a big deal?"

"Nothing's not a big deal. Just go back inside."

"'Nothing's Not a Big Deal' would be a good name for a

band," I told her. I wanted her to look up at me so I could assess the situation, and finally she did, and her nose was red, and I thought she was cold, but then I thought maybe she had been crying, which was weird, because the Duke doesn't cry.

"I just...I just wish you wouldn't do it in front of me. I mean, what is interesting about her? Tell me what is interesting about her, seriously. Or any of them."

"I don't know," I said. "You were talking to Billy Talos."

She looked up at me again and this time held my gaze as she spoke. "I was telling Billy that I didn't think I could actually go to the stupid formal with him, because I just can't bring myself to stop liking someone else."

The idea crept up on me slowly. I turned toward her, and she said, "I realize that they giggle and I actually laugh, that they show their cleavage and I have none to show, but just so you know, I am also a girl."

"I know you're a girl," I said defensively.

"Really? Does anyone? Because I walk into the D and D and I'm the Duke. And I'm one of the three wise *men*. And it's gay to think that James Bond is hot. And you never *look* at me like you look at girls, except...whatever. Whatever whatever whatever. When we were walking here right before the twins came, I thought for one second that you *were* looking at me like I was an actual female, and I was, like, hey, maybe Tobin is not the world's biggest superficial jackass, but then you go and I'm breaking up with Billy and I look up and you're talking to some girl like you'd never talk to me and whatever."

And then, belatedly, I got it. The thing that I was trying to unthink was a thing that the Duke had also thought. We were trying to unthink the same thought. The Duke liked me. I looked down. I had to think it through before I looked at her. Okay. *Okay,* I decided, *I will look at her and if she is looking at me, I will take one good look at her and then I will look down again and reassess. One look.*

I looked over at her. Her head was cocked toward me, her eyes unblinking, containing all of the colors. She sucked her chapped lips into her mouth and then let them go, and there was one strand of her hair coming out from under her hat, and her nose was rosy red, and she sniffled. And I didn't want to stop looking at her, but finally I did. I looked back down at the snowy parking lot beneath my feet.

"Will you say something, please?" she asked.

I spoke into the ground. "I always had this idea that you should never give up a happy middle in the hopes of a happy ending, because there is no such thing as a happy ending. Do you know what I mean? There is so much to lose."

"Do you know why I wanted to go? Why I wanted to go back up that hill, Tobin? I mean, surely you know it's not because I cared if Keun had to hang out with the Reston twins or because I wanted to see you fawn over cheerleaders."

"I thought because of Billy," I said.

She was really looking at me now, and I could see her breath all around me in the cold, surrounding me. "I wanted us to have an adventure. Because I love that crap. Because I'm not whatever-her-name-is. I don't think it's oh so hard to walk four miles in the snow. I want that. I love that. When we were at your house watching the movie, I wanted it to snow more. More and more! It makes it more interesting. Maybe you aren't like that, but I think you are."

"I wanted that, too," I said, half interrupting her, still not looking for fear of what I might do if I looked. "For it to keep snowing."

"Yeah? Cool. So, cool. And so what if more snow makes a happy ending less likely? So the car might get messed up—so what! So we might ruin our friendship—so what? I've kissed guys where nothing was at stake, and all it ever made me want to do was to have a kiss where *everything*—"

I looked up at about the "nothing was at stake," and I waited all the way until the "everything" and then I couldn't wait anymore, and my hand was on the back of her head, and then her lips on mine, the cold air gone and replaced with the warmth of her mouth, soft and sweet and hash-brown-tastic, and I opened my eyes and my gloves touched the skin of her face pale from the cold, and I had never before had a first kiss with a girl I loved. When we parted, I looked at her, bashful, and said, "Wow," and then she laughed and pulled me back

toward her and then from above and behind us, I heard the
ding-dong of the Waffle House door opening.

"HOLY. CRAP. WHAT. THE. HELL. IS. HAPPENING."

I just looked up at JP, trying to wipe the goofy smile off
my face.

"KEUN!" JP shouted. "GET YOUR FAT KOREAN ASS
OUT HERE."

Keun appeared at the doorway, looking down at us. JP
shouted, "TELL THEM WHAT YOU JUST DID TO
EACH OTHER!"

"Um," I said.

"We kissed," the Duke said.

"That's kinda gay," Keun said.

"I AM A GIRL."

"Yeah, I know, but so is Tobin," Keun said.

JP was still shouting, seemingly unable to modulate
his voice. "AM I THE ONLY PERSON PROFOUNDLY
CONCERNED ABOUT THE WHOLE MAKEUP OF
OUR GROUP? WILL NO ONE THINK OF THE GOOD
OF THE GROUP?!"

"Go gawk at cheerleaders," the Duke said.

JP looked at us for a while and then he smiled. "Just don't
get all gooey with each other." He turned around and walked
inside.

"Your hash browns are getting cold," I said.

"If we go back in, no flirting with cheerleaders."

"I only did it to get your attention," I confessed. "Can I kiss you again?" She nodded and I did, and there was no second-kiss drop-off whatsoever. I could have kept going forever, but finally, through the kiss, she said, "I actually really do want my hash browns," and so I opened the door and she ducked beneath my arm and we ate dinner at three A.M.

We hid in the back amid the giant steel refrigerators, our time interrupted only occasionally by JP coming back to give us the hilarious details of his and Keun's aborted attempts to engage the cheerleaders in conversation. And then the Duke and I fell asleep together on the red tile of the Waffle House kitchen, my shoulder as her pillow and my jacket as mine. JP and Keun woke us up at seven, and Keun briefly broke his vow never to abandon the cheerleaders and drove us to the Duke and Duchess. It turned out that Tinfoil Guy drove the tow truck for them, and so Tinfoil Guy gave us a tow, and I jacked the car up in the driveway so the axle wouldn't break and just put the wheel in the garage, and then the Duke and I went over to her house and opened presents, and I tried not to make it incredibly obvious to her parents how incredibly gooey I felt about the Duke, and then my parents came home and I told them the car got jacked when I was trying to drive the Duke home, and they yelled at me about it, but not for too long because it was Christmas and they had insurance and it was just a car. I called the Duke and JP and Keun that evening after the cheerleaders had finally left the Waffle House and everyone had eaten their Christmas dinners. They all came over, and we watched two James Bond movies and then stayed up half the night recounting our escapades. And then we all fell asleep, all four of us in four sleeping bags, like we'd been doing forever, and nothing was different except that I didn't actually fall asleep, and neither did the Duke, and we just kept looking at each other, and then finally got up at, like, four thirty and walked a mile in the snow to Starbucks, just the two of us. I overcame the confusing French of the Starbucks ordering system and managed to get a latte, which contained the caffeine I so sorely needed, and then the Duke and I were sitting next to each other in plush purple chairs, sprawled out all over those chairs, as tired as I had ever been, so tired I could barely even smile. And we were talking about nothing, which she was still so good at, and then there was a pause, and she looked over at me with sleepy eyes and said, "So far so good," and I said, "God, I love you," and she said, "Oh," and I said, "Good oh?" and she said, "Best oh ever," and I put the latte down on a table, awash in the happy middle of my greatest adventure.

The Patron Saint of Pigs
lauren myracle

For Dad, Sarah Lee, and the lovely mountain town of Brevard, NC . . . all chock-full of grace

Chapter One

*B*eing me sucked. Being me on this supposedly gorgeous night, with the supposedly gorgeous snow looming in five-foot drifts outside my bedroom window, double-sucked. Add the fact that today was Christmas, and my score was up to triple-suck. And add in the sad, aching, devastating lack of Jeb, and *ding-ding-ding!* The bell at the top of the Suckage Meter couldn't ring any louder.

Instead of jingle bells, I had suckage bells. Lovely.

Well, aren't you a merry little figgy pudding, I said to myself, wishing Dorrie and Tegan would hurry up and get here. I didn't know what figgy pudding was, but it sounded like the sort of dish that sat cold and alone at the end of the buffet table because no one wanted it. Like me. Cold and alone and probably lumpish.

Grrrrrr. I hated feeling sorry for myself, which was why I'd called Tegan and Dorrie and begged them to come over. But they weren't here yet, and anyway, I couldn't *help* but feel sorry for myself.

Because I missed Jeb so much.

Because our breakup, which was only a week old and as raw as an open wound, was my own stupid fault.

Because I'd written Jeb a (pathetic?) e-mail asking him please, please, please to meet me at Starbucks yesterday so we could talk. But he never showed up. Didn't even call.

And because, after waiting at Starbucks for nearly two hours, I hated life and myself so much that I trudged across the parking lot to Fantastic Sam's, where I tearfully told the stylist to lop my hair off and dye what was left of it pink. Which she did, because why did she care if I committed hair suicide?

So of course I felt sorry for myself: I was a brokenhearted, self-loathing, plucked pink chicken.

"Addie, wow," Mom had said yesterday afternoon when I'd finally come home. "That's...a pretty major haircut. And you got it colored. Your beautiful blonde hair."

I gave her a why-don't-you-shoot-me-now look, which she answered with a tilted head warning that said, *Watch it, sweetie. I know you're hurting, but that doesn't give you permission to take it out on me.*

"Sorry," I said. "I guess I'm just not used to it yet."

"Well...it is a lot to get used to. What inspired you to do it?"

"I don't know. I needed a change."

She put down her whisk. She was making Cherries Jubilee, our family's traditional Christmas Eve dessert, and the tang of the mushed-up cherries made my eyes prickle.

"Did it by any chance have to do with what happened at Charlie's party last Saturday?" she asked.

Heat rose to my cheeks. "I don't know what you mean." I blinked. "Anyway, how do *you* know what happened at Charlie's party?"

"Well, sweetie, you've cried yourself to sleep almost every night—"

"No, I haven't."

"And of course, you've been on the phone with either Dorrie or Tegan pretty much twenty-four/seven."

"You've been listening to my calls?" I cried. "You eaves-dropped on your own daughter?!"

"It's hardly 'eavesdropping' if you have no choice."

I gaped at her. She pretended to be so motherly in her Christmas apron, making Cherries Jubilee from an old family recipe, when really she was...she was...

Well, I didn't know what she was, just that it was wrong and bad and evil to listen in on other people's conversations.

"And *don't* say 'twenty-four/seven,'" I said. "You're too old to say 'twenty-four/seven.'"

Mom laughed, which pissed me off more, especially since she then suppressed her amusement and regarded me in that Mom-way of, *She's a teenager, poor thing. She's bound to go through heartache.*

"Oh, Addie," she said. "Were you punishing yourself, sweetie?"

"Oh my God," I said. "That is *so* not the right thing to say to someone about her new haircut!" And then I'd fled to my room to bawl in private.

Twenty-four hours later, I was still in my room. I'd come out for Cherries Jubilee last night and for the opening of presents this morning, but I hadn't enjoyed it. I certainly hadn't been filled with the joy and magic of Christmas. In fact, I wasn't sure I believed in the joy and magic of Christmas anymore.

I rolled over and grabbed my iPod from my bedside table. I selected my "Gray Day" playlist, which was made up of every single melancholy song that ever existed, and hit *play*. My iPenguin gloomily flapped her wings as "Fools in Love" hummed from her plastic body.

Then I returned to the main menu and scrolled through until I reached "Photos." I knew I was entering dangerous territory, but I didn't care. I highlighted the album I wanted and punched the button to open it.

The first picture to come up was the very first picture I ever took of Jeb, snapped sneakily using my cell phone a little over a year ago. It had been snowing that day, too, and in the picture, there were snowflakes caught in Jeb's dark hair. He was wearing a denim jacket even though it was *freezing*, and I remember wondering if maybe he and his mom didn't have much money. I'd heard that the two of them had moved to Gracetown from the Cherokee Reservation, which was about a hundred miles from here. I thought that was cool. He seemed so exotic.

Anyway, Jeb and I had sophomore English together, and he was heart-stoppingly hot with his jet-black ponytail and smoky eyes. He was also wa-a-a-ay serious, which was a new concept for me, since I had a tendency to be a big ol' spaz. Every day, he bent over his desk and took notes while I snuck peeks at him, marveling at how shiny his hair was and how his cheekbones were the most beautiful things I'd ever seen. But he was reserved to the point of possible aloofness, even when I was my bubbliest self.

When I discussed this extremely problematic issue with Dorrie and Tegan, Dorrie suggested that maybe Jeb felt uncomfortable in this tiny mountain town where everyone was real Southern, real Christian, and real white.

"There's nothing wrong with any of those things," I said defensively, being all three.

"I know," Dorrie said. "I'm just saying that *possibly* the guy feels like an outsider. *Poss*ibly." As one of two—count 'em, *two*—Jewish kids in the entire high school, I suppose she knew what she was talking about.

Well, that got me wondering if maybe Jeb *did* feel like an outsider. Could that be why he ate lunch with Nathan Krugle, who was definitely an outsider with his all–*Star Trek*, all-the-time T-shirt collection? Could that be why, in the mornings before the school was unlocked, Jeb leaned against the wall with his hands in his pockets instead of joining the rest of us and dishing about *American Idol*? Could that be why he didn't succumb to my charms in English, because he felt too *uncomfortable* to open up?

The more I thought about it, the more I worried. Nobody should feel like an outsider in their own school—especially not someone as adorable as Jeb, and especially since we, his fellow classmates, were all so nice.

Well, at least me and Dorrie and Tegan and our other friends. We were *very* nice. The stoners weren't so nice. They were rude. And not Nathan Krugle, as Nathan was a bitter person who held grudges. I wasn't all that psyched about what crazy ideas Nathan might be planting in Jeb's head, to be honest.

And then, one day as I was obsessing over all of this for the thousandth time, I shifted from worried to huffy, because *really*. Why was Jeb choosing to spend time with Nathan Krugle over me?

So that day in class, I jabbed him with my pen and said, "For heaven's sake, Jeb. Would you just *smile*?"

He jumped, knocking his book to the floor, and I felt terrible. I thought, *Smooth, Addie, why don't you blow a bugle in his ear next time?*

But then his lips quirked up, and amusement flickered in his eyes. Something else, too—something that made my heart beat faster. A flush reddened his face, and he bent down quickly to pick up his book.

Oh, I realized with a pang. *He's just shy.*

Leaning against my pillow, I gazed at the picture of Jeb on my iPod until the sting of it grew too strong.

I punched the center button, and the next picture popped up. It was of the Great Hollyhock Blitzkrieg, which took place last Christmas Eve, only a couple of weeks after I told Jeb to smile, for heaven's sake. Since Christmas Eve was one of those days that lasted forever, with all the waiting and finger drumming for Christmas itself, a group of us had tromped to Hollyhock Park in order to get out of our houses for a while. I made one of the guys call Jeb, and miraculously, he agreed to come with us.

We ended up having a snowball fight, boys against girls, and it was awesome. Dorrie, Tegan, and I made a snow fort and set up a snowball-distribution system that involved Tegan packing, me stacking, and Dorrie pummeling our enemies with dead-on accuracy. We dominated the guys until Jeb cut around behind us and tackled me, using his body to drive me into our snowball pile. Snow went up my nose, and it hurt like heck, but I was too exhilarated to care. I rolled over, laughing, and his face was *right there*, inches from mine.

That was the image captured in the photo, this time taken by Tegan on her cell phone. Jeb was wearing his denim jacket again—the faded blue so sexy against his dark skin—and he was laughing, too. What I remembered, as I looked at our happy faces, was how he didn't get off me right away. He braced himself on his forearms so that he wasn't squishing me, and his laugh softened into a question that made my stomach quivery.

After the snowball fight, Jeb and I went out for mocha lattes, just the two of us. I was the one who suggested it, but Jeb said yes without a moment's hesitation. We went to Starbucks, and we sat in the matching purple armchairs at the entrance of the store. I was giddy; he was bashful. And then he grew less bashful, or perhaps just more determined, and he reached over and took my hand. I was so surprised I spilled my coffee.

"For heaven's sake, Addie," he said. His Adam's apple jerked. "Can I just kiss you?"

My heart went crazy, and suddenly I was the shy one, which was nuts. Jeb took my cup from my hand and put it on the table, then leaned in and brushed his lips over mine. His eyes, when at last he drew back, were as warm as melted chocolate. He smiled, and I melted into a swirl of chocolate, too.

It was the most perfect Christmas Eve ever.

"Hey, Addie!" my little brother called from downstairs, where he and Mom and Dad were playing with the Wii that Santa brought him. "Want to box with me?"

"No, thanks," I called.

"How about tennis?"

"No."

"Bowling?"

I groaned. Wii did not make me say "Wee!" But Chris was eight. He was only trying to cheer me up.

"Maybe later," I called.

"Okay," he said, and his footsteps retreated.

I heard him tell our parents, "She said no," and my melancholy deepened. Mom and Dad and Chris were downstairs together, merrily strapping on nunchucks and punching each other in the face, while here I was, gloomy and alone.

And whose fault is that? I asked myself.

Oh, shut up, I replied.

I scrolled through more pictures:

Jeb posing cheesily with a Reese's Big Cup, because he knew it was my favorite and he'd brought it for me as a surprise.

Jeb in the summer, shirt off, at Megan Montgomery's pool party. God, he was beautiful.

Jeb looking sudsy-adorable at a car wash Starbucks held as a fund-raiser. I gazed at the picture of him, and my insides went soft. That had been such a fun day—and not just fun, but cool, too, because it was for a good cause. Christina, my shift manager at Starbucks, had gone into labor early, and our store wanted to help with the hospital bills not covered by insurance.

Jeb volunteered to pitch in, and he was a total stud. He arrived at nine and stayed through three, scrubbing and slaving away and looking pretty much like he should be in one of those beefcake Hottest Guys in the Universe calendar. He went way beyond what boyfriend duty required, and it made my heart happy. After the last car pulled out of the parking lot, I wrapped my arms around Jeb and tilted my face toward his.

"You didn't have to work so hard," I said. I breathed in his soapy smell. "You had me at the very first car."

I was going for flirtatious, along the lines of the scene in *Jerry Maguire* when Renée Zellweger told Tom Cruise, "You had me at 'hello.'" But Jeb furrowed his brow and said, "Oh, yeah? Uh, good. But I'm not sure what you mean."

"Ha-ha," I said, assuming he was fishing for more praise. "I just think it's sweet that you stayed the whole time. And if you were doing it to impress me...well, you didn't have to. That's all."

His eyebrows went up. "You thought I washed those cars to *impress* you?"

My cheeks grew warm as it dawned on me that he wasn't kidding. "Uh...not anymore."

Embarrassed, I tried to pull away. He didn't let me. He

kissed the top of my head and said, "Addie, my mom raised me on her own."

"I know."

"So I know how hard it can be. That's all."

For a moment, I felt pouty. Which was totally lame. But while I knew that Jeb's wanting to help Christina was a good thing, I wouldn't have minded if at least part of his motivation had to do with me.

Jeb pulled me close. "I'm glad I impressed you, though," he said, and I could feel his lips on my skin. I could also feel the warmth of his chest through his wet shirt. "There's nothing I want more than to impress my girl."

I wasn't *quite* ready to be teased out of my sulk. "So you're saying I'm your girl?"

He laughed, as if I'd asked out loud if the sky was still blue. I didn't let him off the hook but instead stepped backward out of his embrace. I looked at him, like, *Well?*

His dark eyes grew serious, and he took both of my hands in his. "Yes, Addie, you're my girl. You'll be my girl forever."

In my bedroom, I squeezed shut my eyes, because it was too hard, that memory. Too hard, too painful, too much like losing a slice of myself, which, in fact, I had. I pressed the off button on my iPod, and the screen went black. The music stopped, and my iPenguin stopped dancing. She made her sad you're-turning-me-off? sound, and I said, "You and me both, Pengy."

I sank into my pillow and stared at the ceiling, rehashing just how things had gone wrong between Jeb and me. How I'd stopped being his girl. I knew the obvious answer *(bad, yuck, didn't want to go there)*, but I couldn't help obsessively analyzing what got us to that point, because even before Charlie's party, things were less than great between us. It wasn't that he didn't love me, because I knew he did. As for me, I loved him so much it hurt.

What tripped us up, I think, was the way we showed our love. Or, in Jeb's case, the way he didn't show it—at least, that was how it felt to me. According to Tegan, who watched a lot of Dr. Phil, Jeb and I spoke different love languages.

I wanted Jeb to be sweet and romantic and affectionate, like he had been at Starbucks when he kissed me that first time last Christmas Eve. I ended up getting a job at that same Starbucks the month after that, and I remember thinking, *Sweet, we'll get to relive our kiss again and again and again.*

But we didn't, not one single time. Even though he stopped by all the time, and even though I always broadcasted with my body language that I wanted him to kiss me, the most he would do was reach across the counter and tug the strings of my green apron.

"Hey, coffee girl," he'd say. Which was cute, but not… enough.

That was just one thing. There were others, too, like how I wanted him to call and say good night every night, and how he felt awkward because his apartment was so small. "I don't want my mom hearing me be all mushy," he'd said. Or how other guys were totally fine holding their girlfriends' hands in the school halls, but whenever I grabbed Jeb's hand, he gave me a fast squeeze and then let go.

"Do you not like touching me?" I'd said.

"Of course I do," he said. His eyes got that look in them that I guess I'd been trying to stir up, and when he spoke, his voice was raw. "You know I do, Addie. I love being alone with you. I just want us to actually be *alone* when we're alone."

For a long time, even though I noticed all that stuff, I mostly kept it to myself. I didn't want to be a whiner-baby girlfriend.

But around our six-month anniversary (I gave Jeb a play-list of the most romantic songs ever; he gave me nothing), something turned sour inside me. It sucked, because here I was with this guy I loved, and I wanted things to be perfect between us, but I couldn't do it all on my own. And if that made me a whiner-baby girlfriend, well, tough.

Like, with the sixth-month-anniversary thing. Jeb could tell I wasn't happy, and he kept asking and asking why, and finally I said, "Why do you think?"

"Is it because I didn't get you anything?" he said. "I didn't know we were doing that."

"Well, you should have," I muttered. The next day he gave me a quarter-machine necklace with a heart on it, only he took it out of the plastic egg and put it in an actual jewelry box. I was underwhelmed. The *next* day, Tegan pulled me aside and told me that Jeb was worried I didn't like the present, because I wasn't wearing it.

"It came from the Duke and Duchess," I said. "The exact same necklace is in the quarter machine by the exit. It's, like, one of win-this! display necklaces."

"And do you know how many quarters Jeb had to feed in before he did?" Tegan said. "Thirty-eight. He had to keep going back and getting change from the customer-service desk."

A heaviness descended. "You mean...?"

"He wanted you to have that particular one. With the heart."

I didn't like the way Tegan was staring at me. I shifted my gaze. "That's still less than ten dollars."

Tegan was silent. I was too afraid to look at her. Finally, she said, "I know you don't mean that, Addie. Don't be a jerk."

I didn't *want* to be a jerk—and of course I didn't care how much a present cost. But I did seem to want more from Jeb than he could give, and the longer we went on like that, the crappier we both felt.

Flash-forward several months, and guess what? I was still making him feel crappy, and vice versa. Not always, but way more often than was, like, healthy or whatever.

"You want me to be someone I'm not," he said, the night before we broke up. We were sitting in his mom's Corolla outside

Charlie's house, but we hadn't gone in yet. If I could go back to that night and *never* go in, I would. In a heartbeat.

"That's not true," I told him. My fingers found the gash on the side of the passenger seat and wormed into the foam rubber.

"It is true, Addie," he said.

I changed tactics. "Okay, even if I do, why is that necessarily bad? People change for each other all the time. Take any love story, any great love story at all, and you'll see that people have to be willing to change if they're going to make things work out. Like in *Shrek*, when Fiona tells Shrek that she's sick of his burping and farting and everything. And Shrek's like, 'I'm an ogre. Deal with it.' And Fiona says, 'What if I can't?' So Shrek takes that potion that turns him into a hunky prince. He does it out of love for Fiona."

"That's in *Shrek Two*," Jeb said. "Not the original."

"Whatever."

"And then Fiona realized she didn't want him to be a hunky prince. She wanted him to turn back into an ogre."

I frowned. That wasn't how I remembered it.

"The point is, he was willing to change," I said.

Jeb sighed. "Why does the guy always have to be the one to change?"

"The girl can, too," I said. "Whatever. All I'm saying is that if you love someone, you should be willing to show it. Because, Jeb, this is our one shot at life. *Our one shot.*" I felt the familiar tightening of despair. "Can't you just *try*, if for no other reason than because you know how important it is to me?"

Jeb stared out the driver's-side window.

"I…I want you to follow me onto a plane and serenade me in the first-class cabin, like Robbie did to Julia in *The Wedding Singer*," I said. "I want you to build a house for me, like Noah did for Allie in *The Notebook*. I want you to fly me across the ocean at the prow of an ocean liner! Like the guy in *Titanic*, remember?"

Jeb turned. "The guy who drowned?"

"Well, I don't want you to *drown*, obviously. It's not about drowning. It's about you loving me enough to be *willing* to drown, if you had to." My voice caught. "I want…I want the big gesture."

"Addie, you know I love you," he said.

"Or even the medium gesture," I said, unable to let it go.

Frustration and anguish warred with each other on his face. "Can't you just trust in our love, without asking me to prove it every single second?"

Apparently not, as demonstrated by what happened next. No, not "what happened." *What I did.* Because I sucked and I *was* a jerk, and because I downed thirty-eight quarters worth of beer shots, if not more. Or maybe not thirty-eight, but a lot. Not that I can blame it on that, either.

Jeb and I went inside to the party, but we went our own

ways because we were still fighting. I ended up in the basement with Charlie and some other guys, while Jeb stayed upstairs. I heard later that he joined some theater geeks who were watching *An Affair to Remember* on Charlie's parents' flatscreen TV. It was such a horrible irony that it would have been funny, except it totally wasn't.

In the basement, I played quarters with the guys, and Charlie egged me on because Charlie was the devil. When the quarters game broke up, Charlie asked me if we could go somewhere to talk, and like an idiot, I stumbled obediently after him to his older brother's room. I was a little surprised, because Charlie and I had never had a heart-to-heart before. But Charlie was part of the group of guys we hung out with. He was arrogant and smarmy and pretty much an overall asshat, to steal a term from a Korean guy at school, but that was just Charlie. Since he looked like a Hollister model, he could be an asshat and get away with it.

In his brother's room, Charlie sat me down on the bed and told me he needed advice about Brenna, a girl from our grade he sometimes hooked up with. He looked at me in an I-know-I'm-cute-and-I'm-going-to-work-it way and said how lucky Jeb was to be dating someone as great as me.

I snorted and said something like, "Oh, yeah, whatever."

"Are you guys having problems?" he asked. "Tell me you guys aren't having problems. You guys are golden."

"Uh-huh, that's why Jeb's upstairs doing God knows what, and I'm down here with you." *Why am I down here with you?* I remember wondering. *And who shut the door?*

Charlie pushed for details, charming and sympathetic, and when I got teary, he moved in close to comfort me. I protested, but he pressed his mouth to mine, and eventually I submitted. A guy was paying me all sorts of attention—a really cute and charismatic guy—and who cared that he didn't mean it?

I did. Even during the moment of betraying Jeb, I cared. I've replayed that moment again and again, and that was the part that killed me. Because what was I thinking? Jeb and I were having problems, but I still *loved* him. I loved him then and I loved him now. I would always love him.

Only yesterday, when he never showed up at Starbucks, he sent the message loud and clear that he no longer loved me back.

Chapter Two

A ping on my windowpane intruded into my pity party. It took me a minute to pull myself back to reality. There was another ping, and I craned up from my bed to see a heavily bundled Tegan and an even more heavily bundled Dorrie standing atop a drift of snow. They beckoned with mittened hands, and Dorrie called in a glass-muted voice for me to come out.

I clambered to my feet, and the strange lightness of my head reminded me of my hair disaster. Crud. I looked around, grabbed my throw blanket off my bed, and put it over me like a hood. Holding the fabric beneath my chin, I walked to the window and jerked it up.

"Get your booty on the dance floor!" Dorrie hollered, the sound of her suddenly much louder.

"That's not a dance floor," I said. "That's snow. Cold, frozen snow."

"It's so beautiful," Tegan said. "Come see." She paused, regarding me quizzically from beneath her striped wool hat. "Addie? Why do you have a blanket on your head?"

"Ehhh," I said, waving them off. "Go home. I'm a bummer. I'll bum you out."

"Oh, don't *even*," Dorrie said. "Exhibit A: You called and said you were having a crisis. Exhibit B: Here we are. Now get down here and experience this glory of nature."

"I'll pass."

"It'll cheer you up, I swear."

"Impossible. Sorry."

She rolled her eyes. "*Such* a baby. C'mon, Tegan."

They high-stepped out of my sight, and a couple of seconds later, the doorbell rang. In my bedroom, I adjusted my blanket to make it more of an official turban-y thing. I sat on the edge of my bed and pretended to be a nomadic desert wanderer with startling green eyes and a desolate expression. After all, I knew all about desolation.

Parental chatter floated up from the hall—"Merry Christmas! You girls walked all that way in the snow?"—and Dorrie and Tegan annoyingly chose to reply. Their happy voices made happy Christmas chitchat, making me grouchier and grouchier until I wanted to yell down, "Hey! Girlies! The wretched soul you're here to comfort? *She's up here!*"

Finally, two sets of stockinged feet jogged up the stairs. Dorrie burst in first.

"Whew," she said, lifting her hair off her neck and airing herself out. "If I don't sit down, I'm going to *plotz*."

Dorrie loved saying "I'm going to *plotz*." It was her catchphrase; it meant she was going to explode. She also loved Cheerwine, bagels, and pretending she was from the Old Country, which was where Jewish people lived before they came to America, I guess. Dorrie was big into her Jewishness, going so far as to call her awesome curly hair a "Jew fro." Which shocked me the first time she said it, and then made me laugh. Which was pretty much Dorrie in a nutshell.

Tegan came in behind Dorrie with flushed cheeks. "Omigosh, I'm totally sweating," she said, peeling off the flannel button-down she wore over her T-shirt. "Getting here about killed me."

"You're telling me," Dorrie said. "Five thousand miles I trudged to get from my house to yours!"

"And by that you mean…twenty feet?" Tegan said. She turned to me. "Think that's about right, twenty feet from Dorrie's house to mine?"

I gave her a steely-eyed look. We were not here to discuss the foot-by-foot boringness of how far apart their houses were.

"So what's with the headdress?" Dorrie asked, dropping down beside me.

"Nothing," I said, because it turned out I didn't want to discuss that, either. "I'm cold."

"Uh-huh, sure." She yanked the blanket from my head, then made a sound of strangled horror. "*Oy*. What have you done?"

"Gee, thanks," I said sourly. "You're as bad as my mom."

"Whoa," Tegan said. "I mean... *whoa*."

"I'm assuming this is your crisis?" Dorrie said.

"Actually, no."

"Are you sure?"

"*Dorrie*." Tegan swatted her. "It's...cute, Addie. It's very brave."

Dorrie snorted. "Okay, if someone says your hairstyle is brave? You pretty much want to go back and demand a refund."

"Go away," I said. I pushed at her with my feet.

"Hey!"

"You are being mean to me in my time of need, so you're no longer allowed on the bed." I put some muscle into it, and off she thunked.

"I think you broke my tailbone," she complained.

"If your tailbone's broken, you'll have to sit on an inflatable doughnut."

"I'm not sitting on an inflatable doughnut."

"I'm just saying."

"*I'm* not being mean to you in your time of need," Tegan interrupted. She nodded at the bed. "May I?"

"I suppose."

Tegan took Dorrie's original spot, and I stretched out and put my head in her lap. She stroked my hair, gingerly at first, and then with more assurance.

"So…what's going on?" she said.

I didn't speak. I wanted to tell them, but at the same time I didn't. Forget my hair—the true crisis was so much worse that I didn't know how to get the words out without bursting into tears.

"Oh, no," Dorrie said. Her face mirrored what she must have seen on mine. "Oh, *bubbellah*."

Tegan's hand stilled. "Did something happen with Jeb?"

I nodded.

"Did you see him?" Dorrie asked.

I shook my head.

"Did you talk to him?"

I shook my head again.

Dorrie's gaze shifted upward, and I felt something pass between her and Tegan. Tegan nudged my shoulder to make me sit up.

"Addie, just tell us," she said.

"I'm so stupid," I whispered.

Tegan put her hand on my thigh to say, *We're here. It's okay.* Dorrie leaned over, resting her chin on my knee.

"Once upon a time…" she prodded.

"Once upon a time Jeb and I were still together," I said

miserably. "And I loved him, and he loved me. And then I screwed up big-time."

"The Charlie Thing," Dorrie said.

"We know," Tegan said, giving me several comforting pats. "But that happened a week ago. What's the new crisis?"

"Other than your hair," Dorrie said.

They waited for me to reply.

They waited some more.

"I wrote Jeb an e-mail," I confessed.

"No," Dorrie said. She bashed her forehead against my knee, *bam-bam-bam.*

"I thought you were giving him space to heal," Tegan said. "You said the kindest thing you could do was stay away, even if it was super-hard. Remember?"

I shrugged helplessly.

"And not to be a downer, but I thought Jeb was hanging out with Brenna now," Dorrie said.

I glared at her.

"I mean, no, of course he isn't," she amended. "After all, it's only been a week. But she's going after him, right? And as far as we know, he's not exactly pushing her away."

"Bad Brenna," I said. "Hate Brenna."

"I thought Brenna got back together with Charlie," Tegan said.

"Of course we hate Brenna," Dorrie said to me. "That's not

the issue." She turned to Tegan. "We *wanted* her to get back with Charlie, but it didn't take."

"Oh," Tegan said. She still looked confused.

I sighed. "Remember how braggy Brenna was the day before winter break? How she was going on and on about how she was going to see Jeb during vacation?"

"I thought we thought she was just trying to make Charlie jealous," Tegan said.

"We did," Dorrie said, "but still. If there were actual *plans* involved…"

"Ahh," Tegan said. "Got it. Jeb's not a 'plan' kind of guy, not unless he means it."

"I don't want Jeb having plans with *any*one—especially Brenna." I scowled. "Fake white-girl dreadlocks."

Dorrie exhaled through her nose. "Addie, can I tell you something you're not going to want to hear?"

"I'd rather you didn't."

"She's going to anyway," Tegan said.

"I realize that," I replied. "I'm just saying I'd rather she didn't."

"It's the holidays," Dorrie said. "Holidays make people lonely."

"I'm not lonely because of that!" I protested.

"Yes, you are. Holidays bring out neediness like nothing else—and for you it's a double whammy, because this would have been your and Jeb's one-year anniversary. Am I right?"

"Yesterday," I admitted. "On Christmas Eve."

"Oh, Addie," Tegan said.

"Do you think couples all over the world get together on Christmas Eve?" I said, wondering this for the first time. "Because it's all…Christmasy and magical, only then it's not, and everything sucks?"

"So the e-mail you sent him," Dorrie said in a let's-not-get-distracted tone. "Was it a 'Merry Christmas' kind of thing?"

"Not exactly."

"Then what did it say?"

I shook my head. "Too painful."

"Just tell us," Addie urged.

I got off the bed. "Nope, nuh-uh. But I'll pull it up. You can read it yourselves."

Chapter Three

*T*hey followed me to my desk, where my white MacBook waited cheerfully, pretending it wasn't a participant in my disgrace. Puffy Chococat stickers decorated its surface, which I should have scraped off after Jeb and I broke up, since Jeb was the one who gave them to me. But I couldn't bear to.

I flipped the computer open and clicked on Firefox. I went to Hotmail, pulled up my "Saved" folder, and dragged the cursor to the e-mail of shame. My stomach knotted. *Mocha lattes?* read the subject line.

Dorrie slid into the computer chair and squished over to make room for Tegan. She pressed the mouse-bar thingie, and the e-mail I wrote two days ago popped onto the screen, dated December 23:

Hey Jeb. I'm sitting here scared, typing these words. Which is crazy. How can I be scared talking to YOU? I've written so many versions of this, and deleted them all, and I'm just sick of myself in my own brain. No more deleting.

Although there is something I wish I *could* delete—and you know what it is. Kissing Charlie was the biggest mistake of my life. I'm sorry. I'm so so sorry. I know I've told you that again and again, but I could keep telling you forever and it wouldn't be enough.

You know how in movies, when someone does something really stupid like fooling around behind his girlfriend's back? And then he says, "It was nothing! She was nothing!" Well, what I did to you wasn't nothing. I hurt you, and there's no excuse for what I did.

But Charlie *is* nothing. I don't even want to talk about him. He came on to me, and it was like...this rush, that's all. And you and I, we'd had that stupid fight, and I was feeling needy or whatever, or maybe just pissed, and it felt good, all that attention. And I didn't think about you. I just thought about me.

It's really not fun saying all of this.

It makes me feel like crap.

But what I want to tell you is this: I screwed up big-time, but I learned my lesson.

I've changed, Jeb.

I miss you. I love you. If you give me another chance, I'll give you my whole heart. I know that sounds corny, but it's true.

Do you remember last Christmas Eve? Never mind. I

know you do. Well, I can't stop thinking about it. About
you. About us.

Come have a Christmas Eve mocha with me, Jeb. Three
o'clock at Starbucks, just like last year. Tomorrow's my
day off, but I'll be there, waiting in one of the big purple
chairs. We can talk...and hopefully more.

I know I deserve nothing, but if you want me, I'm
yours.

xoxo,
me

I could tell when Dorrie finished reading, because she
turned and looked at me, biting her lip. As for Tegan, she
made a sad *ohhhh* sound, got up out of the chair, and hugged
me tight. Which made me cry, only it wasn't crying so much
as a spasm of weeping that took me totally by surprise.

"Honey!" Tegan cried.

I wiped my nose on my sleeve. I took a heaving breath.

"Okay," I said, giving them a watery smile. "I'm better."

"No, you're not," Tegan said.

"No, I'm not," I agreed, and lost it all over again. My tears
were hot and salty, and I imagined them melting my heart.
They didn't. They just made it mushy around the edges.

Big breath.

Big breath.

Big, trembly breath.

"Did he write back?" Tegan asked.

"At midnight," I said. "Not last night's midnight, but the midnight before Christmas Eve." I swallowed and blinked and swiped again at my nose. "I checked my e-mail, like, every hour after I sent him the message—and nothing. So I was like, *Give it up. You suck, and of* course *he didn't write back.* But then I decided to check one last time, you know?"

They nodded. Every girl on the planet was familiar with one-last-time e-mail checks.

"And?" Dorrie said.

I leaned over them and tapped on the keyboard. Jeb's reply came up.

Addie... he'd written, and I could feel the complicated Jeb-silence inside that dot-dot-dot. I could imagine him thinking and breathing, his hands hovering over the keyboard. Finally—or at least, that was how I pictured it—he'd typed in, *We'll see.*

"'We'll see'?" Dorrie read aloud. "That's all he said, 'We'll see'?"

"I know. Classic Jeb."

"Hmm," Dorrie said.

"I don't think 'we'll see' is bad," Tegan said. "He probably didn't know *what* to say. He loved you so much, Addie. I bet he got your e-mail, and at first his heart lifted up, and then, because he's Jeb—"

"Because he's a *guy,*" Dorrie interjected.

"He said to himself, *Hold on. Be careful.*"

"Stop," I said. It was too painful.

"And maybe that's what his 'we'll see' meant," Tegan said anyway. "That he was thinking about it. I think that's good, Addie!"

"Tegan..." I said.

Her expression faltered. She went from hopeful to uncertain to worried. Her eyes flew to my pink hair.

Dorrie, who was quicker on the uptake with these things, said, "How long did you wait at Starbucks?"

"Two hours."

She gestured at my hair. "And after that, that's when you...?"

"Uh-huh. At the Fantastic Sam's across the street."

"Fantastic *Sam's?*" Dorrie said. "You got your breakup haircut at a place that gives out Dum-Dums and balloons?"

"They didn't give me a Dum-Dum or a balloon," I said glumly. "They were about to close. They didn't even want to give me an appointment."

"I don't get it," Dorrie said. "Do you know how many girls would have died for your hair?"

"Well, if they're willing to dig through a trash can for it, they can have it."

"Honestly, the pink is growing on me," Tegan said. "And I'm not just saying that."

"Yes, you are," I said. "But who cares? It's Christmas, and I'm all alone—"

"You're not alone," Tegan argued.

"And I'll *always* be alone—"

"How can you be alone when we're right here next to you?"

"And Jeb..." My voice hitched. "Jeb doesn't love me anymore."

"I can't believe he didn't come!" Tegan said. "That just doesn't sound like Jeb. Even if he didn't want to get back together, don't you think he'd at least show up?"

"But why doesn't he want to get back together?" I said. *"Why?"*

"Are you sure it's not some kind of mistake?" she pressed.

"Don't," Dorrie warned her.

"Don't what?" Tegan said. She turned to me. "Are you absolutely positive he didn't try to call you or anything?"

I grabbed my phone off my bedside table. I tossed it to her. "Look for yourself."

She went to my call history and read the names out loud. "Me, Dorrie, home, home, home *again*—"

"That was my mom, trying to figure out where I was, since I was gone for so long."

Tegan frowned. "Eight-oh-four, five-five-five, three-six-three-one? Who's that?"

"Wrong number," I said. "I answered, but no one was there."

She pressed a button and lifted the phone to her ear.

"What are you doing?" I asked.

"Whoever it was, I'm calling them. What if it was Jeb calling from someone else's phone?"

"It wasn't," I said.

"Eight-oh-four is Virginia's area code," Dorrie said. "Did Jeb take some mystery trip to Virginia?"

"No," I said. Tegan was the one grasping at straws, not me. Still, when she held up her finger, my pulse quickened.

"Um, hi," Tegan said. "May I ask who's calling?"

"You're the one who's calling, you doof," Dorrie said.

Tegan blushed. "Sorry," she said into the phone. "I mean, um, may I ask who's *speaking*?"

Dorrie waited for about half a second. "Well? Who is it?"

Tegan fluttered her hand, meaning, *Shush, you're distracting me.*

"Me?" she said to the mystery person on the other end of the line. "No, because that's insanity. And if I *had* thrown my cell phone into a snowbank, why would I—"

Tegan drew back and held the phone several inches from her ear. Tiny voices spilled out from the speaker, sounding like Alvin and the Chipmunks.

"How old are you guys?" Tegan said. "And hey, quit passing the phone around. All I want to know... Ex*cuse* me, could we get back to..." Her jaw dropped. "No! Absolutely not. I'm hanging up now, and I think you should...go play on the swing set."

She shut the phone. "Can you believe that?" she asked Dorrie and me indignantly. "They're eight years old—eight!—and they want me to tell them how to French-kiss a guy. They are seriously in need of deprogramming."

Dorrie and I looked at each other. Dorrie turned to Tegan and said, "The person who called Addie was an eight-year-old girl?"

"There wasn't just one. There was a whole gaggle, all yapping away. Yap, yap, yap." She shook her head. "I sure hope we weren't that annoying when we were that age."

"Tegan?" Dorrie said. "You're not giving us much to work with, babe. Did you find out why this gaggle of eight-year-olds called Addie?"

"Oh. Sorry. Um, I don't think it was them, because they said it wasn't actually their phone. They said they found it a few hours ago, after some girl flung it in a snowbank."

"Come again?" Dorrie said.

My palms felt itchy. I didn't like the sound of this girl. "Yeah, please tell us what the heck you're talking about."

"Well," Tegan said, "I'm not convinced they knew what they were talking about, but what they *said* was that the girl—"

"The phone-flinging girl?" Dorrie interrupted.

"Right. That she was with a guy, and that they were *in*

loooooove, which the eight-year-olds knew because they saw the guy 'plant a juicy one' on the girl. And then they asked me to teach them how to French-kiss!"

"You can't teach someone to French-kiss over the phone," Dorrie said.

"Plus, they're eight! They're babies! They don't need to be French-kissing, period. And 'plant a juicy one'? Please!"

"Um, Tegan?" I said. "Was the guy Jeb?"

The giggliness went out of her. I could see it happen. She bit her lip, flipped my phone back open, and hit redial.

"I am not here to chat," she said, right off the bat. She held the phone away from her head, wincing, then drew it back. "No! *Shhh!* I have one question and one question only. The guy with the girl...what did he look like?"

Chipmunk chatter burbled from the phone, but I couldn't make out the words. I watched Tegan's face and gnawed my thumbnail.

"Uh-huh, okay," Tegan said. "He did? Aw, that's so cute!"

"Tegan," I said through gritted teeth.

"Gotta go, bye," Tegan said, snapping shut the phone. She turned to me. "Most definitely not Jeb, because this guy had curly hair. So...yay! Case solved!"

"What made you say, 'Aw, that's so cute'?" Dorrie asked.

"They said that the guy did this dorky happy dance after kissing the phone-flinging girl, and that he thrust his fist into the air and yelled, 'Jubilee!'"

Dorrie drew back and made an okay-that's-weird expression.

"What?" Tegan said. "Wouldn't you want some guy yelling 'jubilee' after kissing you?"

"Maybe they'd just had dessert," I said.

They looked at me.

I looked back at them. I flipped my palms up, like, *C'mon, guys*. "With cherries? Cherries Jubilee?"

Dorrie turned back to Tegan. "No," she said. "I wouldn't want some guy yelling 'jubilee' about my cherry."

Tegan giggle-snickered, then stopped when she saw that I wasn't.

"But it wasn't Jeb," she repeated. "Isn't that good?"

I didn't answer. I didn't want Jeb kissing strange girls in Virginia, but if the eight-year-old Kissing Patrol *had* somehow possessed news of Jeb—well, I would very much have appreciated hearing it. Just say the guy they saw *didn't* have curly hair, and instead of kissing some girl, he was, like...locked in a Porta-Potty or something. If the Kissing Patrol had told Tegan that, then yes, it would have been good news, because it would have meant Jeb had an excuse for not meeting me.

Not that I wanted Jeb to be locked in a Porta-Potty, obviously.

"Addie? Are you okay?" Tegan asked.

"Do you believe in the magic of Christmas?" I asked.

"Huh?" she said.

"I don't, 'cause I'm Jewish," Dorrie said.

"Yeah, I know," I said. "Never mind, I'm just being dumb."

Tegan looked at Dorrie. "Do you believe in the magic of Hanukkah?"

"What?"

"Or, I know! Angels!" Tegan said. "Do you believe in angels?"

Now Dorrie and I both stared at her.

"You brought it up," Tegan said to me. "The magic of Christmas, the magic of Hanukkah, the magic of the holiday season..." She held her hands out, palms up, as if the answer was obvious. *"Angels."*

Dorrie snorted. Not me, though, because I guess maybe that was where my lonely heart was headed, even if I didn't want to say the word.

"Last year on Christmas Eve, after Jeb kissed me at Starbucks, he came over and watched *It's a Wonderful Life* with Mom and Dad and Chris and me," I said.

"I've seen that movie," Dorrie said. "Jimmy Stewart almost jumps off a bridge because he's so depressed about his life?"

Tegan pointed at me. "And an *angel* helped him decide not to. Yes."

"Actually, he wasn't an angel yet," Dorrie said. "Saving Jimmy Stewart was his test to *become* an angel. He had to make Jimmy Stewart realize his life was worth living."

"And he did, and everything worked out, and the angel got his wings!" Tegan finished. "I remember. It was at the end, and there was this silver bell on the Christmas tree, and out of nowhere the bell went *ting-a-ling-a-ling* without anyone touching it."

Dorrie laughed. "'*Ting-a-ling-a-ling*'? Tegan, you kill me."

Tegan plowed on. "And Jimmy Stewart's little girl said, 'Teacher says, every time a bell rings, an angel gets his wings.'" She sighed happily.

Dorrie swiveled the computer chair so that she and Tegan faced me. Tegan lost her balance but grabbed the arm of the chair and righted herself.

"Christmas magic, Hanukkah magic, *It's a Wonderful Life*?" Dorrie said to me. She lifted her eyebrows. "You going to connect the dots for us?"

"Don't forget angels," Tegan said.

I sat down on the end of my bed. "I know I did a terrible thing, and I know I really, really, really hurt Jeb. But I'm *sorry*. Doesn't that count for anything?"

"Of course it does," Tegan said sympathetically.

A lump formed in my throat. I didn't dare look at Dorrie, because I knew she'd roll her eyes. "Well, if that's true"—it was suddenly hard to get the words out—"then where's *my* angel?"

Chapter Four

"Angels, schmangels," Dorrie said. "Forget angels."

"*No*, don't forget angels," Tegan said. She flicked Dorrie. "You pretend to be such a Grinch, but you don't mean it."

"I'm not a Grinch," Dorrie said. "I'm a realist."

Tegan got up from the computer chair and sat beside me. "Just because Jeb didn't call you, that doesn't necessarily mean anything. Maybe he's on the reservation, visiting his dad. Didn't he say the res has crappy cell service?"

Jeb had taught us to call the reservation "the res," which made us feel tough and in-the-know. But hearing Tegan say it just deepened my despondency.

"Jeb did go to the res," I said. "But he's back. And how I know this is because evil Brenna *just happened* to come to Starbucks on Monday, and she *just happened* to trot out Jeb's entire Christmas break schedule while waiting in line to order. She was with Meadow, and she was all, 'I'm so bummed Jeb's not here. But he's coming in on the train Christmas Eve—maybe I'll go meet him at the station!'"

"Is that what made you write the e-mail?" Dorrie asked. "Hearing Brenna talk about him?"

"It's not what *made* me, but it might have had something to do with it." I didn't like the way she was looking at me. "So?"

"Maybe he got stuck in the storm," Tegan suggested.

"And he's *still* stuck? And he dropped his phone in a snow-drift like the kissing girl, and that's why he hasn't called? And he doesn't have access to a computer because he had to build an igloo to spend the night in and he doesn't have elec-tricity?"

Tegan gave a nervous shrug. *"May*be."

"I can't get my head around it," I said. "He didn't come, he didn't call, he didn't e-mail. He didn't do anything."

"Maybe he needed to break your heart the way you broke his," Dorrie said.

"Dorrie!" Fresh tears sprung to my eyes. "That's an awful thing to say!"

"Or not. I don't know. But, Adds...you hurt him *really* bad."

"I know! I just said that!"

"Like deep, wounding, forever bad. Like when Chloe broke up with Stuart." Chloe Newland and Stuart Weintraub were famous at Gracetown High: Chloe for cheating on Stuart, and Stuart for being unable to get over her. And guess where their breakup occurred? Starbucks. Chloe was there with another guy—in the bathroom! So skanky!—and Stuart showed up, and I got to be there for it all.

"Whoa," I said. My heart started thumping, because I had been so mad at Chloe that day. I'd thought she was so...*heartless*, cheating on her boyfriend like that. I told her to leave, that's how worked up I was, and Christina had to give me a little talk afterward. She informed me that in the future, I was not to throw out Starbucks customers just for being heartless bitches.

"Are you saying..." I tried to read Dorrie's expression. "Are you saying I'm a *Chloe?*"

"Of course not!" Tegan said. "She's not saying you're a Chloe. She's saying Jeb is a Stuart. Right, Dorrie?"

Dorrie didn't immediately answer. I knew she had a soft spot for Stuart, because every girl in our grade had a soft spot for Stuart. He was a nice guy. Chloe treated him like dirt. But Dorrie's protectiveness went even deeper, I think, because Stuart was the other Jewish kid at our school, so he and she sort of had a bond.

I told myself that was the reason she brought Stuart and Chloe up. I told myself she didn't *mean* to compare me to Chloe, who, in addition to being a coldhearted bitch, wore red lipstick that was totally the wrong shade for her skin.

"Poor Stuart," Tegan said. "I wish he'd find someone new. I wish he'd find someone who deserves him."

"Yeah, yeah," I said. "I'm all for Stuart finding true love. Go, Stuart. But Dorrie, I ask you again: Are you saying I'm the Chloe in this scenario?"

"*No,*" Dorrie said. She squeezed shut her eyes and rubbed her forehead, as if she'd developed a headache. She dropped her hand and met my gaze. "Adeline, I love you. I will always love you. But…"

Prickles shot up and down my spine, because any sentence that combined "I love you" and "but" could not be good. "But what?"

"You know you get wrapped up in your own dramas. I mean, we all do, I'm not saying we don't. But with you it's practically an art form. And sometimes…"

I rose from the bed, taking the blanket with me. I rewrapped it around my head and clutched it beneath my chin. "Yes?"

"Sometimes you worry more about yourself than you do about others, kind of."

"Then you *are* saying I'm a Chloe! You're saying I'm a heartless, self-absorbed *bitch*!"

"Not heartless," Dorrie said quickly. "Never heartless."

"And not a"—Tegan dropped her voice—"*you know.* You are not that *at all.*"

It didn't escape me that neither of them denied the "self-absorbed" bit. "Oh my God," I said. "I'm having a *crisis*, and my best friends gang up and attack me."

"We're not attacking you!" Tegan said.

"Sorry, can't hear you," I said. "Too busy being self-absorbed."

"No, you can't hear us because you have a blanket over your ears," Dorrie said. She strode over to me. "All I'm saying—"

"La-la-la! Still can't hear you!"

"—is that I don't think you should get back together with Jeb unless you're sure."

It was insane how fast my heart was going. I was safe in my room with my two best friends, and I was terrified of what one of them was about to say to me.

"Sure of what?" I managed.

Dorrie pulled down my hood. "In your e-mail, you said you've changed," she said carefully. "But I'm just wondering if you really have. If you've, you know, looked inside yourself to figure out what you even *need* to change."

Spots popped in my brain. It was extremely possible that I was hyperventilating, and I would soon faint and hit my head and *die*, and the blanket clutched around me would turn red with blood.

"Leave!" I told Dorrie, pointing at the door.

Tegan shrank into herself.

"Addie," Dorrie said.

"I'm serious—just go. And Jeb and I *didn't* get back together, did we? *Because he didn't show up.* So who cares if I've 'really' changed? It doesn't frickin' matter!"

Dorrie held her hands up. "You're right. I suck. That was completely bad timing."

"You're telling me. You're supposed to be my friend!"

"She *is* your friend," Tegan said. "Could you stop bickering? Both of you?"

I turned away, and as I did, I caught a glimpse of my reflection in my dresser mirror. For a second I didn't recognize myself: not my hair, not my scowl, not my anguished eyes. I thought, *Who is that crazy girl?*

I felt a hand on my shoulder.

"Addie, I'm sorry," Dorrie said. "I was talking out of my butt like I always do. I just—"

She broke off, and this time I did *not* say, "You just what?"

"I'm sorry," she said again.

I dug my fingers into the fibers of my throw blanket. After several long seconds, I gave a tiny nod. *But you still suck*, I said in my head, even though I knew she didn't.

Dorrie squeezed my shoulder, then released me. "We probably should get going, huh, Tegan?"

"I guess," Tegan said. She fooled with the hem of her T-shirt. "Only I don't want us to end the night on a bad note. I mean, it's Christmas."

"It's already ending on a bad note," I muttered.

"No, it's not," Dorrie said. "We made up. Right, Addie?"

"I wasn't talking about *that*," I said.

"Stop," Tegan said. "I have something good to tell y'all—something that has nothing to do with sadness or broken hearts or arguing." She gave the two of us a pleading look. "Will you listen?"

"Of course," I said. "Well, *I* will. Can't speak for Grinch here."

"I would love to hear something good," Dorrie said. "Is it about Gabriel?"

"Gabriel? Who's Gabriel?" I said. Then I remembered. "Oh! Gabriel!" I didn't look at Dorrie, because I didn't want her using this as proof that I thought only about myself or whatever.

"I got the most amazing news right before we came over," Tegan said. "I just didn't want to bring it up while we were still dealing with Addie's crisis."

"I think we're done with Addie's crisis," Dorrie said. "Addie? Are we done with your crisis?"

We will never be done with my crisis, I thought.

I sat down on the floor and tugged Tegan to make her sit beside me. I even made room for Dorrie. "Tell us your good news," I said.

"My news *is* about Gabriel," Tegan said. She smiled. "He's coming home tomorrow!"

Chapter Five

"I have his bed all set up," Tegan said. "I have a special Piglet stuffed animal to make him feel comfortable, and I have a ten-pack of grape Dubble Bubble."

"Ah, yes, because Gabriel loves grape Dubble Bubble," Dorrie said.

"Do pigs eat gum?" I said.

"They don't eat it, they chew it," Tegan said. "And I have a blanket for him to snuggle on, and a leash, and a litter box. The only thing I don't have is any mud for him to roll around in, but I figure he can roll in the snow, right?"

I was still hung up on the gum bit, but I pulled myself out of it. "Why not?" I said. "Tegan, that is so awesome!"

Her eyes were bright. "I'm going to have my own pig. I'm going to have my very own pig, and it's all thanks to y'all!"

I couldn't help but smile. In addition to being impossibly endearing, there was something else that gave Tegan her distinctive Tegan-ness.

She had a thing for pigs.

A really *big* thing for pigs, so I guess if she said pigs chewed gum, well, then pigs chewed gum. Tegan, of all people, would know.

Tegan's room was Pig Central, with porcelain pigs and china pigs and carved wooden pigs on every surface. Every Christmas, Dorrie and I gave her a new pig for her collection. (Tegan and I gave Dorrie Hanukkah gifts, too, of course. This year we ordered her a T-shirt from this cool site called Rabbi's Daughters. It was white with black baby-doll sleeves, and it read, GOT CHUTZPAH?)

Tegan has wanted a real pig forever, but her parents always said no. Actually, because her dad fashions himself a comedian, his standard response was to snort and say, "When pigs fly, Sugar Lump."

Her mom was less annoying, but equally unyielding.

"Tegan, that cute little piglet you're dreaming about is going to grow up to weigh eight hundred pounds," she said.

I could see her point. Eight hundred pounds—that was like *eight* Tegans all balanced on top of each other. It might not be such a good idea to have a pet that weighed eight times as much as you did.

But then Tegan discovered—drumroll, please!—the *teacup*

pig. They are beyond cute. Tegan showed Dorrie and me the Web site last month, and we oohed and ahed over the pictures of teensy-weensy piggies that seriously fit inside a teacup. They grow to weigh a maximum of five pounds, which is a twentieth of Tegan's weight, and which is a much better proposition than an eight-hundred-pound porker.

So Tegan talked to the breeder, and then she made her parents talk to the breeder. While all that talking was going on, Dorrie and I did some talking to the breeder of our own. By the time Tegan's parents gave their official okay, the deed was done: the last of the breeder's teacup piglets was paid for and reserved.

"You guys!" Tegan squealed when we told her. "You're the best friends ever! But...what if my parents had said no?"

"We had to risk it," Dorrie said. "Those teacup pigs go quick."

"It's true," I said. "They literally fly off the shelves."

Dorrie groaned, which egged me on.

I flapped my wings and said, "Fly! Fly away home, little piggy!"

We'd fully assumed Gabriel *would* have flown home by now, so to speak. Last week, Tegan had gotten word from the breeder that Gabriel was weaned, and Tegan and Dorrie made plans to drive to Fancy Nancy's Pig Farm to pick him up. The pig farm was in Maggie Valley, about two hundred miles away, but they could easily get there and back in a day.

Then came the storm. Bye-bye plan.

"But Nancy called tonight, and guess what?" Tegan said. "The roads in Maggie Valley aren't so bad, so she decided to drive on up to Asheville. She's spending New Year's there. And since Gracetown's on the way, she's going to swing by and drop Gabriel off at Pet World. I can get him tomorrow!"

"The Pet World across from Starbucks?" I said.

"Why there?" Dorrie said. "Couldn't she bring him straight to your house?"

"No, because the back roads haven't been cleared," Tegan said. "Nancy's buddies with the guy who owns Pet World, and he's going to leave a key for her. Nancy said she'd put a note on Gabriel's carrier that says, *Do Not Adopt This Pig Out Except To Tegan Shepherd!*"

"'Adopt this pig out'?" I said.

"That's pet-store-speak for 'sell,'" Dorrie said. "And thank goodness for Nancy's note, since no doubt there'll be thousands of people storming the pet store, desperate to buy a teacup piglet."

"Shut up," Tegan said. "I'll drive into town and get him the very second the snowplow comes through." She made praying hands. "Please, please, please let them get to our neighborhood early!"

"Dream on," Dorrie said.

"Hey," I said, struck by an idea. "I'm opening tomorrow, so Dad's letting me take the Explorer."

Dorrie made muscle arms. "Addie has Explorer! Addie no need snowplow!"

"You're darn straight," I said. "Unlike—*ahem*—the wimpy Civic."

"Don't be mean to the Civic!" Tegan protested.

"Ooh, sweetie, we kind of have to be mean to the Civic," Dorrie said.

"*Any*way," I interrupted, "I would be happy to pick up Gabriel if you want."

"Really?" Tegan said.

"Is Starbucks even going to be open?" Dorrie asked.

"Dude," I said. "Neither rain nor snow nor sleet nor hail shall close the doors of the mighty Starbucks."

"Dude," Dorrie shot back, "that's the mailman, not Starbucks."

"But unlike the mailman, Starbucks actually means it. They'll be open, I guarantee it."

"Addie, there are nine-foot drifts out there."

"Christina said we'll be open, so we'll be open." I turned to Tegan. "So yes, Tegan, I will be driving into town far too early tomorrow morning, and yes, I can pick up Gabriel."

"Yay!" Tegan said.

"Hold on," Dorrie said. "Aren't you forgetting something?"

I wrinkled my forehead.

"Nathan Krugle?" she said. "Works at Pet World, hates your guts?"

My stomach plunged. In all the talk of pigs, I'd forgotten entirely about Nathan. How could I have forgotten about Nathan?

I lifted my chin. "You are so negative. I can totally handle Nathan—*if* he's even working tomorrow, which he probably won't be, since he's probably off at a *Star Trek* convention or something."

"Already you're making excuses?" Dorrie said.

"*Nooo.* Already I'm demonstrating my complete and utter lack of self-absorption. Even if Nathan is there, this is about Tegan."

Dorrie looked dubious.

I turned to Tegan. "I'll take my break at nine and I'll be the first person through Pet World's doors, 'kay?" I strode to my desk, ripped off a *Hello Kitty* sticky note, and scrawled, *Do Not Forget Pig!* on it with my purple pen. I marched to my bureau, pulled out tomorrow's shirt, and slapped the sticky note on it.

"Happy?" I said, holding up the shirt for Tegan and Dorrie to see.

"Happy," Tegan said, smiling.

"Thank you, Tegan," I said grandly, suggesting with my tone that Dorrie could stand to learn a little lesson from such a trusting friend. "I promise I won't let you down."

Chapter Six

*T*egan and Dorrie bade their farewells, and for about two minutes I forgot my heartbreak in the midst of our good-byes and hugs. But as soon as they were gone, my shoulders slumped. *Hi*, said my sadness. *I'm ba-a-ack. Did you miss me?*

This time my grief took me to the memory of last Sunday, the morning after Charlie's party and the worst day of my life. I'd driven to Jeb's apartment—he didn't know I was coming—and at first he was happy to see me.

"Where'd you run off to last night?" he said. "I couldn't find you."

I started crying. His dark eyes filled with worry.

"Addie, you're not still mad, are you? About our fight?"

I tried to answer. Nothing came out.

"It wasn't even a fight," he reassured me. "It was a...nothing."

I cried harder, and he took my hands.

"I love you, Addie. I'll try to be better about showing it. All right?"

If there'd been a cliff up there in his bedroom, I'd have flung myself off it. If a dagger had been lying on his dresser, I'd have plunged it in my chest.

Instead, I told him about the Charlie Thing.

"I'm so sorry," I said, blubbering. "I thought we'd be together forever. I wanted us to be together forever!"

"Addie..." he said. He was still trying to catch up, but right that second, what he was reacting to—and I knew this because I knew Jeb—was the fact that I was upset. *This* was his most pressing concern, and he squeezed my hands.

"Stop it!" I said. "You can't be nice to me, not when we're breaking up!"

His confusion was terrible. "We're breaking up? You...you want to be with Charlie instead of me?"

"No. God, no." I jerked away. "I cheated on you, and I ruined *everything*, so"—a sob choked out—"so I have to let you go!"

He still wasn't there. "But...what if I don't want you to?"

I could hardly breathe for crying, but I remember thinking—no, *knowing*—that Jeb was so much better than me. He was the greatest, most wonderful guy in the world, and I was an absolute shit who didn't even deserve to be stepped on by him. I was an asshat. I was as big an asshat as Charlie.

"I have to go," I said, moving toward the door.

He grabbed my wrist. His expression said, *Don't. Please.*

But I had to. Couldn't he see that?

I wrenched away and made myself say the words. "Jeb... it's over."

He hardened his jaw, and I was perversely glad. He *should* be furious at me. He *should* despise me.

"Go," he said.

So I did.

And now...here I was. I stood by my bedroom window, watching Dorrie and Tegan grow smaller and smaller. The moonlight made the snow look silver—all that snow—and just looking at it made me cold.

I wondered if Jeb would ever forgive me.

I wondered if I would ever stop feeling so miserable.

I wondered if Jeb felt as miserable as I did, and I surprised myself by realizing that I hoped he didn't. I mean, I wanted him to feel a little miserable, or even fairly miserable, but I didn't want his heart to be a frozen lump of regret. He had such a good heart, which made it so confusing that he didn't show up yesterday.

Still, it wasn't Jeb's fault that I screwed up, and wherever he was, I hoped his heart was warm.

Chapter Seven

"Brrr," Christina said as she unlocked the front door to Starbucks at four thirty the next morning. Four frickin' thirty! The sun was an hour and a half from rising, and the parking lot was a ghostly landscape, broken up here and there by snow-covered cars. Christina's boyfriend honked as he pulled onto Dearborn Avenue, and Christina turned and waved. He drove off, and it was us, the snow, and the unlit store.

She pushed open the door, and I hurried in behind her.

"It's freezing out there," she said.

"You're telling me," I said. The drive from my house had been treacherous, even with snow tires and chains, and I passed at least a dozen cars abandoned by less gutsy drivers. In one snowbank there was an imprint of an entire SUV or some other monster vehicle. How was that possible? How did some idiot driver not see a six-foot wall of snow?

Until the snowplow came, there was no way Tegan would be driving *any*where in her wimpy Civic.

I stomped to dislodge the clumps of snow, then tugged off my boots and padded sock-footed to the back room. I flipped the six switches by the heating vent, and the store blazed with light.

We are the Christmas star lit by the angels, I thought, imagining how this one spot of brightness must look from anywhere else in the pitch-black town. *Only Christmas is over, and there were no angels.*

I pulled off my hat and coat and slipped on my black clogs, which matched my black pants. I resecured the DO NOT FORGET PIG! sticky note to my Starbucks shirt, which read, YOU CALL IT, WE'LL MAKE IT. Dorrie made fun of my T-shirt, just as she made fun of everything Starbucks, but I didn't care. Starbucks was my safe place. It was also my sad place, since it housed so many Jeb memories.

Even so, I found solace in its smells and routines—and especially its music. Call it "corporate" or "canned" or whatever, but the Starbucks CDs were good.

"Hey, Christina," I called, "care for a little 'Hallelujah'?"

"Heck yeah," she called back.

I stuck in the *Lifted: Songs of the Spirit* CD (which, yes, Dorrie gagged at) and selected track seven. Rufus Wainwright's voice filled the air, and I thought, *Ah, the sweet sound of Starbucks.*

What Dorrie failed to appreciate—along with the squillions of other Starbucks scoffers—was that the people who worked at Starbucks were still *people*, just like everyone else. Yes, Starbucks was owned by some hotshot Starbucks daddy, and yes, Starbucks was a chain. But Christina lived here in Gracetown just like Dorrie did. So did I. So did the rest of the baristas. So what was the big deal?

I walked out of the back room and started unpacking the pastries left by Carlos, the food-delivery guy. My attention kept getting pulled to the purple chairs at the front of the store, and tears made the reduced-fat blueberry muffins go blurry.

Stop it, I commanded myself. *Get a frickin' grip, or it's going to be a very long day.*

"Whoa," Christina said, her feet appearing in front of me. "You cut your hair."

I lifted my head. "Um...yeah."

"And dyed it pink."

"That's not a problem, is it?"

Starbucks had a Don't Ask, Don't Tell appearance code that prohibited nose rings, other facial piercings, and visible tattoos—meaning you could have tattoos and piercings, you just couldn't show them. I didn't think there was anything in the guidelines that said you couldn't have pink hair, though. Then again, the topic had never come up.

"Hmm," Christina said, studying me. "No, it's fine. Surprised me is all."

"Yeah, me, too," I said under my breath.

I didn't intend for her to hear me, but she did.

"Addie, are you okay?" she asked.

"Of course," I said.

Her gaze shifted to my shirt. She frowned. "What pig are you not supposed to forget?"

"Huh?" I looked down. "Oh. Uh…nothing." I suspected that pigs were probably prohibited in Starbucks, too, and I saw no reason to get Christina all worked up by explaining the whole story. I'd keep Gabriel hidden in the back room after I picked him up, and she would never have to know.

"Are you sure you're all right?" she said.

I smiled brightly and peeled off the sticky note. "Never better!"

She went back to prepping the coffee station, and I folded the note in half and stuck it in my pocket. I lugged the pastries to the glass case, put on a pair of plastic gloves, and started loading the trays. Rufus Wainwright's cover of "Hallelujah" filled the store, and I hummed along. It was almost pleasant, in a life-sucks-but-at-least-there's-good-music sort of way.

But as I listened to the lyrics—truly listened, instead of just letting them float over me—the almost-pleasant feelings went away. I'd always thought this was an inspirational song about God or something, because of all the hallelujahs. Only it turned out there were words before and after the hallelujahs, and those words were hardly uplifting.

Rufus was singing about love, and how love couldn't exist without faith. I grew still, because what he was saying sounded way too familiar. I listened some more, and was horrified to realize that the whole song was about a guy who was in love, only the person he loved betrayed him. And those heartbreakingly sweet hallelujahs? They weren't inspirational hallelujahs. They were...they were "cold and broken" hallelujahs—it said so right there in the chorus!

Why had I ever liked this song? This song sucked!

I went to change the CD, but it switched to the next track before I got there. A gospel version of "Amazing Grace" filled the store, and I thought, *Well, it's a heck of a lot better than a broken hallelujah.* And also, *Please, God, I sure could use some grace.*

Chapter Eight

*B*y five A.M., our morning prep was done. At 5:01, our first customer rapped on the glass door, and Christina walked over to officially unlock it.

"Merry day-after-Christmas, Earl," she said to the burly guy waiting outside. "Didn't know if we'd see you today."

"You think my customers care what the weather's like?" Earl said. "Think again, darlin'."

He trundled into the store, bringing with him a gust of frigid air. His cheeks were ruddy, and he wore a red-and-black hat with earflaps. He was huge, bearded, and looked like a lumberjack—which worked out nicely since he *was* a lumberjack. He drove one of those semis you never wanted to get behind on one of the many mountain roads around here, since, first of all, the weight he pulled meant he maintained a speed of a rip-roaring twenty miles an hour, and, second of all, the back of his open trailer was filled with logs. *Massive* logs, stacked five or six high. Logs, should the trailer restraints snap, that would roll off the truck and smush you as flat as a crushed to-go cup.

Christina crossed back behind the bar and got the steamer going. "Must be nice to be needed, though, huh?"

Earl grunted. He tromped over to the cash register, squinted at me, and said, "What'd you do to your hair?"

"I cut it," I said. I watched his face. "And dyed it." When he still didn't say anything, I added, "Do you like it?"

"What's it matter?" he replied. "It's your hair."

"I know. But…" I found I didn't know how to finish my sentence. Why *did* I care if Earl liked it or not? Eyes down, I took his money. He always got the same drink, so there was no further discussion required.

Christina swirled a generous galaxy of whipped cream onto Earl's raspberry mocha, drizzled the cream with bright red raspberry syrup, and topped the whole thing off with a white plastic lid.

"Here you go," she announced.

"Thank you, ladies," he said. He raised his cup in a toast, then strode out the door.

"You think Earl's lumberjack buddies tease him about getting such a girly drink?" I asked.

"Not more than once," Christina said.

The door jangled, and a guy held it open for his girlfriend. At least, I assumed she was his girlfriend, because they had that coupley look to them, all goofy and love struck. I immediately thought of Jeb—I'd gone, what, two seconds without his crossing my mind?—and felt lonely.

"Wow, more early birds," Christina commented.

"More like *late birds* is my guess." The guy, whom I recognized from school, had bleary eyes and an up-all-night sway to his posture. I thought I recognized the girl, too, but I wasn't sure. She couldn't stop yawning.

"Could you quit that?" the guy said to Yawning Girl. Tobin, his name was Tobin. He was one grade above me. "You're giving me a complex."

She smiled. She yawned again. Was her name Angie, maybe? Yeah, Angie, and she was nongirly in a way that made me feel *too* girly. I doubted she meant to, though. I doubted she even knew who I was.

"That's just great," he said. He appealed to me and Christina, spreading his arms. "She thinks I'm boring. I'm *boring* her—can you believe it?"

I kept my expression pleasant but noncommittal. Tobin wore scruffy sweaters and was friends with the Korean guy who said "asshat," and he and all of his buddies were intimidatingly clever. The kind of clever that made me feel cheerleader-dumb, even though I wasn't a cheerleader, and even though I personally didn't think cheerleaders *were* dumb. Not all of them, anyway. Chloe-the-Stuart-dumper, maybe.

"Hey," Tobin said, pointing at me. "I know you."

"Um, yeah," I said.

"But your hair wasn't always pink."

"Nope."

"So you *work* here? That's wild." He turned to the girl. "She works here. She's probably worked here for years, and I never knew it."

"Spooky," the girl said. She smiled at me and kind of tilted her head, as if to say, *I know I know you, and I'm sorry I don't know your name, but "hi" anyway.*

"Can I get drinks started for you guys?" I asked.

Tobin scanned the menu board. "Ah, Christ, this is the place with the messed-up sizes, isn't it? Like, *grandé* instead of large?" He stretched it out all stupid and fake-French, and Christina and I shared a look.

"Why can't you just call it a large?" he asked.

"You could, except *grandé* is a medium," Christina said. "*Venti* is large."

"*Venti*. Right. For the love of God, can't I order in plain English?"

"Absolutely," I told him. It was a delicate balance: keeping the customer happy, but also, when needed, calling him on his crap. "It might confuse me, but I'll figure it out."

Angie's lips twitched. It made me like her.

"No, no, no," Tobin said, holding his hands up and making a show of recanting. "When in Rome and all that. I'll, uh...let me think...can I get a *venti* blueberry muffin?"

I had to laugh. His hair was sticking up, he looked utterly exhausted, and yes, he was acting like a tool. I was fairly sure he didn't know my name, either, despite the fact that we'd gone to the same elementary school, middle school, and high school. Yet there was something sweet about him as he looked at Angie, who was laughing along with me.

"What?" he said, bewildered.

"The sizes are for drinks," she said. She put her hands on his shoulders and aimed him toward the pastry case, where six identically plump muffins sat at attention. "The muffins are all the same."

"They're muffins," Christina agreed.

Tobin blustered, and at first I assumed it was more of his act. *Hapless counter-culture-boy, thrust against his will into Big Bad Starbucks.* Then I noticed his rising blush, and I realized something. Tobin and Angie...their togetherness was new. New enough that being touched by her still came as a glorious, blush-worthy surprise.

Another wave of loneliness flooded through me. I remembered that skin-tingling exhilaration.

"This is my first time in a Starbucks," Tobin said. "Seriously. My first time ever, so be gentle with me." His hand fumbled for Angie's, and their fingers locked. She blushed, too.

"So...just a muffin?" I asked. I slid back the glass door of the pastry case.

"Never mind, I no longer want your stinking muffin." He pretend-pouted.

"Poor baby," Angie teased.

Tobin gazed at her. Sleepiness, and something else, softened his features.

"Um, how about your biggest-size latte," he said. "We can share."

"Sure," I said. "You want any syrup in that?"

He shifted his attention back to me. "Syrup?"

"Hazelnut, white chocolate, raspberry, vanilla, caramel... " I said, ticking them off.

"Hash brown?"

For a second I thought he was making a joke at my expense, but then Angie laughed, and it was a private-joke kind of laugh, but not in a mean way, and I realized maybe everything wasn't *always* about me.

"Sorry, no hash-brown syrup."

"Uh, okay," he said. He scratched his head. "Then, um, how about—"

"A cinnamon dolce white mocha," Angie told me.

"Excellent choice." I rang it up, and Tobin paid with a five and then stuffed a bonus five in the "Feed Your Barista" jar. Maybe he wasn't such a tool after all.

Still, when they went to the front of the store to sit down, I couldn't help thinking, *Not the purple chairs! Those are Jeb's and my chairs!* But of course the purple chairs were the ones they chose. After all, they were the softest and the best.

Angie dropped into the chair closest to the wall, and Tobin sank into its mate. In one hand, he held their drink. With his other, he reclaimed Angie, lacing his fingers through hers and holding on tight.

Chapter Nine

By six thirty, the sun was officially on the rise. It was pretty, I suppose, if you liked that sort of thing. Fresh starts, new beginnings, the warming rays of hope...

Yeah. Not for me.

By seven, we had an actual morning rush, and the demands of cappuccinos and espressos took over and made my brain shut up, at least for a while.

Scott swung by for his customary chai, and, as always, he ordered a to-go cup of whipped cream for Maggie, his black lab.

Diana, who worked at the preschool down the road, stopped in for her skinny latte, and as she dug around in her purse for her Starbucks card, she told me for the hundred-billionth time that I needed to change my picture on the "Meet Your Baristas" board.

"You know I hate that photo," she said. "You look like a fish with your lips puckered like that."

"I like that picture," I said. Jeb had snapped it last New Year's Eve, when Tegan and I were goofing around pretending to be Angelina Jolie.

"Well, I don't know why," Diana replied. "You're just such a pretty girl, even with this"—she waved her hand to indicate my new hairstyle—"*punk* look you've got going on."

Punk. Good Lord.

"It's not punk," I said. "It's pink."

She found her card and held it aloft. "Aha! Here you go."

I swiped it and returned it, and she wagged it in my face before going to claim her drink.

"Change that picture!" she commanded.

The Johns, all three of them, came in at eight and took up residence at their customary corner table. They were retired, and they liked to spend their mornings drinking tea and working through their Sudoku books.

John Number One said my new hair made me look foxy, and John Number Two told him to stop flirting.

"She's young enough to be your granddaughter," John Number Two said.

"Don't worry," I replied. "Anyone who uses the word *foxy* has pretty much taken himself out of the running."

"You mean I was in the running till then?" John Number

One said. His Carolina Tar Heels baseball cap perched high on his head like a bird's nest.

"No," I said, and John Number Three guffawed. He and John Number Two knocked their fists together, and I shook my head. *Boys.*

At eight forty-five, I reached for the strings of my apron and announced that I was going on break.

"I have a quick errand to run," I told Christina, "but I'll be right back."

"Wait," she said. She grabbed my forearm to keep me with her, and when I followed her gaze, I understood why. Entering the store was one of Gracetown's finest, a tow truck driver named Travis who wore nothing but tinfoil. Tinfoil pants, tinfoil jacket-shirt-thing, even a cone-shaped tinfoil hat.

"Why oh why does he dress like that?" I said, and not for the first time.

"Maybe he's a knight," Christina suggested.

"Maybe he's a lightning rod."

"Maybe he's a weather vane, here to predict the winds of change."

"Ooo, nice one," I said, and sighed. "I could use a wind of change."

Travis approached. His eyes were so pale they looked silver. He didn't smile.

"Hey, Travis," Christina said. "What can I get you?" Usually,

Travis just asked for water, but every so often he had enough change for a maple scone, his favorite pastry. Mine, too, actually. They looked dry, but they weren't, and the maple icing rocked.

"Can I have a sample?" he said gruffly.

"Of course," she said, reaching for one of the sample cups. "What would you like a sample of?"

"Nothing," he said. "Just the cup."

Christina glanced at me, and I trained my eyes on Travis to keep from laughing, which would be mean. If I looked closely, I could see lots of "me"s in his jacket-shirt-thingy. Or rather, fragments of me, broken up by the crinkles in the foil.

"The eggnog latte is good," Christina suggested. "It's our seasonal special."

"Just the cup," Travis repeated. He shifted in agitation. "I just want the cup!"

"Fine, fine." She handed him the cup.

I pulled my gaze away from the "me"s, which were mesmerizing.

"I can't believe you're dressed like that, especially today," I said. "Please tell me you've got a sweater on under that tinfoil."

"What tinfoil?" he said.

"Ha-ha," I said. "For real, Travis, aren't you cold?"

"I'm not. Are you?"

"Um, *nooo*. Why would I be cold?"

"I don't know. Why would you?"

I half laughed. Then stopped. Travis regarded me from beneath his craggy brows.

"I wouldn't," I said, flustered. "I'm not. I'm totally, completely comfortable, *temperature-wise*."

"'*Temperature-wise*,'" he scoffed. "It's always about you, isn't it?"

"What?! I'm not...talking about me! I'm just telling you that I'm not cold!"

The intensity of his gaze made me feel itchy.

"Okay, maybe I'm talking about me *this very second*," I said. "But it's not *always* about me."

"Some things never change," he said scornfully. He strode off with his doll-size cup, but at the door, he turned for one last parting shot. "And don't bother asking for a tow. I'm off duty!"

"Well," I said. He'd actually hurt my feelings, but I didn't want to let on. "That was interesting."

"I don't think I've ever heard Travis deny anyone a tow before," Christina said. "Seriously, I think you're the first."

"Please don't sound so impressed," I said faintly.

She laughed, which was what I wanted. But as she refilled the napkin container, Travis's words came back to me: *It's always about you, isn't it?*

It was disconcertingly similar to what Dorrie said to me last night: *Have you truly looked inside yourself? Do you even know what you need to change?*

Or something like that.

"Hey, um, Christina...?"

"Yeah?"

"Is there something wrong with me?"

She glanced up from the napkins. "Addie, Travis is nuts."

"I know. But that doesn't mean everything he says is nuts, necessarily."

"*Ad*die."

"Chris*ti*na."

"Just tell me the truth: Am I a good person? Or am I, like, too self-absorbed?"

She considered. "Does it have to be either/or?"

"Ouch." I drew my hand to my heart and staggered back.

She grinned, thinking I was being Funny Addie. And I was, I guess. But I also had the strangest fear that the universe was trying to tell me something. I felt as if I were teetering on the edge of a great chasm, only the chasm was in myself. I didn't want to look down.

"Look lively," Christina told me. "Here come the seniors."

Sure enough, the Silver Sneakers van had pulled up outside Starbucks, and the driver was carefully helping his load of senior citizens navigate the sidewalk. They resembled a line of well-bundled bugs.

"Hi, Claire," Christina said as the first of the seniors jingled through the door.

"Nippy, nippy!" Claire said, slipping off her colorful hat.

Burt made his way straight to the counter and ordered a shot in the dark, and Miles, shuffling in behind him, called out, "You sure your ticker can handle it, old man?"

Burt thumped his chest. "Keeps me young. That's why the ladies love me. Right, Miss Addie?"

"Absolutely," I said, putting the universe on hold as I grabbed a cup and handed it to Christina. Burt had the biggest ears I'd ever seen (maybe because he'd had eighty-odd years to grow them?), and I wondered what the ladies thought of them.

As the line grew, Christina and I fell into our crunch-time roles. I took orders and manned the register while she worked her magic with the steamer.

"Grande latte!" I called.

"Grande latte," she repeated.

"Venti soy toffee nut mocha single shot no whip!"

"Venti soy toffee nut mocha single shot no whip."

It was a dance. It pulled me out of myself. The chasm still gaped within me, but I had to tell it, *Sorry, caz, no time.*

The last of the seniors was Mayzie, with her gray braids and a beatific smile. Mayzie was a retired folklore professor, and she dressed all hippy-dippy in battered jeans, an oversize striped sweater, and a half dozen beaded bracelets. I loved that about her, that she dressed more like a teenager than an old lady. I mean, I didn't want to see her in super-low-rise Sevens and a thong, but I thought it was cool that she did her own thing.

No one was waiting behind her, so I rested my hands on the counter and allowed myself a breath of air.

"Hey, Mayzie," I said. "How you doing today?"

"I'm terrific, hon," she said. Today she was wearing purple jingle bell earrings, and they tinkled when she tilted her head. "Ooo, I *like* your hair."

"You don't think I look like a plucked chicken?"

"Not at all," she said. "It suits you. It's spunky."

"I don't know about that," I said.

"Well, I do. You've been moping around for too long, Addie. I've been watching. It's time you grew into your next self."

There it was again, the prickling sense of standing on a precipice.

Mayzie leaned closer. "We are all flawed, my dear. Every one of us. And believe me, we've *all* made mistakes."

Heat rushed to my face. Were my mistakes so public that even my customers knew? Did the Silver Sneakers gang discuss my hookup with Charlie over bingo?

"You've just got to take a good hard look at yourself, change what needs to be changed, and move on, pet."

I blinked at her dumbly.

She lowered her voice. "And if you're wondering why I get to tell you this, it's because I've decided to pursue a new profession: Christmas angel."

She waited for my reaction, her eyes bright. It was strange

that she would bring up the whole "angel" thing after I'd talked about angels with Dorrie and Tegan last night, and for a teeny-tiny fraction of a second I actually wondered if she *was* my angel, here to save me.

Then cold, hard reality thudded back down, and I hated myself for being such a fool. Mayzie was no angel; today was just the Day of the Nut Jobs. Apparently, everyone had eaten too much fruitcake.

"Don't you have to be dead to be an angel?" I said.

"Now, Addie," she scolded. "Do I look dead to you?"

I looked at Christina to see if she was catching this, but Christina was over by the exit, putting a new bag in the trash can.

Mayzie took my lack of response as permission to continue. "It's a program called Angels Among Us," she said. "I don't have to get a degree or anything."

"There's not really a program called that," I said.

"Oh, yes, yes. It's offered at Gracetown's Center for the Heavenly Arts."

"Gracetown doesn't have a Center for the Heavenly Arts," I said.

"I sometimes get lonely," she confided. "Not that the Silver Sneakers aren't wonderful. But sometimes they're a bit"—she dropped her voice to a whisper—"well, *boring*."

"Ohhh," I whispered back.

"I thought becoming an angel might be a nice way to connect with others," she said. "Anyway, to get my wings, I just have to spread the magic of Christmas."

I snorted. "Well, I don't believe in the magic of Christmas."

"Sure you do, or I wouldn't be here."

I drew back, feeling somehow as if I'd been tricked. Because how was I supposed to respond to that? I shook myself and tried another tactic. "But...Christmas is over."

"Oh, no, Christmas is never over, unless you want it to be." She leaned on the counter and propped her chin on her palm. "Christmas is a state of mind."

Her gaze dropped below the level of the counter. "Goodness gracious," she said.

I looked down. "What?"

The top corner of the folded-up sticky note was sticking out of my jeans pocket, and Mayzie reached across the counter and plucked it free. The gesture was so unexpected, I just stood there and let her.

"'Do not forget the pig,'" Mayzie said after unfolding the note. She tilted her head and peered at me like a little bird.

"Oh *crud*," I said.

"What pig are you not supposed to forget?"

"Uh"—my mind was jittery—"it's for my friend, Tegan. What drink can I get started for you?" My fingers itched to untie my apron strings so I could go on break.

"Hmm," Mayzie said. She tapped her chin.

I tapped my foot.

"You know," she said, "sometimes when we forget to do things for others, like this *Tegan*, it's because we're too wrapped up in our own problems."

"Yes," I said vigorously, hoping to dissuade further discussion. "You want your usual almond mocha?"

"When actually, what we need to forget is ourselves."

"Yes again. I hear ya. Single shot?"

She smiled as if I amused her. "Single shot, yes, but let's mix it up this time. Change is healthy, right?"

"If you say so. So what'll it be?"

"A toffee nut mocha, please, in a to-go cup. I think I'll take in some air before Tanner comes back for us."

I relayed Mayzie's order to Christina, who had slipped back behind the counter. She whipped it up and slid it over.

"Keep what I said in mind," Mayzie said.

"I'm pretty sure I will," I said.

She giggled merrily, as if we were in cahoots. "Bye, now," she called. "See you soon!"

As soon as she was gone, I tore off my apron.

"I'm going on break," I told Christina.

She handed me the steamer. "Rinse this out for me, and you're officially free to go."

Chapter Ten

I set the steamer in the sink and twisted the faucet. As I waited impatiently for it to fill, I turned and leaned against the sink's edge. I drummed my fingers against its metal rim.

"Mayzie says I need to forget myself," I said. "What do you think that means?"

"Don't ask me," Christina said. Her back was to me as she blew out the steam wand, and I watched the puff of steam rise above her shoulders.

"And my friend Dorrie—you know Dorrie—she kind of said the same thing," I mused. "She said I always have to make things be about me."

"Well, I won't argue with you there."

"Ha ha," I said. I grew uncertain. "You're kidding, right?"

Christina looked over her shoulder and grinned. Her eyes widened in dismay, and she gestured furiously. "Addie, the... the..."

I twisted around to see a sheet of water spill over the edge of the sink. I jumped back, yelping, *"Ahhh!"*

"Turn it off!" Christina said.

I fumbled with the faucet, but water continued to pour into and over the sink.

"It's not working!"

She pushed me aside. "Get a rag!"

I dashed to the back room, grabbed a rag, and dashed back. Christina was still twisting the faucet, and water was still pouring onto the floor.

"See?" I said.

She glared.

I wormed in and pressed the rag to the sink's edge. A second later it was soaked, and I had a flashback to the time I was four and couldn't turn the bathtub off.

"Crap, crap, crap," Christina said. She gave up on turning the water off and applied pressure to the spurting faucet. It squirted past her fingers in an umbrella-shaped arch. "I have *no idea* what to do!"

"Oh, God. Okay, um"—I scanned the store—"John!"

All three Johns looked up from their corner table. They saw what was happening and hurried over.

"Can we come behind the counter?" John Number Two asked, because Christina was hard-core about customers not coming behind the counter. Starbucks policy.

"Of course!" Christina cried. She blinked as the water sprayed her shirt and face.

The Johns took charge. Johns One and Two came to the sink, while John Number Three loped toward the back room.

"Move aside, ladies," John Number One said.

We did. Christina's apron was soaked, as was her shirt. And her face. And her hair.

I pulled a stack of napkins from the dispenser. "Here."

She took them wordlessly.

"Um...are you mad?"

She didn't respond.

John Number One hunkered down by the wall and did studly things with the pipes. His Tar Heels cap bobbed as he moved.

"I didn't do anything, I swear," I said.

Christina's eyebrows rose to her hairline.

"Well, fine, I forgot to turn the water off. But that shouldn't have caused the whole system to break down."

"Musta been the storm," John Number Two said. "Probably burst one of the outside pipes."

John Number One grunted. "Just about got it. If I could only"—more grunts—"get this one valve...*durn it!*"

A stream of water nailed him between the eyes, and I clapped my hand to my mouth.

"Don't think you got it," John Number Two observed.

The water chugged from the pipe. Christina looked like she was about to cry.

"Oh God, I am so sorry," I said. "Please make your face go back to normal. Please?"

"Why, look at that," John Number Two said.

The gurgling sounds slowed. A drop of water trembled on the rim of the pipe, then sploshed to the floor. After that, nothing.

"It stopped," I said in amazement.

"I disconnected the main line," John Number Three announced, emerging from the back room with a towel.

"You did? That is so cool!" I exclaimed.

He tossed the towel to John Number One, who dabbed at his pants.

"You're supposed to mop the floor, not your pants," John Number Two said.

"I already *did* mop the floor," John Number One grouched. "With my pants."

"I better call an actual plumber," Christina said. "And Addie...I think you should take your break."

"Don't you want me to help clean up?" I said.

"I want you to take your break," she said.

"Oh," I said. "Um, yeah, sure. That's what I was *going* to

do before, but then Crazy Travis showed up, and then Crazy Mayzie—"

She pointed toward the back room.

"It's just that you were the one who asked me to stay. I mean, who cares, right? But it *was*—"

"Addie, please," Christina said. "Maybe it isn't about you this time, but it sure feels like it. I need you to go."

We stared at each other.

"Now."

I jumped and headed for the back room.

"Don't worry," John Number Three said as I passed him. "She'll be over it by the next time you break something." He winked, and I smiled wanly.

Chapter Eleven

I sloughed off my wet shirt and borrowed a new one from the shelf. It was for Starbucks' DoubleShot and read, BRING ON THE DAY. Then I fished my cell from my cubby and punched in Dorrie's speed dial.

"*Hola*, cookie," she said, picking up on the second ring.

"Hi," I said. "Do you have a minute? I've had the weirdest day, and it just keeps getting weirder, and I have *got* to talk to someone about it."

"Did you get Gabriel?"

"Huh?"

"I said, did you get—" She broke off. When she spoke again, her voice was overly controlled. "Addie? Please tell me you remembered to go to Pet World."

My stomach slammed down to my feet, like an elevator

whose cables broke. I quickly closed my phone and grabbed my coat from the hook. As I was leaving, my phone rerang. I knew I shouldn't answer, I *knew* I shouldn't answer...but I gave in and answered anyway.

"Listen," I said.

"No, you listen. It's ten thirty, and you promised Tegan you'd go to Pet World at nine o'clock on the dot. There's no excuse you can give that'll justify why you're still at Starbucks futzing around."

"That's not fair," I argued. "What if...what if an iceberg fell on my head and left me in a coma?"

"*Did* an iceberg fall on your head and leave you in a coma?"

I pressed my lips together.

"Uh-huh, well, let me ask you this: Whatever your reason really is, does it have to do with you and some ridiculous new crisis?"

"No! And if you'd stop attacking me and let me tell you all the weird stuff that's happened to me, you'd understand."

"Do you even hear yourself?" she said incredulously. "I ask if it's about some new crisis, and you say 'No, and by the way, let me tell you about my new crisis.'"

"I didn't say that." *Did I?*

She exhaled. "Not cool, Addie."

My voice went small. "Okay, you're right. But, um...it has

been an unusually bizarre day, even for me. I just want you to know that."

"Of course it was," Dorrie said. "And of course you forgot about Tegan, because it's always, always, *always* about you." She made an impatient sound. "What about the sticky note that said *Do Not Forget Pig*? Didn't that ring any bells for you?"

"An old lady stole it from me," I said.

"An old lady…" She broke off. "Yeah, uh-huh. It's not that you spaced it; an old lady had to steal it from you. It's *The Addie Show* all over again. Every channel, every network."

That stung. "It's not *The Addie Show*. I just got side-tracked."

"Go to Pet World," Dorrie said, sounding tired. She hung up.

Chapter Twelve

Sunlight glinted on the snow as I hurried down the road and over to Pet World. The sidewalks were mostly clear, but there were spots here and there where the shoveled-off drifts had crumbled down, and my boots made *oomph* sounds as I trudged through those deeper stretches.

As I *oomphed*, I kept up a running monologue inside my brain about how *The Addie Show* was *not* on every channel. *The Addie Show* wasn't on the monster-truck channel, and it wasn't on the pro-wrestling channel. It most certainly wasn't on whatever channel aired *Let's Go Fishing with Orlando Wilson*, and I was tempted to call Dorrie back and tell her that. "Is it called *Let's Go Fishing with Adeline Lindsey*?" I'd say. "Why, no! It's not!"

But I didn't, because no doubt she'd find a way to turn that into an example of my being self-absorbed, too. Worse, she'd probably be right. A better plan was to get Gabriel in my hot little hands—well, my cold little hands—and *then* call Dorrie. I'd say, "See? It turned out okay." And then I'd call Tegan and let Gabriel *oink* into the phone or something.

Or, no. I'd call Tegan first, to spread the joy, and *then* I'd call Dorrie. And I wouldn't say, "Ha-ha," because I was bigger than that. Yeah. I was big enough to admit my wrongs, and I was big enough to stop cowering when Dorrie scolded me, since the new, enlightened me would need no scolding.

My cell rang from within my bag, and I cowered. *Holy crud, does the girl have ESP?*

A worse possibility entered my mind: *Maybe it's Tegan.*

And then a wildly unworse possibility, stubborn and fluttering: *Or...maybe it's Jeb?*

I fumbled in my bag and snatched out my phone. The display screen said DAD, and I deflated. *Why?* I railed silently. *Why couldn't it have been—*

And then I stopped. I cut that whiny voice off midsentence, because I was sick of it, and it wasn't doing me any good, and anyway, shouldn't I have some say over the endless thoughts running through my head?

In my brain—*and* in my heart—I experienced a sudden absence of static. *Wow.* I could get used to that.

I hit the ignore button on my phone and dropped it back

into my bag. I'd call Dad later, after I'd made things right.

Eau de hamster hit me as I stepped inside Pet World, as well as the unmistakable scent of peanut butter. I paused, closed my eyes, and said a prayer for strength, because while eau de hamster was to be expected in a pet store, the smell of peanut butter could mean only one thing.

I approached the cash register, and Nathan Krugle glanced up midchew. His eyes widened, then narrowed. He swallowed and put down his peanut butter sandwich.

"Hello, Addie," he said distastefully, á la Jerry Seinfeld greeting his nemesis, Newman.

No. Wait. That would make *me* Newman, and I was *so* not Newman. Nathan was Newman. Nathan was a super-skinny, acne-pocked Newman with a taste for shrunken T-shirts inscribed with *Star Trek* quotes. Today his shirt said, YOU WILL DIE OF SUFFOCATION IN THE ICY COLD OF SPACE.

"Hello, Nathan," I replied. I pushed my hood off, and he took in my hair. He semi-snorted.

"Nice haircut," he said.

I started to say something back, then restrained myself. "I'm here to pick up something for a friend," I said. "For Tegan. You know Tegan."

I'd thought the mention of Tegan, with her bottomless sweetness, might distract Nathan from his vendetta.

It didn't.

"Indeed I do," he said, his eyes gleaming. "We go to the same school. The same *small* school. Surely it would be hard to ignore someone in a school that small?"

I groaned. Here it came, again, as if we hadn't spoken for four years and still had to process that one regrettable incident. Which we didn't. We had processed it many times, and yet apparently the processing was one-sided.

"But wait," he said in the robotic voice of a bad infomercial host. "*You* ignored someone in a school that small!"

"Seventh *gra*-ade," I said in a gritted-teeth, singsong voice. "Many many *years* ago."

"Do you know what a Tribble is?" he demanded.

"Yes, Nathan, you've—"

"A Tribble is a harmless creature desperate for affection, native to the planet Iota Geminorum Four."

"I thought it was Iota Gemi-blah-blah Five."

"And *not* that many years ago"—he arched his brows to make sure I understood his emphasis—"I was such a Tribble."

I slumped next to a rack of dog treats. "You were not a Tribble, Nathan."

"And like a specially trained Klingon warrior—"

"Please don't call me that. You know I really hate being called that."

"—you obliterated me." He noticed the location of my elbow, and his nostrils flared. "Hey," he said, snapping his fingers repeatedly at the offending body part. "Don't touch the Doggy de Lites."

I jerked upright. "Sorry, I'm sorry," I said. "Just as I am very sorry I hurt your feelings *four years ago*. But. And this is important. Are you listening?"

"In galactic terms, four years is but a nanosecond."

I made a sound of exasperation. "I didn't get the note! I swear to God, I never saw it!"

"Sure, sure. Only, know what I think? I think you read it, tossed it, and promptly forgot it, because if it has to do with anyone else's woes, it doesn't matter, right?"

"That's not true. Listen, can we just—"

"Shall I recite the note's contents?"

"Please don't."

He gazed into the distance. "And I quote: 'Dear Addie, will you go steady with me? Call me with your answer.'"

"I didn't get the note, Nathan."

"Even if you didn't want to go steady, you should have called."

"I would have! But I didn't get the note!"

"The heart of a seventh-grade boy is a fragile thing," he said tragically.

My hand itched toward the tidy rows of Doggy de Lites. I wanted to peg a pack at him.

"Okay, Nathan?" I said. "Even if I did get the note—*which*

I didn't—can't you let it go? People move on. People grow. People *change*."

"Oh, please," he said coldly. The way he regarded me, as if I were lower than a straw wrapper, reminded me that he and Jeb were friends. "People like you don't change."

My throat closed. It was too much, that he would come down on me in the same way that everyone else on the planet had.

"But..." It came out wavery. I tried again, and in a voice that wobbled despite my best intentions, I said, "Can't anyone see I'm trying?"

After a long moment, he was the one who finally dropped his eyes.

"I'm here to pick up Tegan's pig," I said. "Can I just have him, please?"

Nathan's brow furrowed. "What pig?"

"The pig that was dropped off last night." I tried to read his expression. "Teeny-tiny? With a note that said, *Do not sell to anyone but Tegan Shepherd*?"

"We don't 'sell' animals," he informed me. "We adopt them out. And there was no note, just an invoice."

"But there *was* a pig?"

"Well, yes."

"And it was really, really small?"

"Maybe."

"Well, there should have been a note attached to the pet

carrier, but it doesn't matter. Can you just get him for me?"

Nathan hesitated.

"Nathan, oh my God." I envisioned Gabriel alone through the cold night. "Please tell me he didn't die."

"What?! *No.*"

"Then where is he?"

Nathan didn't reply.

"Nathan, come on," I said. "This isn't about me. It's about Tegan. Do you honestly want to punish her because you're pissed at me?"

"Someone adopted him," he muttered.

"I'm sorry. What's that?"

"Some lady, she adopted the pig. She came in about half an hour ago and forked over two hundred dollars. How was I supposed to know he wasn't for sale—I mean, adoption?"

"Because of the note, you idiot!"

"I didn't *get* the note!"

We realized the irony of his protest at the same time. We stared at each other.

"I'm not lying," he said.

There was no point pushing the issue. This was bad, bad, bad, and I had to figure out how to fix it, not get all over Nathan for something that was too late to change.

"Okay, um, do you still have the invoice?" I said. "Show me the invoice." I held out my hand and wiggled my fingers.

Nathan jabbed the cash register, and the bottom drawer

sprung open. He drew out a wrinkled piece of pale pink paper.

I grabbed it. "'One teacup piglet, certified and licensed,'" I read aloud. "'Two hundred dollars.'" I flipped it over, zeroing in on the neatly penned message at the bottom. "'Paid in full. To be picked up by Tegan Shepherd.'"

"Damn," Nathan said.

I flipped it over again, looking for the name of who rebought Tegan's pig.

"Bob gets in new animals all the time," Nathan said defensively. "They show up and I, you know, adopt them out. Because it's a pet store."

"Nathan, I need you to tell me who you sold him to," I told him.

"I can't. That's private information."

"Yes, but it's Tegan's pig."

"Um, we'll give her a refund, I guess."

Technically, it was Dorrie and I who should get the refund, but I didn't mention that. I didn't care about the refund.

"Just tell me who you sold him to, and I'll go explain the situation."

He shifted, looking incredibly uncomfortable.

"You do have the person's name, right? Who bought him?"

"No," he said. His eyes darted to the open drawer of the cash register, where I saw the tail end of a white credit-card slip.

"Even if I did know, there's nothing I could do," he continued. "I can't reveal the details of customer transactions. But I don't know the lady's name anyway, so, um...yeah."

"It's okay. I understand. And...I do believe you about not seeing the note."

"You do?" he said. His expression was bewildered.

"I do," I said truthfully. I turned to leave, and as I did, I hooked the toe of my boot under the Doggie de Lite display rack and tugged. The rack toppled, and cellophane bags tumbled to the floor, bursting open and spilling dog treats everywhere.

"Oh, no!" I cried.

"Aw, crap," Nathan said. He came around from behind the counter, knelt, and started piling up the bags that were still intact.

"I am *so* sorry," I said. As he fished for a stray dog cookie, I leaned over the counter and plucked the white receipt. I shoved it into my pocket. "You must hate me even more now, huh?"

He paused, straightening up and propping one hand on his knee. He did a weird thing with his lips, as if he were going through some sort of struggle.

"I don't *hate* you," he said at last.

"You don't?"

"I just don't think you realize, sometimes, how you affect people. And I'm not just talking about me."

"Then...who are you talking about?" I was very aware of the receipt in my pocket, but I couldn't walk away from a comment like that.

"Forget it."

"No way. Tell me."

He sighed. "I don't want this to go to your head, but you're not *always* annoying."

Gee, thanks, I wanted to say. But I held my tongue.

"You've got this...light about you," he said, turning red. "You make people feel special, like maybe there's a light in them, too. But then if you never call them, or if you, you know, kiss some asshole behind their back..."

My vision blurred, and not just because Nathan was suddenly saying things that instead of being rude were dangerously close to sweet. I stared at the floor.

"It's just cruel, Addie. It's really cold." He gestured at a bag of Doggy de Lites by my boot. "Pass me that, will you?"

I bent down and picked it up.

"I don't mean to be cold," I said awkwardly. I handed him the Doggy de Lites. "And I'm not trying to make excuses." I swallowed, surprised by how much I needed to say this to someone who was Jeb's friend and not mine. "But sometimes I need someone to shine a little light on me, too."

The muscles of Nathan's face didn't move. He let my comment hover between us, just long enough for regret to start pressing in.

Then he grunted. "Jeb's not exactly the most demonstrative guy," he acknowledged.

"You think?"

"But get a grip. When it comes to you, he's totally whupped."

"*Was* whupped," I said. "Not anymore." I felt a tear, and then another, make its way down my cheek, and I felt like a fool. "Yeah. I'm going now."

"Hey, Addie," Nathan said.

I turned.

"If we get another teacup pig, I'll call you."

I looked past his acne and his *Star Trek* shirt and saw just plain Nathan, who, as it turned out, wasn't always annoying, either.

"Thanks," I said.

Chapter Thirteen

As soon as I was ten feet away from the pet store, I fished out the pilfered receipt. On the "item" line, Nathan had scrawled, *pig.* Where the credit-card info was printed, it said, *Constance Billingsley.*

I swiped away my tears with the back of my hand and took a steadying breath. Then I sent a psychic message to Gabriel: *Don't worry, little guy. I'll get you to Tegan, where you belong.*

First, I called Christina.

"Where are you?" she said. "Your break ended five minutes ago."

"About that," I said. "I'm having a bit of an emergency, and before you ask, no, this is not an Addie moment. This particular emergency is about Tegan. I have to do something for her."

"What do you have to do?"

"Uh, something important. Something life-or-death, although don't worry, no one's actually going to *die*." I paused. "Except me, if I don't get it done."

"Addie," Christina said. Her tone that suggested I pulled this kind of crap all the time, which I did not.

"Christina, I'm not fooling around, and I'm not being dramatic just to be dramatic. I swear."

"Well, Joyce just clocked in," she said grudgingly, "so I suppose the two of us can cover things."

"Thank you, thank you, thank you! I'll be back in the quickest jiffy possible." I started to hang up, but Christina's tinny voice said, "Wait—hold on!"

I raised the phone back to my ear, antsy to be on my way. "What?"

"Your friend with the dreads is here."

"Brenna? *Ugh*. Not my friend." I had a horrible thought. "She's not with anyone, is she?"

"She's not with Jeb, if that's what you're asking."

"Thank God. Then why are you telling me?"

"Just thought you'd be interested. Oh, and your dad came by. He said to tell you he took the Explorer."

"He...*what*?!" My gaze flew to the north end of the parking lot. There was a rectangle of smushed snow where I'd parked the Explorer. "Why? Why in the world did he take my car?"

"*Your* car?"

"His car, whatever. What was he thinking?"

"No idea. Why, do you need it for your *thing*?"

"Yes, I need it for my thing. And now I have no clue how I'm going to—" I broke off, because ranting to Christina wouldn't help.

"Never mind, I'll figure it out," I said. "Bye."

I hit the end button, then called my voice mail.

"You have three new messages," the recording said.

Three? I thought. I'd only heard my phone ring once—although I guess things got kind of loud when the Doggy de Lites came crashing down.

"Addie, it's Dad," Dad said on message number one.

"Yes, Dad, I know," I said under my breath.

"I rode into town with Phil, because your mom needs some groceries. I'm taking the Explorer, so don't worry if you look out and see that it's gone. I'll swing by to pick you up at two."

"Nooooo!" I cried.

"Next message," my phone informed me. I bit my lip, praying that it was Dad saying, "Ha-ha, just kidding. I didn't take the Explorer; I just moved it. Ha-ha!"

It wasn't Dad. It was Tegan.

"Hola, Addikins!" she said. "Do you have Gabriel? Do ya, do ya, do ya? I cannot *wait* to see him. I found a heat lamp down in the basement—remember that year my dad was trying to grow those tomatoes?—and I set it up so Gabriel will stay warm in his little bed. Oh, and while I was down there, I found my old American Girl stuff, including a Barcalounger that is just the right size for him. And a backpack with a star on it, though I'm not sure he'll need a backpack. But you never know, right? Okay, um, *call me*. Call me *as soon as you can*. The snowplow is two streets over, so if I don't hear from you, I'll just head on over to Starbucks, 'kay? Bye!"

My stomach sank all the way to my toes, and I stood there dumbly as my voice mail announced the final message. It was Tegan again. "Oh, and Addie?" she said. "Thank you. Thank you *so* much."

Well, *that* made me feel better.

I shut my phone, cursing myself for not going to Pet World at the crack of nine like I'd planned. But rather than whimper pathetically, I had to deal with it. The old me would have stood here feeling sorry for myself until I got frostbite and my toes fell off, and good luck finding strappy heels to wear on New Year's Eve then, buster. Not that I had anywhere to go wearing strappy heels. But whatever.

The new me, however, was not a whimperer.

So. Where could I get a last-minute pig-rescue car?

Chapter Fourteen

Christina? Not an option. She got dropped off this morning by her boyfriend, per usual. Joyce, the barista whose shift just started, was also without car. Joyce walked to work no matter what the weather was like and wore one of those personal pedometers to measure how many steps she took.

Hmm, hmm, hmm. Not Dorrie and not Tegan, because (a) their street was still being plowed (hopefully), and (b) no way was I going to tell them why I needed said car.

Not Brenna, heaven forbid. If I asked her to take me to the south end of town, she'd drive north just to spite me. *And* she'd blast her reggae-emo-fusion crap, which sounded like drugged-out ghouls.

Which left only one person. One evil, charming, too-handsome-for-his-own-good person. I kicked a whump of snow, because he was the last person in the world I ever wanted to call, ever ever ever.

Well, guess what? I told myself. *You're going to have to suck it up for the sake of Tegan. Either that, or say bye-bye to Gabriel forever.*

I flipped opened my phone, scrolled through my contacts, and jabbed CALL. I clenched my toes inside my boots as I counted rings. One ringie-dingie, two ringie-dingies, three ringie—

"Yo, mama!" Charlie said when he picked up. "S'up?"

"It's Addie," I said. "I need a ride, and I'm only asking because I have absolutely no other choice. I'm outside Pet World. Come pick me up."

"Someone's bossy this morning," Charlie said. I could practically hear him waggle his eyebrows. "I like it."

"Whatever. Just come get me, will you?"

He lowered his voice. "What'll you give me in return?"

"A free chai," I said flatly.

"Venti?"

I tightened my jaw, because the way he said it, even "venti" sounded lewd.

"Fine, a venti chai. Have you left yet?"

He chuckled. "Hold on, babe. I'm still in my skivvies. My *venti* skivvies, and not because I'm fat, but because I'm"— ridiculous, loaded pause—*"venti."*

"Just get over here," I said. I started to hang up, then thought of one last thing. "Oh—and bring a phone book."

I hung up, did a shake-it-off shudder, and despised myself all over again for fooling around with such a skeeze. Yes, he was hot—in theory—and once upon a time, I suppose, I'd even found him funny.

But he wasn't Jeb.

Dorrie had summed up the difference between them one night at a party. Not *the* party, but just a normal, pre-breakup party. Dorrie and I were slouching on a sofa, rating a bunch of guys according to their strengths and weaknesses. When we got to Charlie, Dorrie let out a sigh.

"The problem with Charlie," she said, "is that he's *too* charming, and he knows it. He knows he can have any girl in the grade—"

"Not me," I interjected, balancing my drink on my knee.

"—so he sails through life like a typical trust-fund baby."

"Charlie has a trust fund? I didn't know that."

"But what that means, sadly, is that he has no depth. He's never had to work for anything in his life."

"I wish I didn't have to work for anything," I said wistfully. "I wish I had a trust fund."

"No, you don't," Dorrie said. "Are you even listening?" She took my drink, and I made a sound of protest.

"Take Jeb, for instance," Dorrie said. "Jeb is going to grow up to be the kind of man who spends his Saturdays teaching his little boy to ride a bike."

"Or little girl," I said. "Or twins! Maybe we'll have twins!"

"Charlie, on the other hand, will be off playing golf while *his* kid kills people on his Xbox. Charlie will be dashing and debonair, and he'll buy his kid all kinds of crap, but he'll never actually *be* there."

"That is so sad," I said. I reclaimed my drink and took a long sip. "Does that mean his kid will never learn to ride a bike?"

"Not unless Jeb goes over and teaches him," Dorrie said.

We sat. For several minutes, we watched the guys play pool. Charlie's ball hit its mark, and Charlie pulled his fist in by his side.

"That's what I'm talking about!" he crowed. "Ice, baby!"

Jeb looked across the room at me, and his lips twitched. I felt warm and happy, because the message in his eyes was, *You're mine and I'm yours. And thank you for not using expressions like "Ice, baby."*

A twitch of the lips and a loving look…what I wouldn't give to have that back. Instead, I threw it all away for the guy who was rumbling into the parking lot this very second in his ridiculous gray Hummer.

He pulled up short, spraying me with snow.

"Hey," he said, powering down the window. He jerked his chin at my hair and grinned. "Look at you, Pink!"

"Stop smiling at me," I warned him. "Don't even look at

me." I trudged to the passenger side and heaved myself in, straining my quads. I felt like I was climbing into a tank, which, basically, I was.

"Did you bring the phone book?"

He flicked it with his finger, and I saw that it was resting on the seat beside me. I found the residential section and flipped to the Bs. Baker, Barnsfeld, Belmont...

"I'm glad you called," Charlie said. "I've missed you."

"Shut up," I said. "And no, you haven't."

"You're being awfully mean toward someone who's giving you a ride," he said. I rolled my eyes. "Seriously, Adds. Ever since you broke up with Jeb—and I'm sorry about that, by the way—I've been hoping we could, you know, give it a go."

"That's not going to happen, and seriously, shut up."

"Why?"

I ignored him. Bichener, Biggers, Bilson...

"Addie," Charlie said. "I dropped everything to come pick you up. Think you could at least talk to me?"

"I'm sorry, but no."

"Why?"

"Because you're an asshat."

He guffawed. "Since when have you been hanging out with JP Kim?" He shut the phone book, and I just barely managed to keep my finger in it to mark my place.

"Hey!" I said.

"Seriously, why don't you want to go out with me?" he asked.

I lifted my head and glared. Surely he knew how much I regretted our kiss, and how much I hated just being here in this ridiculous Hummer with him. But as I took in his expression, I faltered. Was that...? Oh good grief. Was that *plaintiveness* in those green eyes?

"I like you, Addie, and you know why? 'Cause you're *zesty*." He said "zesty" with the same intentional cheesiness as when he'd said "venti."

"Don't call me zesty," I said. "I am not zesty."

"You're zesty, all right. *And* you're a good kisser."

"That was a mistake. That was me being drunk and stupid." My throat closed, and I had to gaze out the window until I pulled myself together. I turned back and attempted to divert the conversation. "Anyway, what happened to Brenna?"

"Brenna," he mused. He leaned back against the headrest. "Brenna, Brenna, Brenna."

"You're still into her, aren't you?"

He shrugged. "She seems to be...involved with someone else, as I'm sure you know. At least, that's what she tells me. I, myself, can't see it." He swiveled his head. "If you had the choice, would you pick Jeb over me?"

"In a heartbeat," I said.

"Ouch," he said. He gazed at me, and beneath his posturing, I saw that plaintiveness again. "Once, Brenna would have picked me. But I was a cad."

"Um, yeah," I said glumly. "I was there. I was an even bigger cad."

"Which is why we'd be great together. We might as well make lemonade, right?"

"Huh?"

"Out of our lemons," he explained. "Which is us. We're the lemons."

"Yeah, I got the reference. I just…" I didn't finish my sentence. If I had, it would have gone something like, "I just didn't know you saw yourself that way. As a lemon."

He snapped out of it. "So what do you say, Pink? Trixie's having a rocking New Year's Eve party. Want to go?"

I shook my head. "No."

He put his hand on my thigh. "I know you're having a rough time. Let me comfort you."

I pushed him off. "Charlie, I'm in love with Jeb."

"That didn't stop you before. Anyway, Jeb dumped you."

I was silent, because everything he said was true. Except, I wasn't that girl anymore. I refused to be.

"Charlie…I can't go out with you if I'm in love with someone else," I finally said. "Even if he no longer wants me."

"*Whoa,*" he said, drawing his hand to his heart. "Now *that's* rejection." He laughed, and just like that, he was back to being obnoxious Charlie. "What about Tegan? She's hot. Think she'd go to Trixie's party with me?"

"Give me back the phone book," I demanded.

He let go of it, and I pulled it into my lap. I opened it back up, scanned the entries and—*aha!*

"Billingsley, Constance," I read out loud. "108 Teal Eye Court. Do you know where Teal Eye Court is?"

"No clue," he said. "But never fear, Lola is here."

"Do guys *always* name their cars?"

He punched commands into his GPS system. "Quickest way, or most use of highways?"

"Quickest."

He hit SELECT, and a sexy female voice said, "Please proceed to the highlighted route."

"Ahhh," I said. "Hello, Lola."

"She's my girl," Charlie said. He shifted the Hummer into gear and bumped over the ridges of snow, slowing when he reached the parking lot's exit. At Lola's prompting, he took a right, drove half a block, and took another right into the narrow alley behind the stores.

"Prepare for a left turn in point one miles," Lola purred. "Turn left *now*."

Charlie wrenched the wheel to the left, taking the Hummer down a dinky, unplowed cul-de-sac.

There was a bing, and Lola said, "You have reached your destination."

Charlie stopped the Hummer. He turned to me and lifted his eyebrows. "This is where you needed a ride to?"

I was as baffled as he was. I craned my neck to read the street sign at the corner of the cul-de-sac, and sure enough, it said Teal Eye Court. A hundred feet away was the back of the Starbucks. The entire ride had taken thirty seconds, tops.

A laugh rolled out of Charlie.

"Shut up," I said, willing myself to stop blushing. "You didn't know where it was either, or you wouldn't have had to use Lola."

"Don't you tell me you're not zesty," Charlie said. "You are zesty with a capital Z."

I opened the door of the Hummer and hopped out, sinking deep into several feet of snow.

"Want me to wait for you?" he called.

"I think I can make it back on my own."

"You sure? It's a long way back."

I shut the door and started walking.

He rolled down the passenger's-side window. "See you at Starbucks—I'll be waiting for my chai!"

Chapter Fifteen

I waded across the snowy alley to the apartment complex at 108 Teal Court, praying that Constance Billingsley didn't have a little kid, because I didn't know if I could take a baby pig from a little kid.

I also prayed she wasn't blind, or paralyzed, or a dwarf like that lady I saw on the Discovery Channel who was less than three feet tall. I could not take a teeny-tiny pig from a teeny-tiny woman, no way.

Someone had shoveled the walkway leading to the individual apartments, and I climbed over the ridge of packed snow and hopped down to the much less treacherous pavement. One-oh-four, one-oh-six...*one-oh-eight*.

I set my shoulders and rang the bell.

"Why, hello, Addie!" exclaimed the gray-braided woman who opened the door. "What a treat!"

"Mayzie?" I said, befuddled. I glanced at the credit-card receipt. "I'm...uh...looking for Constance Billingsley?"

"Constance May Billingsley, that's me," she said.

My brain struggled to catch up. "But..."

"Now, think about it," she said. "Would you go by 'Constance' if you had a choice?"

"Uh..."

She laughed. "I didn't think so. Now, come inside, I have something to show you. Come, come, come!"

She led me into the kitchen, where on a blue quilt folded several times over sat the most adorable piglet I'd ever seen. He was pink and black and looked soft to the touch. His snout was a funny, squished thing, and his eyes were curious and alert. The curl of his tail said *sproing* even without being stretched and released, and yes, he was just the right size to nestle snugly into a teacup.

He oinked, and my insides went buttery.

"Gabriel," I said. I knelt by the edge of the quilt, and Gabriel stood and trotted over. He nosed my hand, and he was so sweet, I didn't care that I was being slimed with pig snot. Anyway, it wasn't snot. Gabriel had a damp snout, that was all. No biggie.

"What did you call him?" Mayzie said. "Gabriel?"

I looked up to see her smiling quizzically.

"Gabriel," she said, trying it out. She scooped Gabriel up. "Like the Angel Gabriel!"

"Huh?"

She put on an I'll-be-quoting-now face. "'The time has come,' the Walrus said, 'to talk of many things: Of shoes—and ships—and sealing-wax—of cabbages—and kings. And why the sea is boiling hot—and whether pigs have wings.'"

"Okay, I have no idea what you're talking about," I said.

"'And whether pigs have wings,'" Mayzie repeated. "An angel pig, you see? The Angel Gabriel!"

"I don't think my friend was being that deep," I said. "And please don't start talking about angels again. Please?"

"But why not, when the universe has such fun revealing them to us?" She looked at me with pride. "You did it, Addie. I knew you would!"

I put my hands on my thighs and pushed myself up. "What did I do?"

"You passed the test!"

"What test?"

"And so did I," she went on exuberantly. "At least, I think I did. We'll find out soon enough, I suppose."

Something tightened under my ribs. "Mayzie, did you go to Pet World and buy Gabriel on purpose?"

"Well, I didn't buy him on accident," she said.

"You know what I mean. You read my note, my pig note. Did you buy Gabriel just to *mess* with me?" I felt my lower lip tremble.

Her eyes widened. "Sweetie, *no!*"

"I went to Pet World, and Gabriel wasn't there...and do you know how frantic I've been?" I fought back tears. "And I had to deal with Nathan, who hates me." I sniffled. "Only it's possible he doesn't hate me anymore."

"Of course he doesn't," Mayzie said. "How could anyone hate you?"

"And *then* I had to deal with Charlie, which, believe me, you don't want to hear about." I ran the back of my hand under my nose. "Although weirdly enough, I handled it pretty well."

"Go on," Mayzie said encouragingly.

"I think he's even more messed up than I am."

Mayzie looked intrigued. "Maybe he'll be my next case."

With those words, *my next case*, I remembered that Mayzie wasn't my friend anymore, if she ever had been. She was just a kook who had my friend's pig.

"Are you going to give Gabriel back?" I said, keeping my voice as level as I could.

"Why, yes. I was never going to *keep* him." She lifted Gabriel so that she and he were nose to snout. "Although I will miss you, Mr. Gabriel. It was nice having company in this lonely apartment, even for just a while." She nestled him back into the nook of her elbow and kissed the top of his head.

I curled my toes inside my boots. "Are you going to give him back to*day*?"

"Oh, dear. I've upset you, haven't I?"

"Whatever, just let me have Gabriel."

"And here I thought you'd be happy to have an angel looking out for you. Isn't that what you wanted?"

"Enough with the angel bit," I said. "I'm not kidding. If the universe gave me *you* as my angel, then I deserve a refund."

Mayzie chuckled. She *chuckled*, and I wanted to throttle her.

"Adeline, you make things so much harder for yourself than you have to," she said. "Silly girl, it's not what the universe gives *us* that matters. It's what *we* give the universe."

I opened my mouth to tell her how stupid and hokey and woo-woo that was—but then I didn't, because something shifted inside me. *Big* shift, like an avalanche, and I could no longer resist it. The feeling inside of me was so big, and I was so small....

So I let go. I gave myself over to it and let go...and it felt marvelous. So marvelous that I couldn't understand why I'd resisted at all. *So* marvelous, in fact, that I thought, *Holy cow, has this been here all this time? A state of being that isn't tight and tangled and full of me me me?* Because *damn* it felt good. And *damn* it felt pure. And maybe I *could* be full of light, like

Nathan said, and maybe I could just…let that light *be*, and let it shine, and say screw it to being pinchy-squinchy-life-sucks-I-suck-guess-I'll-go-eat-worms. Was that possible in this existence of mine? Could I, Adeline Lindsey…could I evolve?

Mayzie escorted me to the door. "I think it's time for you to get going," she said.

"Uh, okay," I said. But I dragged my feet, because I no longer felt bitter toward her—and, in fact, I felt bad that I was about to be leaving her all alone. I wanted her to feel as expansive inside as I did, and I worried that might be hard in her single-person, soon-to-be-pigless apartment.

"Hey!" I said. "Can I, um, come visit you sometimes? I promise I won't be boring."

"I don't think you could possibly be boring, even if you tried," Mayzie said. "And I would absolutely love it if you came to see me sometimes." To Gabriel, she said, "See what a good heart she has?"

Something else clicked in. "And I'll get your money back from Pet World. I'll explain the whole crazy mess to Nathan."

She chuckled. "If anyone can, you can."

"So…yeah," I said, feeling pretty good about things. "I'll bring you your refund, and I'll bring those chocolate-covered graham crackers you like, too. And we'll have tea, 'kay? We'll have a ladies' tea every week. Or coffee. What do you think?"

"I think that's a splendid idea," Mayzie said. She handed Gabriel to me, and he paddled his legs, searching for purchase. I breathed in the heavenly scent of him. He smelled like whipped cream.

Chapter Sixteen

*G*abriel pressed his snout against my coat as I tromped through the alley snow. I wished the Silver Sneaker van would miraculously appear and pick me up, even though I was sixteen instead of seventy-six. Although, at least I *could* muscle through these drifts. If I were seventy-six? No way.

Gabriel squirmed, and I said, "Hold on, little guy. It won't be long now."

Halfway to Starbucks, I saw Tegan's Civic pull to a stop at the traffic light two blocks down. Eek, she'd be here in, like, two minutes! I picked up my pace, because I wanted to get inside before Tegan arrived. I wanted to settle Gabriel into an actual teacup—or coffee mug—because wouldn't that be the cutest thing in the world?

I used my hip to push through the door, and Christina

looked up from the espresso machine. The other barista, Joyce, wasn't in sight.

"At last!" Christina called. "Can you take these guys' orders?"

She gestured at the guy and the girl standing at the counter, and I did a double take.

"Stuart!" I said, because it was Stuart Weintraub of the Stuart-and-Chloe-heartbreak-forever duo. Only, the girl he was with wasn't Chloe; in fact, she was pretty much the opposite of Chloe with her short bob and cute little cat-eye glasses. She smiled at me kind of shyly, and my heart went *awwwww*, because she looked nice, and she was holding Stuart's hand, and she wasn't wearing bright red lipstick. She did not look like the kind of girl to have skanky bathroom make-out sessions on guys who weren't her boyfriend.

"Hey, Addie," Stuart said. "You cut your hair."

One hand went to my head; the other kept a firm hold on Gabriel, who was trying to snuffle his way out of my coat. "Uh, yeah." I jerked my chin at the girl he was with. "Who's this?" It probably came out abrupt, but good heavens! Stuart Weintraub was not only without Chloe, but also without sad Stuart eyes! I mean, he still had *eyes*, but they were happy eyes now. His happiness made him look super-cute, too.

Yay, Stuart, I thought. *Yay for Christmas miracle happening after all.*

Stuart grinned at the girl and said, "This is Jubilee. Jubilee, this is Addie. She goes to my school."

Awwww, I thought again. *How adorable that he was going out with someone named after a yummy Christmas dessert.* How adorable that he *got* his yummy Christmas dessert—even though he was Jewish or whatever.

"Thanks for that," Jubilee said to Stuart, blushing. To me she said, "Weird name. I know. I'm not a stripper, I promise."

"Uh...okay," I said.

"You can call me Julie," she said.

"Nah, I like Jubilee," I said. Saying her name out loud made a memory ping in my brain. *Tegan...the Kissing Patrol...some un-Jeb guy thrusting his fist into the air...*

"Maybe you could take their order?" Christina prompted, knocking whatever it was right out of my head. Oh, well. Stuart was with a lovely girl named Jubilee, and she wasn't a stripper. That's all that mattered.

"As in, now?" Christina said.

"Uh...*yes!*" I said enthusiastically. Possibly too enthusiastically. "In just a second, 'kay? I just have to do this one teeny thing."

"Addie," Christina warned.

To my right, Tobin stirred in the purple chair. Was he just now waking up? He blinked at me and said, "Whoa. Your name's *Addie?*"

"Um, yep, that's me, Addie," I said, thinking, *See? Knew you didn't know my name.* I juggled Gabriel to keep him hidden under my coat, and he made a funny noise that sounded like *wheep.* "And now I'm just going to *run* to the back—"

Gabriel wheeped again. Louder.

"Addie," Christina said in a trying-not-to-freak voice. "What do you have under your coat?"

"Addster!" Charlie said from the bar. "You gonna set me up with that chai?" He grinned, and I realized why when I saw his arm slung around the girl beside him. Oh my God, this was like Christmas Miracle Central.

"Hi, Addie," the evil Brenna said. "Nice hair." She might have smirked, but I wasn't sure, because she didn't look *quite* as evil as I remembered her. Today she looked more glow-y than snarky. Maybe because of Charlie's arm?

"Seriously," Tobin said. "Your name's Addie?" He nudged Angie, who woke up and rubbed her nose. "Her name's Addie," he told her. "You think she's *the* Addie?"

"*The* Addie?" I asked. What was he talking about? I wanted to push for details, but I got distracted by the sight of Tegan's Civic turning into the parking lot. Dorrie was in the passenger seat, clutching Tegan's shoulder and speaking intently, and I could only imagine what she was saying. Probably something like, "Now, remember, this is Addie we're talking about. It's highly possible she's having some crisis and didn't get Gabriel after all."

"Adeline," Christina said. "That's not...a pig, is it?"

I glanced down to see Gabriel's head peeking out from the top of my zipper. He *wheeped* and looked around.

"Well," I said proudly, since the pig was out of the coat, so to speak. I rubbed Gabriel's ears. "Not just any pig, but a *teacup* pig. Very rare."

Jubilee glanced at Stuart and grinned. "You live in a town where people carry around elf-size pigs?" she said. "And here I thought *my* life was weird."

"Not elf. Teacup," I said. "And speaking of, I need one of the holiday mugs, 'kay, Christina? You can take it out of my paycheck." I headed toward the display shelf, but Tobin stopped me by grabbing my elbow.

"Are you the Addie who goes out with Jeb Taylor?" he asked.

That threw me. Tobin didn't know my name, but he knew I went out with Jeb?

"I'm...well, um..." I swallowed. "Why?"

"Because Jeb gave me a message for you. Crap, I completely dropped the ball."

My heart whacked around in my chest. "He gave you a message? What was the message?"

Tobin turned to Angie. "I'm such an idiot. Why didn't you remind me?"

She smiled drowsily. "That you're an idiot? Okay: you're an idiot."

"Oh, that's great, thanks," he said. She giggled.

"The message?" I managed to say.

"Right!" he said. He turned his attention back to me. "The message was that he got delayed."

"By cheerleaders," Angie contributed.

"I'm sorry?"

"Cheerleaders?" Jubilee said, somewhat manically. She and Stuart came over to where we were standing. "Oh my God, cheerleaders!"

"The cheerleaders were on a train with him, only the train got stuck," Tobin said.

"*I* was on that train!" Jubilee shouted. Stuart laughed the way you do when someone you love is a goofy nut. "And did you say *Jeb*? I gave him a microwavable pizza disc!"

"You gave Jeb a...what?" I said.

"'Cause of the storm?" Charlie asked.

I turned to him in a daze. "Why would she give Jeb a microwavable pizza disc because of the storm?"

"Dude, no," he said. He hopped off his stool and pulled Brenna along with him. They joined us by the purple chairs. "I mean did the *train* get stuck 'cause of the storm, asshat."

Tobin twitched at the word ASSHAT and looked up at Charlie like he'd seen an apparition. Then he shook it off and said, "Uh, yeah. Exactly. And then the cheerleaders abducted Jeb, because they had needs."

Charlie laughed. "Right on."

"Not *those* kind of needs," Angie said.

"Yeah," Brenna said. She jabbed Charlie in the ribs.

"What kind of needs?" I said, feeling lightheaded. In the back of my consciousness, I registered the sound of a car door shutting, and then another. In my peripheral vision, I saw Tegan and Dorrie hurrying toward the store.

"Huh," Tobin said, and he got that inward look of his I was growing familiar with, the one that meant that no answer was forthcoming.

"Well…was there more?" I said, trying a different strategy.

"More what?" Tobin said.

"More to Jeb's message!"

"Oh," Tobin said. "Yes! Yes, there was!" The set of his jaw was purposeful, but after several seconds, he deflated. "Ah, crap," he said.

Angie took pity on me. Her expression went from giddy to kind.

"He said he's coming," she said. "He said you'd know what he meant."

My heart stopped, and the cheerful buzz of Starbucks receded. It was as if someone pressed a mute button on the outside world, or maybe what was going on inside of me was simply drowning everything else out. *He said he was coming? Jeb was coming?!*

A jangling penetrated my consciousness, and in my muddled

state, I had the most random thought: *Every time a bell rings, an angel gets her wings.* Then a burst of cold air brought me back to reality, and I realized it was the bell on the door making such a clatter.

"Addie, you're here!" Dorrie cried, barging toward me in a bright red hat.

Beside her, Tegan beamed. "And *he's* here! We saw him in the parking lot!"

"*I'm* the one who spotted him," Dorrie said. "He looks like he's been out in the wilderness for days, so prepare yourself. To be perfectly honest, *Sasquatch* is what comes to mind. But—"

She broke off, noticing Stuart and Jubilee. "*Stuart's with a girl*," she whispered in a voice loud enough to bring down a house.

"I know!" I whispered back. I grinned at Stuart and Jubilee, who both turned as red as Dorrie's hat.

"Hi, Dorrie," Stuart said. "Hi, Tegan." He put his arm around Jubilee and patted her shoulder, half nervously and half just plain sweetly.

"Gabriel!" Tegan squealed. She rushed over and scooped Gabriel from my arms, which was lucky, as my muscles were wobbly. My whole body was wobbly, because the bell on the door was jingling again,

and it was Jeb,

and he was a total mess,

and sobs rose inside me, and laughter, too, because he really did look like Sasquatch, with straggly hair and wind-chapped cheeks and his strong jaw shadowed with stubble.

His dark eyes darted from person to person, then landed on me. He strode over and crushed me in his arms, and I hugged him with every bit of myself. My cells sang.

"Oh, man, Addie, it's been a crazy couple of days," he murmured into my ear.

"Yeah?" I said, soaking in the glorious, solid realness of him.

"First my train got stuck. Then there were these cheerleaders, and we all ended up in the Waffle House, and they kept making me help them with their lifts—"

"Their *lifts*?" I drew back so I could see his face but kept my arms circled around him.

"And every single one of them left her phone on the train so she could focus on *spirit*, or something. And I tried to use the Waffle House phone, but the manager was like, 'Sorry, no can do. Crisis mode, dude.'"

"Ouch," Tobin said, cringing.

"See what happens when boys get obsessed with cheerleaders?" Angie said.

"Although it's not fair to be prejudiced against *all* cheerleaders," Jubilee said. "Just the ones whose names rhyme with *showy*. Right, Stuart?"

Stuart looked amused.

Jubilee waved at Jeb. "Hi, Jeb."

"Julie," Jeb said. "What are you doing here?"

"Her name's not Julie, it's Jubilee," I whispered helpfully.

"Jubilee?" Jeb repeated. "Whoa."

"No," Christina said, and all eight of us turned to look at her. "I am the one who gets to say *whoa* here, and I'm saying it right now, okay?"

No one responded, so finally I said, "Uh, okay. But come on, it's not *that* weird a name."

She looked pained. "Addie," she said, "I need you to tell me right now: Did you bring a *pig* into my store?"

Ohhhh. Right.

Pig in store...was there any way to put a spin on this?

"He's a really *cute* pig," I said. "Does that count for anything?"

Christina pointed to the door. "The pig has to go. *Now.*"

"Fine, fine," I said. "I just need to give Tegan a cup to put him in."

"Think Flobie'll ever dip into drinkware?" Stuart said to Jubilee under his breath.

"I'm sorry, what's that?" I said.

Giggling, Jubilee elbowed Stuart and said, "Ignore. *Please.*"

Dorrie stepped closer to me. "You did good, Addie," she said. "I doubted you, but I shouldn't have, and...well, you did good."

"Thanks," I said.

"Hello?" Christina said. "Did anyone hear me when I said *the pig needs to go?*"

"Someone needs a refresher in customer service," Tobin said.

"Maybe Don-Keun could help?" Angie said.

Christina glared, and Tegan stepped backward toward the door. "I'm leaving, I'm leaving!"

"Wait!" I said. I released Jeb long enough to grab a snowflake mug from the shelf, which I handed to Tegan. "For Gabriel."

"If the regional manager stops in, I'm fired," Christina said hopelessly. "Pigs are not part of Starbucks policy."

"Here you go, sweetie," Tegan said, tilting Gabriel so that he slipped into the mug. He scrabbled a bit, then seemed to realize the mug was just his size and made a decent house, actually. He sat on his haunches and oinked, and every one of us gave a collective *awwww*. Even Christina.

"Excellent," Dorrie said. "Now come on, we better go before Christina *plotzes*."

I grinned at Jeb, who grinned back. His gaze shifted to my hair, and his eyebrows went up.

"Hey," he said. "You changed your hair."

"Oh, yeah," I said. It seemed like a lifetime ago. That blonde-haired *boo-hoo-hoo* girl who spent Christmas feeling sorry for herself, was that really me?

"Looks nice," he said. He rubbed a lock between his thumb and forefinger. His knuckles slid down, grazing my cheek.

"Addie, I want you," he whispered, and heat flamed to my face. Did he honestly just say that? That he *wanted* me, right here in *Starbucks*?

Then I realized what he meant. He was responding to my e-mail, the part where I said, *If you want me, I'm yours.*

My cheeks stayed warm, and I was glad no one in the store had ESP, because that was a classically self-absorbed misinterpretation. But even if they did have ESP—and how would I know, anyway?—it was certainly no crisis.

I rose on my toes and wrapped my arms around Jeb's neck.

"I'm going to kiss you now," I warned him, since I knew how he felt about being mushy in public.

"No," he said, gently but firmly. "I'm going to kiss you."

His lips touched mine, and a ringing filled my head, sweet and silver and pure. It was probably the bell on the door, jingling as Dorrie and Tegan went out. But I was far too busy to check.